**She'd come to the Pleasure Dom‗
not by her worst enemy!**

By this time, Soledad, her mind spinning with terrible possibilities, had jerked on her one piece regimentals. She knew with awful certainty what had happened. *Damned wormhole dyslexia.* This was the last time she would trust it without more questioning, even if meant asking a passing stranger. With her boots in hand, she shoved past her playmate.

His voice echoed lightly in playfulness. "And just where do you think you're going?"

"Me? I've gotten what I came for. I'm leaving." Sol flashed what she hoped was a convincing grin, twisted her arm, and again tried to get out the door.

"Well, I haven't finished with you yet, Captain," the man clung to her arm, his warm eyes hopeful.

"Oh, may the gods preserve us! Captain Scott." The doorman finally recognized Sol. "I am so terribly sorry. I knew my robot bellhop was malfunctioning. He must have taken you to the wrong room—to Commander Merriweather's room. How can I ever apologize to you?"

The name finally registered with her. Merriweather. Sol's mouth fell open but nothing came out. In shock, she stared at her sexual playmate. Rage choked her. With a mute headshake, she jerked her arm loose from Merriweather's grip and scooted past the doorman.

But before she got out the door, the commander called after her. "Wait. I can't see that an apology is necessary. I don't know about the captain, but I'm satisfied. More than satisfied." Merriweather gave Sol that wicked grin. "I think she is, too. Right, darlin'?"

"Yes . . . well, I must be going. I've a thousand things to do." Sol spit the words from between tight lips and skittered down the hall's slick floors. If she stayed much longer, she'd kill the man who was responsible for the best sex she'd ever experienced—and who was indirectly responsible for her forced retirement. God help her, she hoped he hadn't also fathered her child.

This one is for Dave. I'm sorry you didn't get to read
this, buddy. You were the best fan I'll ever know.
Thanks for all the encouragement. I miss you, pal.

And, thank you, Tom, again, for all your support;
couldn't live without you, my hero.

And another big Thank You to Linda Kichline
and ImaJinn Books for believing in me
and in the passion of my dreams.

Other Books L. F. Hampton

Winged Victory
Winged Darkness

Coming Soon

Forever One
One Heart

Pleasure Dome

* * *

L. F. Hampton

ImaJinn
Books

The Pleasure Dome
Published by ImaJinn Books

10 Digit ISBN: 1-933417-45-5
13 Digit ISBN: 978-1-933417-45-5

10 9 8 7 6 5 4 3 2 1

PUBLISHER'S NOTE:
This book is a work of fiction. Names, characters, places and incidents are products of the author's imagination or are used fictitiously. Any resemblance to actual events or locales or persons, living or dead, is entirely coincidental.

Books are available at quantity discounts when used to promote products or services. For information please write to: Marketing Division, ImaJinn Books, P.O. Box 545, Canon City, CO 81212, or call toll free 1-877-625-3592.

Cover design by Patricia Lazarus

ImaJinn Books
P.O. Box 545, Canon City, CO 81212
Toll Free: 1-877-625-3592
http://www.imajinnbooks.com

One

Soledad Scott, retired warship captain, gazed with feigned disinterest at the fast approaching Straits of Tralarie. Far out near the vast unexplored regions of space, the Straits' asteroids glittered in the cold vacuum like they were diamonds in the rough, but there was nothing new for her to see. She had seen their beauty before, many times in the twenty years of her career in the Spacing Guild. But this time the sight should have been special, and if not for the stomach butterflies that she was trying so hard to ignore, perhaps it would have been.

Scattered among the silent moons, under their protective atmospheric domes, forty-eight fully functional, top of the line pleasure houses awaited her and the other military customers coming there for R&R.

In the packed transport, during the ship's final approach, Sol bumped into the Marine next to her. Her breast grazed his arm, but his gaze remained firmly fixed on the port's view. She thought for a moment that he hadn't noticed the touch, but his cheeks flamed and his neck turned red. Sol wondered if this was his first R&R. Poor baby, his extreme hair cut and innocent blush meant he was obviously new to the service. The transport's deck bucked, and despite Sol's rigid balance, their bodies brushed again. This time the Marine mumbled, "Sorry, Captain."

With a start, Sol realized that she'd worn her uniform. Her red leathers identified her as a warship captain, a rank she no longer held, but rank that set her apart from the other off-duty personnel. She waved a negligent hand at the recruit, and he returned to his window gazing, twin spots of color still staining his smooth cheekbones. Sol went back to her contemplation of her stupidity. This little adventure was surely a mistake from the beginning. Whatever had possessed her to do this? Hell, she wasn't even authorized to wear her leathers anywhere anymore. *Frack 'em.* She snorted the curse to herself, but the Marine recruit edged further away from her as if he'd heard.

She softly sighed. Out here in the Straits, rank didn't matter.
Especially hers.

But no one knew from looking that she no longer held her
rank. The thought burned inside. Earlier, she had choked down
the s-rations that passed for military nutritious food. Now that
food lay like a lead ball in her stomach. Sol gave a mental
headshake at such weakness and flicked on the brochure with
her marked itinerary. All the colorful ads were attractive, but
she was already booked for one place—the Pleasure Dome.
The pretentious name sucked, and the others were no better.
Dante's Circus, Faro's Hump, the Bump and Grind, the Y-Knot,
and the Steel Away—those names surely reflected their type
of business or pleasure. Sol had even used a few of them for
relaxation in the past and knew that their patrons could either
find what they desired or at least find where to obtain it. Females
could even fulfill their dream of conceiving a child without the
encumbrances of an extraneous mate. She shuddered over
that last statement and read the through the advertisement faster.

Males could procure surrogate mothers to bear their
offspring. Foreign species could copulate together in any
fashion, all without the limits of the law. Anything of any sexual
nature could be had here—for the right price. Hiding within
her palm-vid, the ads promised Sol dens of sexual freedoms
that offered something for everyone of every species. She had
sampled a few of those freedoms in the past, but this time she
had something more important in mind. This meeting would be
life changing and scared her as no previous enemy ever had.
She felt her cheeks heat up as hotly as the young recruit's had.
She raised her gaze and connected with the brown-eyed Marine
sitting across from her. This one, obviously more experienced
than the recruit, gave her a thorough, frank appraisal despite
her uniform's rank. Sol didn't hide her smile, although she gave
him a negative headshake. He grinned good-naturedly, shrugged
and turned his attractive attention elsewhere. Too bad. He was
so clearly her type, nonthreatening and easy to please. Sol
sighed deeply. Now was not the time for sideline romances.
The ship was docking, engines dying. *Focus*.

She became part of the crowd jamming the exits. Among

the tired military crews, most of the varied species of broad-shouldered Marines and trim fighter pilots seemed to know where they were going for R&R, and after long and dangerous tours of space duty, all were eager to get there. Sol lagged behind and watched the others, who were obviously more excited to reach their destinations. In the main space port, most travelers avoided physical as well as eye contact with anyone else. If one looked too closely into those tired orbs' reflections, they might catch a glimpse of a weary soul who had seen too much, done too much, and was tired of living. If a little R&R in a protected dome's pleasure palace could restore their joy of life even for a little while, most were eager to seek it in any form. Sol wouldn't judge them. She had led too many Marines into battle to deny them a few days of sexual relaxation.

With her jaw hardened against old memories, Sol finally joined the diverse crowd winding its way like a sensuous snake through Nucleus, the Straits' main space port, toward the shuttles disembarking for said pleasure palaces. She gave a few alien travelers a wider berth due to their overpowering stench or because of their odd appearances. And, thankfully, most of those made their way to shuttles destined for the outer fringe of the Straits where the darker entertainments of the alien variety were located. But the human customers surrounding Sol, those desiring relaxation and/or sexual gratification and opting for the old conventional way of receiving it, boarded the air shuttles for the male and female professional services of the Pleasure Dome. She knew from her booking that the Dome was a human frequented hot spot of the tamer sexual persuasion located on the fifth settlement of the Strait.

The Pleasure Dome guaranteed that the customer comes first—ha! —and that he/she is in the right spot at the right time for their desired pleasure.

Credits back if not satisfied.

* * * *

Soledad wasn't sure about being in the right spot or at the right time. She should have taken the robotic room guide, but she had been confident that she could find her designated room in the Dome's corridors that spread out like a wagon wheel from the centralized check-in desk. Gods above, she had captained galactic star ships for the past twenty years. She could certainly find one little room in a whorehouse.

But now Sol wasn't so confident. She stared at the gaudy, purple-sequined door numbers of room 660 and thought that she had surely lost what little of her mind that remained. At least she thought this was room 660. Or was it 990? She squinted at the sparkling numbers that swirled in her vision, then closed one eye, looked away, then back, making sure that her wormhole dyslexia—that damned affliction left over from staring too long into the swirling abyss—wasn't playing tricks on her. After spacing for the past twenty years, she no longer trusted her reading sight in any kind of distorted light, but this wasn't a new occurrence. Her dyslexia had played tricks on her vision before. But now, in her civilian life, it seemed to be more prevalent than ever. Maybe her human irritation was showing through or perhaps she was just getting old. And, perhaps, she was too old for what she had planned to happen here. Sol snorted at the thought. By the stars, had she become such a *civi* that she was now second-guessing her decisions, doubting herself? What next?

But really, after serving the past twenty years in space, whatever made her think that she should have a child at the age of thirty-eight? Wasn't she too old for that, too? She was certainly too old to captain a war ship any longer. At least, that's what the damned Spacing Guild thought. That fat-assed assistant director had certainly thought she was too old when he turned her out with no more thought than putting a dog out to piss. Memories of her curt dismissal still haunted Sol with sick recrimination.

"Captain Scott, the Guild is very pleased with your performance as Captain of the *Icarus*. Your long record is one of the finest in our history. We hope you will be pleased with your retirement bonus." Dushaw, the longtime assistant director of the Guild, offered Sol a fleshy hand filled with thick fingers that looked like stuffed pink sausages. He arched pointed brows at her blatant refusal of his handshake. Finally, after long moments of pregnant silence, the fake political smile on his lips died. He withdrew his hand, and with watery gray eyes gone as cold and as impersonal as any fish's, he gave a throaty-voiced, "Well," before sitting back down and flipping desk papers to begin the day's next all important business. His gray-haired, spiky buzz-cut remained tilted down, and he never looked up at Sol again. The self-absorbed pencil pusher had dismissed her without another look.

Soledad, teeth grinding and choking on her rage, was summarily escorted out between two solidly muscled, fierce Marine guards dressed in their thick-shouldered, black leather regimentals. But she didn't blame the grim-faced soldiers, they were doing their duty. And, even though Sol knew this day was coming, she had expected to have more time to prepare. The Guild gave her no warning, but then, the Guild never warned about anything. It would drop her into the middle of a deadly war with little more than a two sentence description of who was friendly and who was the enemy. Many a time, on their orders, Sol had led her Marines on dangerous missions that had cost the life of more than one good friend, only to have those enemies become allies through the bribery of the Diplomatic Corps, another self-serving branch of the Guild. Yeah, maybe it was time to retire, before she blasted some important but ignorant government asshole and was retired into space without a suit.

Back on the *Icarus*, Sol had hastily thrown her ragged, ancient books and few personal effects into an old campaign-scuffed duffle bag. Technically, she didn't have to leave until the new captain arrived, but she didn't want to see who would be fulfilling her duties, taking over her ship, and issuing orders to her crew. After leaving her quarters and hastening through the corridors, she heartily lied to her people about the many benefits of retirement, when all she felt like doing was going back to the Spacing Guild's office and punching the insufferable director's soft gut. With her throat muscles as tight as the asteroid-filled Andromeda's Pass, she'd gazed up though misty vision and gave one last salute to the colors. *Icarus*, her beautiful ship, would never be hers again, and she probably would never again see her crew who had become as close as family. Once more she was beginning her life over. Sol felt as if she had lost her identity; no longer was she the confident captain she had been for twenty years.

On the dock, her puzzled but obedient officers on ship's duty that day had raised their arms, snapped their elbows and stiffened their fingers to their foreheads in one last salute. Sol had returned it and left without a backward glance, her spine erect and her long strides steady. A galactic warship's captain shared tears with no one. And, damn it, she'd remain a captain in her heart until she died.

Unconsciously, she had tried hurrying her death wish. After a month-long drinking binge, Te'angel, Sol's big sister, rescued her from an ale and piss joint, slapped her awake and threw her into a sonic shower. Te' then tactfully suggested that perhaps Sol should start a new career, a higher one that gave better rewards, before she killed herself—or Te' did that job for her. It didn't take Te' long to convince Sol into taking on a new and completely diverse career . . . as a mother.

"Well, I personally think you'd make a hella'va mother, Sol. You come from great genes, even as flawed as we are with our diluted Chakkra blood," Te' had smiled her gentle sisterly smile. "And you're certainly strong and self-reliant, with a good pension—and I know firsthand how much you love children."

Te's voice had softened further, and the thin skin around her eyes had crinkled, reflecting the deep love they shared. She'd patted Sol's shoulder. "You've a big heart, honey, so don't waste all that love. Besides, you're not getting any younger, you know, and you need to have your first soon. If you want children, you should get your body in tune with your heart like I did."

Sol had felt the corners of her mouth rise in a wry twist. Te'angel's honest words had been filled with caring, but the age thing had still stung, although Sol laughed it off. Te' was four years older, and she hadn't stopped birthing yet, so Te' certainly believed her own words. And Sol would never do or say anything to hurt her big sister who was actually six inches shorter than Sol and the nearest thing to a mother that Sol had.

And Te' was a great mother. Just ask the Space Academy's breeding program or any of her ten kids.

The thought of those ten kids and their hellacious racket at Te's home gave Sol a shudder before she also remembered the heart-tugging and throat-choking sight of those babies crowded around Te' while she read to them, or the antics of the diverse gang making dinner, baking cookies, or wrapping presents over the holidays. Te's home on Delta Three was always filled with the love and warmth of family. The laughter, the tears, and the honest affection surrounded all who entered. Te' always knew just what to say or to do to smooth over any hurt. But even the stoic Sol cried when Tommy, the oldest of Te's brood, left home for the Space Academy. The agency was only too happy to accept the fifteen-year-old into their flight program, and his brave achievements during the subsequent years had strengthened their greedy acceptance of his other siblings. The next three to leave were even harder for Sol and Te' to let go, but yeah, Sol was sure that she wanted—needed—someone in her life. Someone who made her life count for something. Someone she would love and protect. Someone who would love her in return.

Still, Sol hesitated at the Pleasure Dome's room assigned to her. Here, in this room, her sperm donor awaited. Why hadn't she chosen to do the impersonal breeding the way that Te' did and not even bother with a male? Penises—who needed them anyway? Sol snorted. She was only seeking good, healthy sperm, but she also happened to like the physical exchange in obtaining it, as long as she was in control of the situation. She always chose to experience everything in her own way, on her own terms. Now she wasn't so sure her idea was a sound one.

The door's glitzy numbers continued to blur, spinning and fading in and out of either 660 or 990. Which one was the friggin' right number? Sol sighed. Gods, she must be crazy. And did she really want to live through all the fevers, the whining, and the demands of a child, just to give them up when they were grown? And possibly give them up to the damned Spacing Guild? She only thought on that for a moment.

Oh, hell, yes! She had seen firsthand the love exchanged between Te' and her children in those few times she'd visited them. She felt the need for this. The connected feeling of life and love was stronger now than at any other time in her life. And she told herself that she was only a little frightened of the whole sperm gathering situation. Sex she could handle, sex with a purpose was scary.

Sol gave a slight headshake to wake herself from her musings. Her weakened spirit must be that age-old maternal instinct kicking in after all these years of war. Yeah, Soledad wanted this baby. And if her child desired a career in Space, she would do everything in her power to grant his or her wish. Besides, she had already taken the massive doses of fertility drugs and had undergone weeks of painful treatments, altering her physical system and correcting the sterility demands of spacing. Why not just do this and get it over with? A swift surge of heat swept through her nether regions leaving a tingling behind. The sexual enhancement she had swallowed earlier with a shot of Valtarie wine labeled *tazvidal* was warming her body in all the right places. A shudder raced through her. Her heart rate notched up. Like an irritating itch that needed scratching, her body urged her to hurry. Yep, she was definitely ready in all the right places.

Now, to get her mind in agreement with her body, she took a deep breath and let it out slowly. Soledad Scott, recently retired captain of the galactic warship, *Icarus,* raised her trembling hand, squeezed it into a steady fist, and banged on the ugly-colored, purple door. In her other hand, she held a bottle of properly drugged wine provided by the Pleasure Dome's robotic director. The fertility doctor had suggested its use only to enhance the potency of her eggs' acceptance. Perhaps he was right and she would need the artificial encouragement. It had been awhile since she'd had sex—paid for or otherwise, but according to the tests, she was ripe for fertilization. Yippee!

"Enter. Door's open." The baritone growl that answered her knock sent those fluttering butterflies down Sol's stomach. The deep masculine tone also sent chills up her spine and raised the hair on her arms. *Damned enhancement drug.* As a warship captain, she'd never had such emotional reactions. She was well known for her calm, cool, commanding officer's demeanor. Hormones had turned her to mush. But if she felt this much sexual heat from just his voice, her playmate should give her first rate service. Soledad nudged the door open with the toe of her boot. She peered into the subdued lighting and tried to catch a glimpse of the room's occupant while still shielding herself behind the doorjamb. The dim light from the hall put Sol too much in outline for her comfort, but gave no hint about the man she was meeting. He was supposed to be pleasing to the eye and at least as tall as her six foot stature. The rest of the requirements were in computer numerical printouts of compatible genes, but the technical language looked like so much gibberish to Sol. And she cared little about what the donor looked like anyway. His healthy sperm was the most important thing to consider. That and his willingness to let her control the proceedings. Perhaps she really should have done as Te' always did and had the sperm artificially inseminated. *Too late.* He of the deep voice spoke again.

"Put the wine over there and take off your clothes ." The curt demand came dry and impersonal, just as if he expected Sol to be there for him and his wishes. *The nerve.* After what she was paying, this pleasure treat could at least be polite. Sol was never into the dominating macho trip. *One strike against her donor.* Time to nip this in the bud. She was in charge.

Sol flipped on an energy switch near the door and glared through the fake candlelight that the Dome considered romantic toward the voice's direction. "Hold your slipstream buddy. You're supposed to be of service to me." She wagged her finger at the lump on the bed. "Not the other way around."

The lump sat up. For several seconds, a large, dark-haired man blinked in the sudden light before rising, splendidly naked, from between the golden sheets of the opulent, silk- and brocade-laden bed. Light bounced off his high cheekbones and glittered in his slanted eyes, lending him a foreign cast before he dipped his head and safely dropped his gaze. He looked from the bed back to Sol with a frown. Needless to say, the overdressed, gaudy bed loomed as the focal point of the pleasure room. That is, it had before the man stood up. He, with his arrogant stance, demanded all Sol's attention. Bone-straight black hair tangled over the man's high forehead and dipped to his wide shoulders, while more of it curled in the middle of his broad chest. Between twin circles of flat brown nipples, a line of the sable stuff sprinkled past rippling abs and down his stomach to—Sol jerked her attention back to the safety of his shoulders—those broad shoulders. Yeah, her pleasure toy had enough body hair to be masculine and not look like an ape man, but he was big—much bigger than Sol thought she had specified. He filled the room with his brawny form, and, for a second, Soledad had trouble catching her breath, but not from fear. This sexual attraction rarely happened to her.

Without a word, the man edged closer, frank appraisal in his wide-eyed glance, just as she was sure it was in hers. Sol noted that although he was a large man, he wasn't a bumbling brute; he moved with a natural grace of someone at home in his body—so darkly sensual. Nearly at her side now, he dipped his head at Sol in a brief nod, his gaze puzzled, as if he were trying to figure out something. In the light's soft reflection, Sol noticed his odd eyes—light, icy pale one moment, then a cold, arctic dark of a bottomless lake the next. They seemed at odds with the night-jet color of his hair. And for a quick moment, Soledad thought she glimpsed something swirling behind the brilliant blue, something violent, but she dismissed it as a trick of the fake candlelight's flickering shadows. The damned light did show off his attributes though—only too well.

In her swift inspection, Sol noticed every smooth slab of muscle that flexed across the man's body. And he moved in fluid movement as if just to get her attention. Defying her stare, he deliberately raked back his heavy hair from his forehead—hair that was a shade too long for her taste—then he cocked his head to one side again, patiently waiting while she looked her fill. Between those chiseled cheekbones, Sol noted that his long, aristocratic nose was crooked, probably broken by someone not impressed by that insolent stare that he now used on her. Perhaps he was a professional fighter as well as a sex toy, defiant enough not to have his nose straightened. Soledad liked defiance in a fighter—among other things. Her lips quirked at the idea of some of those other things she was thinking about, thanks to that enhancement drug. But, frankly, the guy fit Sol's idea of the perfect father's size for her child. If he made her libido peak, so much the better. She was enjoying her long perusal. He evidently wasn't. Her playmate had lost his smirk.

A long muscle jerked in his jaw under the darkened shadow of old-fashioned stubble. Odd. He hadn't made use of the spacing luxury of hair removal for his whiskers. That thought brought a hint of strangeness to Sol, since a pleasure toy had access to all the modern oils and depilatories, and a toy wouldn't want to offend a paying customer. This one evidently didn't care about beard burn on his partner, and apparently he also didn't care for her lingering stare.

His snort brought a hot flush to Sol's cheeks before he insolently lowered his glance. Then the corners of his full, sensuous lips turned up. It was his turn to peruse her. His languid gaze slowly traveled from Sol's head to her toes then back again, all uniformed six feet of her.

His stare left prickly heat behind before he said, "Anyway you want it is okay by me . . . Legs."

That mocking voice sent shivers up Sol's spine again, but she didn't change her bored expression. She, too, waited patiently for him to finish looking. Politeness seemed to be the meaning of the day. Soledad evidently met his approval for his arrogant body was on full alert, jutting out like a hunting hound.

At the thick, bobbing sight, another warm flush crawled up Sol's neck, but she shrugged the discomfort away. She set the wine bottle down hard enough to jolt the glasses that waited on the elegant table with its flimsy curved legs. She decided to ignore his reference to her own legs, but speaking of anatomy . . .

Damn, she had seen naked males before, perhaps none as large or as attentive as this specimen, but this wasn't a virgin experience. She'd paid for professional services several times in the past, although not here in the Dome. And sometimes she had paid for services in other places with a more adventuresome male species. Spacing took you to far regions and was a lonely profession, although sometimes not lonely enough.

Crowded ship quarters made for liaisons that could become a problem between shipmates of rank. Long ago, Sol had learned to never mix business with pleasure no matter the attraction. She had slipped only once. And it had been a long time since she had indulged her pleasure or been this attracted. Her sexual adventures were a matter of tension relief, not pleasure, and never with anyone who was dominant. This partner seemed different. Her heart skipped a beat then raced. And this time the results would be more than pleasure. She would leave with a miracle of life in her womb. Somehow, that fact made a world of difference, at least to her. Her partner didn't seem to care about giving up his precious sperm, he was patiently regarding her.

"I want a bath and a massage before . . . anything else." She glared at the man whom the fertility clinic's computer had selected as the perfect father of her child. And he did seem nearly so with his towering height. Again she felt uneasy at his dominance of the room, but she had asked that he be taller than her. Sol studied him further before deciding his unruly hair was a nice shade and suited him with its darkness. His ears were not overly large and lay close to his head. There were those stories about big ears meaning something else was also big. Sol swallowed a snort. She didn't think the size of ears had anything to do with sexual organs.

Suddenly, Sol noted that his expressive, lilting eyes twinkled with a mysterious wickedness—almost as if he'd read her amused thoughts. *Ha. Good luck with that, buddy. No one gets past my guard.* Thanks to her long military training, she had learned how to protect herself from overbearing males. But even then, in her dark past, she had witnessed a rape that she had been helpless to prevent. Never again would she be so hampered, so not in control. And, hopefully, that arrogant, superior look that most males used, as this one did to full advantage, grinning at her with his white teeth that oh so slightly overlapped in front, wouldn't be passed on to her son. Sol watched his lips move and tried not to stare.

"As you wish. One bath coming up." The man gave her a mocking half bow and flashed his firm butt in an arrogant stroll to the sunken marble tub that loomed just to the left of the red- and gold-draped bed. The handles and faucet glowed with the metal richness of false gold, too. But Sol knew that in these outlying settlements, real metal imports were too costly to be used as plumbing fixtures. Actually, most of the room's impressive furnishings were inexpensive imitations of actual ancient art. This part of the Dome seemed to be into an old world theme with the heavy brocade tapestries and large gilded mirrors set against decoratively carved plaster walls. Even the wall lighting flickered off the subtly painted frescos, as if using real candles for illumination. Sol's naked playmate should have looked silly in the elegant room, but he didn't. Rather, he looked as if he belonged, a muscled centurion of Old Rome who owned all the red and gold splendor and was used to living in it, just like he was at home with the luxury of running water. He called to Sol over his shoulder.

"Flowers or spice?" The weathered skin around those all-knowing eyes crinkled in laugh lines. He gave Sol a twisted grin. She suddenly noted silver strands scattered about in the hair at his temples. He was older than what she had first thought, and perhaps older than what she had specified, but by the gods, he was definitely libido lifting. Moisture pooled between her legs at the heated promise in his eyes. The man waited patiently for her answer, still looking as if he already knew what she would say.

"Huh?" Sol's voice sounded thick, and she swallowed against a tight throat.

"For the bath. Flowers or spice." He pointed to the cheap cherub-shaped dispensers of liquid soap. His expressive full lips barely suppressed a smirk. She felt like slapping him.

"Oh. Spice." Sol was still trying to figure out how this guy fit into the idea of a paid pleasure treat. His long body was toned and fit; nothing like how she remembered a pampered sex toy looked when last she visited the Straits ages ago. Oh, she'd expected him to be good looking but more . . . soft . . .

and not so decidedly male. Not that she was threatened by him, she told herself. Men seldom posed a threat to her. The ones that tried never lasted long.

"Do you need help undressing?" The man now stood at her shoulder, then slipped behind her so close that Sol felt the heat of his words breathed on her neck. And he deliberately exhaled low, warm breaths. Delicate shivers slipped through Sol, tickling her stomach. One of his heavy arms curved around her middle. Her pulse leaped. He curled her closer. She grabbed his broad wrist and stopped his advance. For the moment, she just held his wide wrist bones in her two hands, not knowing why she had stopped him other than he was taking the lead. And going too fast.

Arrogantly, he ignored her hint, and on another low exhale, he slowly drew Sol back inch by inch until she rested full against his length. She felt him flush to her back, every damned hot inch of him. She felt him even through her leather uniform. But more than the sexual heat, unexplained comfort surrounded her within his rough embrace. Such serene pleasure flowed from him that her pulse throbbed as if her blood answered a call from him.

Sol closed her eyes, dropped her head back against his shoulder and surrendered to the pleasure of just being held, confident in the knowledge that she was safe, protected...

What? Sol jerked awake. Whatever was she thinking? Where had she gotten the idea that she could trust this stranger? Soledad Scott allowed no one to stand so close behind her, to hold her in such a submissive posture. She didn't know this man, despite his distracting strength. And she sure as hell didn't trust him. She wanted his sperm and nothing else.

With a practiced dark scowl, she spun her body at right angles to his loose-limbed stance, but he still loomed too close. Then a funny thing happened. As if he knew she didn't want the closeness, he dropped his arm and took a deliberate step back. Some of the stiffness went out of her, but she inexplicably missed his heat, the security of his touch. He regarded her with calm eyes, waited for her to make the next move. Sol noticed that his body's naked skin glistened tight and smooth except for where a series of odd black and white scars marked his ribs and curled around his right bicep. She stared at them thinking she should know what they meant. Oddly they looked like tattoos, a distinct pattern of diamonds and stars spaced and shaped like they meant something. But her head spun when she tried to think. She couldn't quite focus. *Must be the damned drugs.* She had drawn a strange playmate, but she couldn't complain. He still waited patiently with that noncommittal look on his compelling features.

Drawn by that serene gaze, Sol leaned in closer and inhaled more of the scent of cedar woods coming off his heated skin. For a moment, she again lost coherent thought amid the rush of responding hormones. He coughed or spoke.

Sol shook her head free of clouded thoughts in time to hear him repeat his question, something regarding help in undressing. She said, "Yes," at the same time she shook her head no.

Those odd eyes laughed, the crinkles deepening around them at her confusion. He slipped behind her again and reached around for the zipper on her one piece jumpsuit.

Then he hesitated, fingertips poised on the tab. "Yes or no?" he whispered near her ear, his voice husky. He waited for her to speak. Such a gentleman.

Again, Sol felt his expelled breath warm on her neck. She caught the hint of alcohol and the sharp bite of something darker, richer; such a definite masculine odor. She shivered as if with a chill, although the room was fast becoming hot—way too hot. Not daring to trust her voice to remain steady, and not daring to do more, she nodded yes, the back of her head thumping his chin. With her head tilted to the side and further back, Sol neatly fit under his jaw, a rare experience for her. The man was tall, just the perfect height to put . . .

No, she told herself, don't go there—yet. She leaned away and quickly glanced up at his eyes. No surprise. He was watching her intently, the slanted corners of his eyes looking all the more alien and dangerous.

Suddenly, the dark ring in those pale blue irises widened. Sol swore she saw that strange mist swirl in them again before he deftly lowered his lashes. His fingertips lightly brushed against the hollow of her throat before he began the slow slide of her zipper down her front. Her heart rate notched higher when his fingers curved against her skin as if protecting her from the jagged teeth. All noise grew exaggerated in the quiet. The slithering rasp of her zipper was almost as loud as her ragged breathing. Her skin grew overly sensitive, too. His touch burned. His knuckles grazed between her breasts, rough fingertips rubbing against the tender skin. Sparks jumped. Static electricity—or something more?

Sol grabbed his hand, stopping her zipper just below her navel. After a moment, and with that calculating steady look, the man moved the zipper an inch farther down. His teasing, one-sided grin mocked her. She refused to respond with anything other than a glare. Again, another inch exposed and that deliberate brush of knuckles against her belly sent sizzling ripples across her skin, a sensation that she felt all the way down to the juncture between her legs. More moisture gathered there and throbbed.

Yeah, she was ready for fertilization. *Ripe.* Her body was at any rate; her reasoning mind just refused to cooperate. But there should be something more to this miracle of life than just a paid business arrangement. Perhaps she was feeling more hormones than anything else. She felt lost and out of control. She needed a distraction.

"Music," Sol gasped, as if asking for a life preserver.

A deep frown marred the man's forehead. His dark brows arched, "Music?" he echoed. He sounded dumb, perhaps as dumb as she felt.

"Yes, we need music," Sol stated with a series of stupid nods. She needed more time to think. Something didn't fit here, but she couldn't put her finger on the problem. After weeks of being pumped full of repressed hormones, she wasn't thinking like a levelheaded galactic ship's captain.

"We do?" The man still stared at her with a wrinkled brow and wondering gaze. His sex continued to bob and twitch at her. Sol's mouth went dry. She had a hard time speaking.

"Yeah. Something soft."

"Oh, something *romantic.*" He exaggerated the word, nodded and grinned again, a peepshow of those tweaked white teeth. Sol felt like smacking those curved lips. The man managed to irritate her with that superior expression. And why, in this age of perfection and the business he was in, didn't he have those imperfect bottom teeth straightened? His lips twitched again, and she found herself watching his mouth for another glimpse of those maddening teeth. It was safer watching his mouth than looking between his legs.

"It doesn't have to be sappy," she snapped. "I just want to relax."

"Sure, Legs." A corner of his mouth lifted, but not enough. No teeth were exposed. Sol couldn't help watching. She flinched at his next words. "Anything the lady with the great legs wants, she gets."

With another flash of that firm butt, he strode across the room and tuned the sound system, disguised as a Grecian vase, to a stringed melody, then said "No?" to her deepened scowl. A high-pitched, Calaxian mating tune was turned on next, then with raised brows that defied her, he announced with a firm nod, "This is perfect," to a vibrating drum beat and a flirtatious guitar rhythm that sounded vaguely familiar to Sol. After a few minutes, she realized it was *Bolero*, ancient Earth music that fit twentieth century times better than that of ancient Rome. Perhaps he thought the sultry music would be perfect for mating.

Mating—her heart thumped again.

"Fine." Sol sighed, tired of the delaying tactics. She had to get on with this. Her hands itched to touch him. The music played on, caressing her nerves more than she had anticipated. The rhythmic drum beat across her chest with compelling notes. Her nipples tightened and puckered into little points against the material of her suit. *Hormones, again.*

Slowly, the naked man strolled back toward her, almost like a cat balancing on the balls of his feet. Sol realized that he wasn't dancing as much as hypnotizing her with his artless grace. And he knew she watched him while he studied her with that intelligent speculation in his eyes. But he was looking at her face, at her eyes, not at her breasts. Maybe he did have a brain to go along with all that muscle. Despite being a paid arrangement, Sol didn't expect a *wham, bam, thank you, ma'am* military sexual release from him. His studious stare hinted at deeper qualities. She anticipated the chance to experience some of those *deeper* ones.

And for a large man, he moved smoothly, with a natural acceptance of himself. Sol watched the spread of healthy muscles tensing and flexing across his chest as he glided nearer. She was sure he was putting a little extra into his movement just for her benefit. *Arrogant male*. But his brilliant gaze stayed fixed on her face. His fists tightened. That muscle jumped again in his jaw. He wasn't as relaxed as he wanted Sol to think. That thought pleased her. Sol sucked in a breath and unconsciously, bit her lower lip.

"Ahhh," he murmured, and slipped behind her again, that one arm curved around her waist inside her gaping uniform, brushing her exposed skin with the barest touch. And, just as before, his breathing tickled her neck and gave her goose bumps. He curled over her in a looming, dark presence.

He's dangerous, truly dangerous. The sudden insight surprised her, and Sol fought against old training drills of grabbing his arm and flipping him over her shoulder. She realized that here was as dangerous a man as she had ever met, but he had made no threatening moves on her. She shouldn't be afraid of him. He just made her heart flutter with attraction, right?

He swiftly found her jumpsuit's zipper again. And with the stealthy movements of a cat's paw, he unzipped her uniform the rest of the way to the bottom. The suddenness stole Sol's breath. When she caught it again, her rapid intakes raised and lowered her chest. She was so used to being in control, so why did she let this man take the lead and steal her defenses? Well, she wouldn't give up so easily. After all, she was the one in control—or was she? The man gave a quiet chuckle that vibrated through Sol's back to her belly. Still behind her, he slipped hard, calloused palms inside her one piece regimentals. He lightly traced his fingertips across her neck and down the center of her chest, not touching her breasts that ached so for his touch. His fingertips flattened to solid palms. His inquisitive hands left a wide square of heat on her flesh that followed in the wake of their path to her waist. He ventured lower. Sol shivered. Again, that sudden loss of control frightened her. As if he felt and knew her tension, her playmate moved his palms back up in a slow, delicious slide of skin against skin. Then, without a pause, his palms cupped her breasts, cradling them as if weighing their size. Sol wasn't overly endowed and held her breath, feeling uncertain. She breathed out when he hummed that pleased sound again. Then she tensed. Surely she didn't care if her body pleased him. Did she? She was in control.

In defiance, Sol pushed back against him. His quickened breathing sounded ragged. The heated breaths fanned her ear. Sol realized she was now inhaling and exhaling in time with him. Not a good sign of control. She started to lean away. He stopped her with just a slight tightening of his arms, then he flicked the tips of her nipples with his thumbs. Sol gasped.

He ignored her, pressed her tighter against his front and smoothed his palms back down her sides. As he caressed her flat abdomen again, his groan actually sounded as if he approved of her lack of underwear. Sol trembled under the vibrations of his voice. The rough sound tickled her ear. She didn't understand the language he spoke, the curses he muttered. And when had she let her head fall back against his shoulder so submissively?

In a daze, she turned her head closer to his chin. Her lips brushed his neck. His skin tasted of salty male sweat. He shuddered and caressed her breasts again. He touched her so freely, as if he had the right to do so. She should stop him. She knew she should. They were going too fast, things could get quickly out of hand. She wasn't ready for this, but she didn't want him to stop.

His soothing circles on her stomach continued, the pads of his fingers finding all of Sol's sensitive spots, almost as if he read her mind. *Yeah, right there. Do that again. Yeah, that's it. Ahhh, now lower.* He felt perfect—perhaps too perfect.

Sol wondered, suddenly, if she had made a mistake, a very big mistake. This man was too sure of himself, taking such control and going much too fast.

She opened her mouth to protest, but his wonderful hands moved lower still, slipped over her hipbones, mesmerizing with their slow circling caresses until Sol no longer cared what she thought or who controlled whom. Thoughts weren't important; neither was control. She wasn't captain here. She didn't need to be in charge, didn't need to make decisions. She only wanted to feel his smooth, soothing touch.

Drowsy, hypnotic warmth spread over Soledad with the magical slide of his skin against hers. The movement of his rough palms against her flesh and the thrust of his jutting hard member between her butt cheeks made her knees weak. Even through her tough red leathers, she felt his heat, the draw of his body. Her officer's uniform gaped open to his hands. Sol knew her attraction to him was due largely to the enhancement drug she had taken earlier and to her increased hormones, but oh, it felt so good just to feel that wonderful male strength in his touch.

His palms slid up and over her pouting nipples. She almost moaned with the yearning pain they left behind. Faintly, she heard him hiss between his teeth. She felt his chest rise with an inhale then he moved lower on her abdomen, sliding his fingers up and down, to nearly where she wanted them between her legs, before he jerked to a stop. He tensed and spread his fingers over her bare mound. He patted then cupped her tightly, one finger slipping on her wetness.

"You have no pubic hair," he stated, as if the fact was of monumental importance.

"Can't be a spacer captain with hair," Sol murmured, and rolled her head back and forth under his chin. She arched into his fingers. He moved them up her belly, away from her need, so she pushed her butt back into him, wanting to feel his arousal probing against her again.

With a grunt, he held himself away then lifted a handful of her hair in his other fist. His tight grip was just short of being painful, but it felt so erotic. How sick was that? She was clearly not herself, not in control, but for once, she didn't care.

"What about this?" He shook his fistful of red hair, his

voice raw.

A fissure of annoyance erupted within Sol. Impatient to get on with her *business,* she twisted around and glared at him. "I had it enhanced—just for you. For just this moment. Okay?"

The color and texture of her hair was natural. It had just been encouraged to grow rapidly while the doctors had reversed the effects of space command, but her pubic hair had been permanently removed years ago. She'd had no time for personal demands when fighting the Guild's wars. Hygiene cups that took care of the problems of elimination through her battle suit fit better on naked skin. Monthly menses were no problem since she was sterile while serving as a captain in space. Now, her body was a different animal, making demands of its own, and she had no time or patience for twenty questions. This night was all she had paid for. An awful thought occurred to her. She wanted more time. She wanted to make her partner feel as he was making her feel. *Need* shook her with greedy claws. Damn *him* for making her want more than one night, even for a moment.

A serious frown wrinkled the man's stern features, and his speculative eyes went stone-cold for just a moment. In that instant, he looked more alien than human. Sol lost her breath at the dangerous, icy glint that flashed in those blue eyes. Then, before she lost her nerve and complete control of the situation, she reached between his legs. She gripped his balls. He tensed at her touch and hissed a breath. She felt his loss of control and wanted him even more excited. She was the one paying for this so she should be the one calling the shots, so to speak. Under her hands, the man stood rigid, shocked immobile. She gently cupped his turgid length in her palms and caressed his shaft up and down. He lengthened even further under her palms. His eyes closed halfway, dark lashes shadowing his cheeks. The flickering light played off the planes of his face, and Sol's breath caught on the unexpected alien beauty of him. She had little experience with pleasuring men. Normally she took her pleasure where she found it, a quick lay to scratch the itch. This time, however, for some reason she wanted to please her partner. She just wasn't sure how to go about it since she had never taken much time in preliminaries.

Her toy obligingly grunted again when she touched the tip of his cock, and he made no move to stop her so her touch must please him. She marveled at the silky moisture that leaked to her fingers from the dip in the rounded knob, then she proceeded on, trailing light touches down his length and up his stomach, down his legs and up the insides of his thighs. Such perfect satiny skin covered his upper thighs, so smooth, so taut. Sol moved her fingers gently back over the thick head of his cock, not believing that such power could feel so soft and yet be so hard at the same time. She played over that drop of moisture that gathered, twirled the wetness around the thick circle. Her playmate sucked in another quick breath and muttered a foreign curse. His slitted eyes had taken on a dazed look and no longer swirled with secrets.

Boldly, Sol stroked down his shaft, caressing the line under it, and then rubbing his hardened balls. They tightened even more, became heavier at her touch. She squeezed them, and her playmate hissed again, like an angry cat.

Sol grinned. His swollen jewels contained just what she wanted, what she had paid for. They felt loaded, ready. Just behind them, between his butt cheeks, a fleshy rose puckered under her fingertips. Bravely, she probed that sensitive area, too. He groaned again, and tightened his grip on her upper arms. The tight pressure of his long fingers would no doubt leave marks, but she didn't care. She wanted him excited. Wickedly, she pressed her fingertip deeper against his pursed opening to darker pleasures, slipped it the barest fraction inside.

"*Jesu!*" the man sputtered and grabbed her wrists. Her bones ground under his tight grip. Breathing hoarsely, he curved into her, stared at her blindly, then swallowed. He waited a moment then shook his head as if to clear it before he whispered, "No. Don't stop now."

Without another word, he guided her fingers back up and down his shaft. His dark lashes closed over his burning gaze, and he curled his body even closer into hers. Sol felt almost sheltered in his looming heat. His spicy arousal surrounded her with his warm scent. For a moment, she was lost in it, like that of the headiest of incense. She shook her own head free of such thoughts. She had control now, though how they both remained standing was a miracle.

She held the length of him in her two hands and grinned at the sight under her caresses. He was unspeakably lovely and surely ready. Suddenly, she realized that she had never held a man this thick—or this hard—before, as if he were ready to spill at any moment. He was beautifully male, although it really wasn't necessary for him to be beautiful. All she needed was his perfect sperm.

But for some reason, Sol wanted this meeting of the sexes to be special. If everything went as planned, this coupling would create the child she wanted; a child she had put off having for years. And a child from this male would be beautiful, she knew it, just as the computer matched data knew it. She caressed him again, and he arched under her touch. He muttered something and tossed his head from side to side, as if saying no—as if he knew what she was thinking. Through a sparkling gaze, Sol noted the little beads of sweat that shone on the man's full upper lip—his wide, sensuous lips that leaned so close to her own. Further up, his high forehead gleamed, and under the tight skin, thick veins pulsed with life. Beneath his closed eyelids and the broad fan of his dark lashes, she could see his eyes rove restlessly back and forth. A long muscle jumped and flexed in his jaw. Such raw male strength called to Soledad as much as an aphrodisiac could. Under her palm, she felt a surging vein throb in his penis. Power, lots of power, waiting just for her taking. Now was a good time for the finish.

She stood on tiptoe and whispered, "Come to bed."

The man's eyes snapped open. For a moment, his startled gaze stared blankly down at her. Then he cocked his head to one side, took a deep breath, and stopped the movement of her hands with his. His lips curved weakly, one side tweaked higher than the other, mocking her.

"What about your bath?" His husky voice rasped like a harsh rub over week-long whiskers. She couldn't believe that he'd regained his control this quickly. Just who was he?

"It'll wait." Sol drew him closer to the bed until the back of her legs touched the thick brocade spread. She mustn't lose control to him again.

"No." He stepped back from her, took her hand and led her back toward the tub. "I want you to have your bath—and massage." That teasing corner of his mouth lifted, but only a hint of those endearing bottom teeth showed. "And I want to give them to you, Legs."

With that, he swept her up into his arms, which was no mean feat. Sol wasn't a lightweight. Indeed, she had boxed in middleweight division on Rigel Three. No one had carried her anywhere since she was a babe.

Before she got over that wonder, he eased her down next to the tub, letting her body rub his in a deliberately slow, sensuous slide. She felt his cock dance along her leg. He closed his eyes again but only for a moment. Sol delighted in the delicious feel of such hot strength against her body. Her hormones were continuing to clamor, but, when her toes touched the floor, her knees buckled. She clung to her treat's forearms like some fainthearted civilian female instead of a galactic warship captain. He solemnly held her gaze, as if he knew her thoughts and delighted in her reactions. Just who was he to know her so well?

Two

With a light slap of his palm against the fake Italian plaster wall, the candlelight dimmed even further, enhancing the shadows that flickered and glowed. *Bolero* still drummed on, probably set to loop over and over. For some reason, the music urged Sol to hurry before she lost her nerve. And, as if he knew her thoughts, the man quickly stripped Sol's shoulders free of her suit and its shoulder-beribboned gear. He didn't take time to ogle her exposed breasts. Without a word, he knelt between her legs and undid the many buckles on her military boots. With a pinch to her heel, he lifted each foot to strip the boot and free her uniform.

Why hadn't she shopped for *civi* clothes? She didn't know. She also didn't know if the man purposely brushed his head against her bare pelvic area or if it was an accident, but the silky glide of his cool hair against her nakedness sent shivers dancing over her. Breathing became a short commodity. Her skin felt stretched far too tightly. Uncontrolled tremors shook her. She couldn't stop the internal jitters and clamped her teeth together, hoping he wouldn't notice her trembling. He did.

"Cold?" he glanced up with a serious look. His slanted eyes narrowed almost to slits, and he seemed unduly concerned for her comfort. His expelled breath puffed warmly against her thighs—so near. Gooseflesh followed.

"No, I'm not cold." Sol muttered, looking down at his proximity to her intimate parts. His mouth moved so close to her that she felt his warm breath. Sol clenched her fists and fought an uncommon giddiness that overcame her normal staid composure. *Remember you are—were—a Guild warship captain*, she reminded herself. The man grunted and stood up. Sol hid her disappointment.

"Good. But I'll have you even warmer in just a moment." With that, he guided Sol into the steaming tub with an impersonal hand cupped under each of her elbows, just like a gentleman. She stifled the next nervous giggle that threatened to escape.

Him—a gentleman, with his large, brooding dark looks promising the hottest of sexual nights? Besides, chivalrous knights of old didn't run around naked. Or perhaps, they did. This one would have fit right in the way he carefully ushered her into the warmth of the bath. You would think she was someone's fragile treasure by the way he handled her. Good gods above, no one except her sister and her dearest friend cared that much about her.

An unexpected mist blurred Sol's vision, and she snorted. *Damned hormones, again.* With his insistent touch gentle on her shoulders, the man pushed her down until the bubbles crept up to her chin.

In their absence, the bath had shut off automatically when the water reached the sensor in the top of the tub. Tralarie plumbing technology rated among the top few in the Straits, although a lot of customers in the other pleasure houses didn't rank getting wet as one of their sought after pleasures. What wild sexual exploits had this room witnessed in its past? Sol's thoughts swirled.

"Here. Drink your wine." Her pleasure toy shoved a stemmed, silver-etched crystal glass into her hand. Sol took a quick gulp before he tapped his glass to hers from where he sat on the tub's edge.

"To new experiences," he toasted before swallowing a sip. He closed his eyes in appreciation. In a daze, Sol followed the shallow movement of his throat, such a handsome thick throat on such handsome, thick shoulders. Why would he say to new experiences? Sex wasn't new. But she was experiencing new ones with him most assuredly. He had such lovely flat nipples resting among his chest hair, she noted absently. A rosy flush crept up from his chest to cover his face, and she knew he had caught her stare. But Sol couldn't take her eyes from him. With three deep swallows, he finished the rest of his wine in a quick flourish not doing justice to the delicate flavor. Then he watched Sol sip hers, his insolent, tilted gaze never leaving her face except to follow the line of her throat as she swallowed. Sexual heat radiated from his intense look. Soledad barely tasted the wine.

"They don't charge enough for you." The muttered words escaped before Sol knew she had spoken her thought aloud.

"Pardon?" His puzzled stare jerked from her lips to her eyes. What he saw there must have inspired him because he reached out for her with the quickness of a snake's strike. What did he intend? She had to regain control of the situation. Sol scooted backward, splashing water over the side of the tub. "Forget it," she waved her hand, scattering water droplets. *Hormones, again.* She wasn't afraid of him. Good gods, she wasn't some timid church mouse. Look at the size of her hands, for gods' sakes. Those large, scarred hands with their chewed cuticles had handled weapons of war, of mass destruction. Thankfully, the man settled back with his inscrutable brooding look.

After a few moments and with a resigned sigh, followed by another at the water's soothing warmth, Sol relaxed against the curvature of the tub. She felt too tired and too old for this dance of seduction. She watched her playmate through narrowed eyes. Maybe she'd just order him to service her, lick her like an ice treat before filling her aching core with what she craved. She ignored the shiver that raced through her at the thought of his mouth against her flesh. After all, that's what he was being paid for. She closed her eyes.

The heady smell of cinnamon drifted in the spicy bubbles that floated under Sol's chin. The scent reminded her of Te'angel's cookies. Sol hum'mphed a non-captain-like sound and blew the bubbles away—right into the man's face. What?

Her sex toy was opposite her. *In the tub with her.* When had that happened? His deep chuckle startled Sol. The man not only moved with silent animallike grace, but he growled like a jungle cat, too. The vibrations of his low laugh through the water sent shivers up her back. Sol suddenly wondered if she could make him purr in sexual delight. Now, where had that thought come from? And why did she care if he enjoyed himself or not?

Water sloshed. The man edged closer, loomed over her. Overwhelmed her. *Damn it.* She was the paying customer, the one in control. She wasn't ready yet. She raised her hands to stop him, push him away, but beneath her fingertips, solid, wet strength rippled. Smooth shoulders slipped ever so nicely under her touch. Comforting warmth spread, grew into sexual pulsations between Sol's legs. Without a word, he lightly traced the tips of his fingers up and down her sides from under her armpits to her hips then back between her breasts and across the shallow hollow of her belly. He gave an appreciative sigh and repeated the motion until Sol finally relaxed—but not for long. With an experienced touch, her playmate fanned her nipples in a teasing air caress that had her arching into his palms. On a growl, he cupped her breasts and thumbed her hardened nipples before he licked them into the hot core of his mouth. *Ahhh.* Sol's mind fought to accept the intimate touch of a stranger's heat and his tongue against her flesh. Always before, she had only found a release never the pleasure this partner gave. As if he knew this, he swept his mouth over her and sucked heavily on her mouth. Sol lost what little breath she could draw in. Her mind shattered, her control vanished. He left her lips and bit her sensitive neck and then moved lower. In the background, Sol heard water draining from the tub. With each inch of her bare skin that was revealed, her toy laved more of his attention on the exposed area. He expelled a sigh at her navel then slipped further down her stomach, doing his soothing, circling thing with his tongue following his hands.

Finally, he reached the thickened lips between her legs. He breathed on her. Sol cried out and raised her hips. She wept there for his touch. He obliged her and scooped her up to his mouth. With his wide hands cupped under her hips, he lifted her—then he licked. One solid tongue lick full on her flesh. On a cry, Sol arched against his mouth. Without a word, he plunged inside. *Velvet.* His tongue was a velvet whip teasing the walls of her sex, urging her to rise up then settle back, rise up, fall back. But he only gave her a taste of what she craved. Sol wanted more, a deeper penetration. She twisted against his mouth. As if he knew her thought, the man raised his head, and again without speaking a word, he rose back over her. With one long finger sliding up and down her slit then over her hard knot of pleasure, he continued seducing her.

"Tell me what you want, Captain."

Sol moaned and writhed with the wanting. *In—in—put it in!* She wanted to shout at him, but she kept her eyes tightly closed, needing only the sensation to continue. Sol felt his breath hot on her neck. She didn't have to see, didn't want to know, who made her feel this good, this alive. The teasing of his clever fingers stopped. Sol gasped in disappointment.

"Why did you leave spacing?" The question was whispered softly as his lips brushed her neck. The man rose but still curved over her, his mouth next to her ear. His hand crept just up from where she wanted to feel his fingers. He touched the tip of one nipple, as if letting her know he was still there. As if Sol could forget the thick promise that loomed just out of reach. She felt him throbbing against her thigh. "Why?" he repeated."

"Forced retirement. The Guild said I was too old to captain." Sol gave a painful laugh that ended in a near sob, and she wondered why she'd answered his question when all she wanted was for him to move his damned finger—or something better—back into her ache.

With a noticeable flinch, the man hesitated for a moment before he suddenly pulled her out of the empty tub, his strong arms under her butt.

"What are you doing?" she yelped.

"I'm taking you to bed for your massage."

"I don't want a massage."

"You did before."

"Well, I don't now. For gods' sake, finish what you started!"

He paused, then flashed that infuriating crooked grin down at her. His strange eyes twinkled with wicked intent. "And what do you want me to do, my captain?"

Sol bristled at his use of her title. How dare he? She'd rather he stuck to calling her *Legs*. Her vision narrowed, and she snapped, "You know what I want."

"Nope, I don't. You tell me." He set Sol on her feet but held her close, sheltering her in a big towel under his arm. He patted and wrapped her gently like a babe. Then, holding her gaze, he slowly licked his finger and slid that wonderfully thick appendage down her belly and back into her so quickly that she moaned and grabbed his wrist. His hard mouth swallowed the sound of her cry, and he cradled her against his chest. He fought her mouth in a fierce kiss. Sol struggled at first, and then she clung to his lips—lips that grew surprisingly soft and warm, moving over hers in a gentle play of enticement before sliding along her jaw.

"Lick me. Lick my face and taste your sweetness." His wicked whisper compelled her to do just as he ordered. The taste of her arousal burned Sol. It urged her to press herself flush against him. She fisted her hand in the silkiness of his hair, closed her eyes and gave herself up to his treatment when he slipped down to kneel at her feet. And her playmate was thorough, not one bit of her escaped his reach. Never knowing how they ended up on the bed, Sol was drifting in a red haze when he nipped her shoulder just hard enough to get her attention. At her frown, he winked at her and began again.

Sol could tell he was experienced at this, and what she had admitted before, about him being worth a whole lot more money, was apparent in the way he applied his talents—stroking, kneading, licking, nibbling and caressing her, giving and never taking. He was clearly one of the Pleasure Dome's best.

She smothered a frustrated scream. Would he never give her what she wanted? Again, her toy played between her thighs, kissed the tender skin on the inside her legs and licked ever closer to her greater throbbing need. But he was too slow! Much too slow, when he had been moving much too fast before. Sol felt as if she were burning up with the waiting. She fisted the sheets in her palms and pulled at them, but smothered her cries. Finally, after moments of excruciating but tantalizing delay filled with his teasing caresses, he spread her wide. He looked up at her face, deep into her eyes, his sparkling gaze holding hers. Then, without breaking eye contact, he kissed her naked apex with his opened mouth.

When Sol sucked in a much needed breath, he pushed his tongue deep into her aching core and twisted inside her. She screamed. With that single stroke, Sol came, arching up and crying out in muscle-clenching aftermath. Just one thrust of his velvet tongue inside her, and her toy had given her a better release than she had ever experienced. Seizures were still echoing through her body when he poured warm oil on her belly and settled both his big hands in the pool. He spread the oil over her, up her belly and down into the still quivering sex folds of skin. The lubricant heated further on contact, heightening and lengthening the pulsing aftereffects of her orgasm. Never had she felt like this. Would he never finish with her?

Sol swallowed a moan but refused to move away from his delightful touch. She watched him through heavy, narrow-slit eyelids, unable to open her eyes further. She was no closer to reaching her goal of becoming a mother, but from the look of things, her toy still meant to oblige. He was beautiful in full sexual rut. His pale eyes glittered, and sweat glistened over his body, exposing the hills and valleys of curving strength. His sex jutted out like a twitching flag pole, but he ignored it, all the while massaging the oil in a professional, impersonal manner. Sol noted the way that long muscle in his jaw flexed and clenched again. His attentive sex bobbed and jerked between his legs as if seeking her. But here was a man who controlled himself.

And ever the attentive playmate and still ignoring his body's demands, the man dipped his thick finger back between her legs and rubbed soothing moisture in the heated cracks of her sex. He rolled the hard nub of pleasure between his fingers and ignored Sol's repeated gasps. There, between the heavy engorged lips of her vulva, he slipped his finger inside for just the barest moment, thrust and released—just enough to bring her back to the point of arching into his hand. Experienced, he played her like a fine instrument.

Sol could almost feel the pride in his husky voice when he asked, "More, my captain?" Those dark brows rose, and a line of sweat rolled down the side of his face.

She watched it drop off his rigid jaw and nodded, "More. I want what I've paid for." She looked pointedly between his legs and almost missed his puzzled frown.

"Ahhh. You want this?" He rose up on his knees and cupped himself, holding balls and thickened shaft up for her. He loomed dark and shadowy over her. Sol nodded at the awesome sight between his legs, mute to say another word.

"Well. Your wish is my command, Captain."

He gave that faint, one-sided grin and eased down next to her, barely dipping the bed, barely touching her with his heat. *Funny how she felt every sensation.* It felt as if he was touching all of her from the inside out.

"Don't call me captain. Just give it to me." Sol reached for him, and he let her caress him, noticeable light shivers following her hand's path across his skin—light against the dark.

"I'll call you anything I want in this room, Legs." His mocking lips twisted, but his heavy-lidded gaze darkened, grew more heated. "Now, say please." His fingers twitched over Sol before slipping inside and touching overly sensitive walls. She gasped.

"What?" Sol was trying hard to follow the conversation but he was doing such nice things to her slit again. He rolled the hard knot of her pleasure lightly between his fingers then suddenly pinched. She moaned. Delicious sensations renewed and raced through her. They demanded more attention. He didn't move. She could have screamed. This time she wanted more.

"Say please." He had stopped the movement of his hand but still cupped her sex. His fingers drummed a teasing rhythm against her swollen lips. "Captain, you do know that six letter word that polite people use?" He dipped his head and gazed up at her through his dark lashes.

"I'm not polite, in case you haven't noticed." Sol arched into his touch. Again he wiggled his finger inside her. Her thighs clenched, and her hips came clear off the mattress.

The man groaned and nuzzled her throat. His lips tickled her neck. "Believe me, I've noticed, Captain." He smiled and faint dimples appeared in his cheeks. "But I like you anyway." He kept the pressure on between her legs, sliding his long fingers in and out. Sol's cheeks heated, hearing the slick noise they made.

"It's not required that you like me," Sol muttered into the curve of his shoulder. She opened her mouth and licked his skin. He shivered. His neck tasted of salt; his scent was a heady enticement of fully aroused male.

"Ahhh," he breathed under her tongue. "Only fuck you, huh?" His wicked whisper tickled her ear.

"Yeah. Only that." Sol nearly whispered the words back and wondered why they were speaking so softly, then she didn't care about anything but him. Even his masculine voice tugged at her. His fingers left her heat, but before she voiced her disappointment, he chuckled to her darkly.

"Well, I can do that. I can fuck you." He cupped her hip and slid just the tip of himself into her throbbing flesh. God, just that thick bit felt so good. Sol's muscles tightened. Her head dropped back—but he withdrew. His absence left her cold, bereft.

"Now, say please for me," he murmured against the hollow of her throat.

Moist chills followed in the heat of his lips' wake. He held himself poised. Sol trembled, but noted that he was shaking in her arms as badly as she. "Okay, please. Damn you. Please— please—*please!*" The last "please" came out in a shout that coincided with his fierce lunge. Such solid, hot strength filled her, moved thickly against her inner walls. He groaned and ground himself deeper. Sol lost her breath. He gave it back in a fierce kiss that left her breathless . . . again.

And again, she heard a foreign curse before he spoke in universal. "Take it all, Captain," he muttered, plunging and retreating, his muscles straining under his control. Sol clawed his broad back, drew him closer to her core. She gripped his wide hipbones and pulled him tighter against her. Never had she felt anything this wild, this good; never had she experienced the hot dance of torrid sex this flawlessly, this beautifully. They moved in a perfect waltz of uncontrolled intercourse—on and on they went throughout the night. Gods, she had to find out what drug the chemist had put in the wine.

Sol experimented that night with sexual pleasures and positions she had never imagined, some that she knew had to be illegal if not by law then by nature. She had never felt so alive, so aware of everything—every scent, every touch, and every sound. They imprinted themselves on her memory like nothing had ever before. And nothing should ever be that good. If it was due only to the drug and hormones, then why did the same act feel even better in the morning, when she awakened sober to find her treat working at her pleasure again?

"Come on, give it up, Captain. Give it to me," the man panted into her ear. He raised her hips with his big hands, spread her wide and slid his thick shaft in and out. He fondled and licked the nipples of both her breasts before nipping one with a bite from crooked bottom teeth that was just shy of being painful. Her playmate claimed her so neatly, so fully, that finally, Sol did give it up again with a scream that echoed a banging on their door.

"Commander! Commander Merriweather, open up! There has been a terrible mistake!"

Three

Calm blue eyes, with their swirling, slanted secrets, regarded Sol for several moments amid the urgent pounding before her companion of the night wrapped a sheet around his middle and stalked to the door. He jerked it open and growled, "What?" at the startled doorman.

"I'm most terribly sorry, Commander, but there has been a mistake with your partner." With a backward hand wave, the bumbling man dressed in a red-lettered Dome uniform, indicated a well-endowed blonde that stood behind him. "Elise was your partner for last night." The blonde gave her fingers a twittering wiggle. Sol's companion grunted his reply.

"Well, I'm satisfied with the one I got." His shoulders filled the doorway, loomed over the Dome's employee.

"But . . . but . . . she's not even one of ours." The bellman's voice fairly squeaked.

"I. Don't. Care."

By this time, Soledad, her mind spinning with terrible possibilities, had jerked on her one piece regimentals. *Shit— shit—shit,* she mumbled to herself. She knew with awful certainty what had happened. *Damned wormhole dyslexia.* This was the last time she would trust it without more questioning, even if meant asking a passing stranger. With her boots in hand, she shoved past her playmate, only to have him grab her by the upper arm. His grip was strong but not painfully so. It had been tighter last night. Even his voice had been rougher. It echoed lightly now in playfulness.

"And just where do you think you're going?"

"Me? I've gotten what I came for. I'm leaving." Sol flashed what she hoped was a convincing grin, twisted her arm, and again tried to get out the door. She was sore between her legs, and her stomach was doing back flips. *Too late now, stupid, stupid, stupid.*

"Well, I haven't finished with you yet, Captain," the man clung to her arm, his warm eyes hopeful.

"Oh, may the gods preserve us! Captain Scott." The doorman finally recognized Sol. "I am so terribly sorry, sir. I knew my robot bellhop was malfunctioning. He must have taken you to the wrong room—to Commander Merriweather's room. How can I ever apologize to you?"

The name finally registered with her. Merriweather. Sol's mouth fell open but nothing came out. In shock, she stared at her playmate. She finally understood the identity of her sexual toy. Rage choked her. She couldn't look at him. With a mute headshake, she jerked her arm lose from Merriweather and scooted past the doorman. But before she got out the door, the commander called after her. He had no idea that she wanted nothing better than to skewer him. His rough voice still teased.

"Wait. I can't see that an apology is necessary. I don't know about the captain, but I'm satisfied. More than satisfied." Merriweather turned and gave Sol that wicked grin that exposed just the tips of his bottom teeth. Why had she thought them endearing earlier? He chuckled, "I think she is, too. Right, darlin'?" She ignored the pleading that lay in his pale eyes.

"Yes . . . well, I must be going. I've a thousand things to do." Sol spit the words from between tight lips and dodged the next lunge Merriweather made toward her. She skittered down the hall's slick floors and looked back only once. If she stayed much longer, she'd kill the man who was responsible for the best sex she'd ever experienced—and who was indirectly responsible for her forced retirement. God, help her, she hoped he hadn't also fathered her child.

The last thing she saw was the room's door latch that snagged the sheet that the commander had wrapped around himself when he ran out the door after her. The handle stripped him neatly. The giggling blonde stopped laughing at the naked sight of what she had missed and turned a deep frown on the doorman, who was attempting to stop the commander from racing down the hall. Sol didn't hear the rest of the conversation. She knew a little of what was being revealed. Time was of the essence. She had a terrible decision to make—and possibly an awful mistake to correct.

* * * *

"Wait! You don't understand, Commander. We have a problem. Captain Scott was a maternity client."

"A *what?*" Gabriel Merriweather, Commander of the Guild Diplomatic Corps, skidded to a sudden halt. If he had the power, he would have fried the doorman with his gaze. His glare must have been sufficient because the Dome's employee hurriedly whined, his thin voice ringing high and loud in the corridor.

"She—the captain—Captain Scott paid for a—a sperm donor." The last word squeaked past the man's throat that Gabe now held tightly in his fist. Thoughts whirled in his head and all the events of the past night played forward. Damn it, he should have known. Oh gods, he had known something was amiss from the start, but he hadn't wanted the night to end. Now he had to face the truth. Words barely got past the obstruction in his throat.

"And I paid for a sterile playmate, so what you're telling me is basically that she—Captain Scott—stole my sperm for procreation." He shook the Dome's employee like a rag doll. "That about right?"

The man nodded, and Gabe dropped him back to his knees.

"Well, she can't have it." He jabbed a finger in the doorman's face and roared, "Get her back here, and tell her she can't have it." Bands of warrior red anger flashed behind his eyes. He felt his nostrils flare under the deep breaths that he drew. He calmed his breathing, fighting to reach his center. He hadn't been this upset in a decade. His Chakkra bloodlines demanded that his anger be freed, but within moments, he had snuffed out his rage. The doorman, oblivious to how close to death he had come, puffed out his chest at Gabe and shook his head.

"I'm afraid we can't do that, Commander. The sperm— you gave it to her willingly. We—" The Dome's employee pointed to the blonde then back to his chest. "—we both heard you say you were more than satisfied with . . . well, the service you received, so our contract was fulfilled. Our hands are tied." For further emphasis, he turned his empty palms up then prudently hobbled on his knees out of range. Gabe thought that particularly wise of him. At the moment, Gabe's temper teetered on the edge of violence. He only managed to control his half-breed Chakkra warrior side by using his empathic ability. The doorman was clearly terrified. Fear came off him in waves. The idea that he had caused such fear made Gabe feel sick. He felt the man cringe at his words.

"You will have the captain's address ready for me by the time I get dressed. Is that clear?" Gabe didn't shout, he didn't rave, all he did was glare at the Dome's employee who backed farther down the hall with the blonde tugging on his arm, trying to keep up. Both looked wide-eyed and nodded silently before turning and running to the end of the corridor. They obviously knew that he wasn't a man to be trifled with. How wrong he was.

Gabe later learned that Elise, the Pleasure Dome's best playmate, put in for a transfer to Faro's Hump and caught the first ship out. And, for some unknown reason, the manager of the Pleasure Dome also felt compelled to take an indefinite vacation. But Gabe would make someone pay for this mistake. No matter how long it took he would find Captain Soledad Scott and correct the problem.

Four

"What do you mean, you can't find her? How hard can it possibly be to find one retired captain of the Spacing Guild?" Gabriel, who never yelled, yelled at his assistant's reflection on his wrist com link. "I want the address of her next of kin," he growled from between clenched teeth then added in a much lower and better controlled tone. "And, Tetra...I want it yesterday."

"Yes, Boss," the wrinkled green face on his link managed to squeak before Gabe disconnected. How could Captain Soledad Scott have just disappeared? Gabriel knew he should have stopped the sexual charade when he had discovered his playmate was a Guild retired captain, but by then, he was in too deep—so to speak. He hadn't wanted to stop, would never have stopped, even if the Dome's protection had shattered over his head. It was as if his tainted blood had found an answering kinship with her. Never had his empathy talents been so totally blanketed and in such sexual heat. More than that, Captain Scott had rendered complete warmth and comfort from the outside battery of emotions that normally bombarded him in a place like the Pleasure Dome. No one had ever granted him such peace—and responded with such sexual enjoyment. Soledad Scott was unique.

In the beginning, all Gabe could do was wallow in the silence and the serenity Captain Scott had offered. He knew he should have identified himself. Law dictated that he had to state that he was a registered empath, a half-breed Chakkra, but surely she knew. Didn't she? She had stared long enough at the registration tattoos on his chest and arm. And the captain was old enough and militarily experienced enough to know she was a tranq, a person who neutralized an empath's ability to read all emotions except those of deepest nature. In return for the comfort the captain offered, all Gabe had wanted was to bring a little happiness into her sad eyes—and maybe get off on doing it. But her projected suffering had eaten through her tranquility, eaten away his problems, until all Gabe felt was the captain's great need, her raging desire, the sucking pull of her heated satin walls. Those emotions had only heightened his own.

But the connection was more than physical. Even now he couldn't get her out of his mind. For weeks he had searched the Straits for the retired Captain Soledad Scott only to find nothing. The damned manager of the Pleasure Dome had also disappeared, and the robotic staff left in his place gave no information except to eagerly press more colorful brochures of their special "extra" services that were available for the right price. And for some reason, they were eager to give him a discount.

Good gods almighty, Gabriel couldn't believe he had ever gone to the Dome in the first place. Due to his empathic abilities and the swamp of sexual influences that swept over him in the confines of such an emotion-racked place, he had never before frequented the brothels of the Straits. The roaring savage of his Chakkra blood held too much influence over his sex drive. Most of the time, Gabriel held control over it. But the pleasure he had received with Captain Scott nearly undid him. She somehow possessed the ability to draw his empathy and swallow his pain, and she had certainly relieved the awful numbness of his last failed mission. In her company, the icy cold isolation was gone. Even back in the midst of conflicting outside emotions, Gabriel still felt alive again, definitely alive. For one night, the captain had muted the external fields and raised him to such sexual heights with her demanding spirit that he forgot his own regrets and recriminations. And Gabe's spirits, along with his sex drive, had definitely needed lifting. He had been too attuned with failure.

The treaty he had negotiated between the Illrullians and the Narhanyahs had collapsed almost before the first month ended, resulting in the Illrullians being nearly wiped out. And Gabriel felt responsible for every death—had heard and felt each and every scream in his head. At the peace conference table before the massacre, he'd known that the agreement between the two worlds was too shaky. He couldn't exactly read their thoughts, but his empathy senses never lied about the emotions being projected. Deceit reigned rampant in the room, with a hollow, sour smell. The Narhanyahs had concealed something behind their smooth, bland expressions. Gabe should have insisted on more time with the leaders, but the Guild refused to allow for anymore delays. He had done as the Guild governor ordered; coerced them into a treaty that was worthless.

As a result, the Illrullians were dead or, at least, dead for another twenty years until their surviving young could rebel against the Narhanyahs who had enslaved them. And rebel they would. The grim little fighters would claw their way out of the ashes of their defeat like the proverbial phoenix. Another war was inevitable, and this time, they would blame the Diplomatic Corps instead of the Spacing Guild for their lying interference. Again, Gabe had failed to bring a lasting peace. The taste of that defeat had rested like cold ashes in his mouth.

Damn the Guild and their meddling ways. He should have fought the governor harder for the right to negotiate a lasting settlement. Well, he hoped the governor was suffering guilt as badly as he. He had told her that the failure rested with her.

Gabe kicked an offending desk chair that interrupted his long strides out of his way. The chair's adaptable mold fitted itself into a "U" from his boot print. It would stay that way until he sat again. He glared at its offensive sight and continued his pacing, at least as much as he could in the cramped confines of his miserly office. With all its expensive shielding, he could afford nothing bigger—not that he wanted larger quarters. He rarely stayed here. His savage nature longed for open vistas where he could roar at the skies in private. He knew better than to keep his beast confined for too long.

Where was Captain Scott? Gabe knew he should be working, but thoughts of the captain kept him from thinking straight. Her vision in his head haunted his days at work as well as his nights. Never had he met anyone who had such a soothing effect on him and was such an itching irritant at the same time. It was as if the captain was a part of him, attuned to his thoughts as well as his body. Without her, he felt as if he was missing a limb. He obsessed over her smell on his skin, refusing to bathe for days. When he had brought the captain pleasure that night, he'd only heightened his own. Never had he felt such release, as if all his self doubts and recriminations fled at her touch. She shouldn't have that power over him, no one he knew did. And the captain wasn't in the Guild's Registry as a tranq or a person with Chakkra blood. He had checked that the first thing upon reaching his office. Then why did she affect him so? *Damn it.* Soledad Scott was soothing and, conversely, upsetting at the same time.

And she had tasted so sweet. Gabriel thought he could still taste her on his tongue. *Ahhh, gods.* He flushed hotly at the thoughts of the things they had done together in the night. He wasn't a notable lover. The few females he had taken in the past were quick to tell him so. But the captain had brought out the best—or possibly the worst—in him. His Chakkra blood sang under her touch. Her need had urged Gabriel to perform inventive sexual acts he'd only fantasized of doing and had never been brave enough to try. She had responded to every one of them. And just the thought of those acts—of remembering her response—made him hard again. Gabe cursed, adjusted the bite of his pants and walked off his stiffened cock in jerking paces—back and forth. He tried to focus on his next assignment. Hell, there was always work to be done in the Corps, diplomatically trying to keep the Universe's varied species from killing each other or from blowing up the entire surrounding area. Surely he had plenty to focus on.

But despite all that turmoil, all Gabriel could think about was Captain Soledad Scott. All he saw in his mind was her strong, sensitive face, with those dark, troubled eyes that flashed a golden hue not unlike that of the aged whiskey he loved. All he saw was her toned and muscled body and those long, long legs that went up nearly to her neck. And that bare mound of hers. *Jesu!* Gabe swallowed his next curse. He would never forget the feel of her, the smell and the sweet taste. She had been like a ripe, sweet fruit in his mouth. And he had loved soothing her with his tongue, with his hands, with his cock. In some places on her long body, her skin had felt so perfectly smooth, but beneath, in the deeper tissues, Gabe had sensed the scar tissue ridge line of healed battle wounds. That thought sickened him, that she had been hurt. The captain welded such strength, but inside, she oozed such hot passion and tenderness. Gabe broke out in a sweat just thinking about her. And just that one thought was enough to make him rock hard again. The rise of his pants cut into his groin.

Good gods, he hadn't been this randy since his early Academy days. Being able to read women, at least most women, was both an asset and a curse. With Captain Scott, Gabe got just enough reading to tantalize and still have her remain a mystery. A mystery he longed to solve.

The feeling had to be lust. Empty Chakkra lust. It couldn't be anything permanent. Gabe didn't have the time or the inclination for anything permanent. But if it was just lust that kept her image alive, why did he still see the shadows in her eyes? Why did he long to make them disappear? He knew he had pleasured her. He had seen it, and by the good gods, he had felt it—more than once. Just where the hell was she?

Thanks to his Mulanian aide, Tetra, Gabe had spent the entire *morning after* going over the captain's thick military records. He was surprised by her brilliant war tactics for one so young. She had won her captain bars at the age of eighteen, the youngest officer of that rank in the Guild's history. And throughout her twenty-year career, she had never failed to use the best strategy to avoid excessive loss of life, almost as if she knew that the Diplomatic Corps would be doing their damnedest to create a peaceful settlement.

And the medals she had earned were astounding. Soledad Scott became the most decorated captain in the fleet's history, but never once did she use her record for advancement. The reason why she was retired at a captain's rank instead of being promoted and moved up in associated services was not stated in her records. Someone or something had kept her from advancement. But he, Gabriel Merriweather, was indirectly responsible for the captain's retirement at the age of thirty-eight.

Years ago, as a new ambassador anxious for recognition, Gabe had recommended his captain-replacement idea to

Dushaw, the assistant director who had the governor's ear. The governor liked Gabe's recommendations that due to slower synaptic responses in humans over thirty-five years of age, they should be replaced with younger officers. A Guild captain must make snap decisions based on conditions at hand—those in the Guild's best interests. But the real reason for their displacement was that if the captains remained too long in service, the mature officers began to think too much on their own. Independent thinking was dangerous, forbidden. The Guild wanted unquestionable, blind obedience to their orders, but most of the early retired officers were given a chance to move up in the ranks in other branches. Captain Scott must have done something rebellious for her not to have been transferred and advanced further in associated services. *Hmmm.*

Gabe tapped the screen again, just to make sure, but no further documentation was forthcoming. Having spent the night with the captain and getting sketchy memory impressions from her deepest emotions, he knew she didn't want a life without the stars. He had felt the brunt of her simmering rage, her grief at the loss of command. If she had stayed with him, Gabe would have helped her somehow, despite her age. Hell, he was Commander of the Diplomatic Corp. He could have used her as *his* captain.

Gabe grinned at the thought. Come to think of it, he had used her as *his* captain. Heat bloomed on his neck and across his shoulders, but he ignored the returned hardening of his body. He was getting used to being in a constant state of full arousal. He frowned as a firm fact taunted him. Soledad Scott had been at the Dome for procreation purposes. She had gotten what she'd contracted for at the Pleasure Dome. Gabe's sperm count was potent. That's why he was always careful to request sterile partners, especially human females, but Scott shouldn't have gotten his tainted genes. Well, Gabe consoled himself. The captain would probably abort once she knew he was a half-breed Chakkra. No one wanted that connection to those savage warriors who were elusive mercenaries isolated from all but their home world.

But out of curiosity, Gabe circumvented protocol and

searched the Pleasure Dome's fertility bank files. He found that he did meet many of the other requirements that Sol had listed. Certainly not his Chakkra blood, nor his independent nature—he'd much rather say independent than jack-assed stubbornness—weren't on the list. But he was very, very close to the captain's specifications. He didn't know why that thought pleased him. He didn't want children when he couldn't even bring lasting peace to two ignorant species that had fought for centuries. Not when his Chakkra nightmares haunted him with visions of his mother and father and their violent deaths.

Children, anyone's children, should be born to a better life, one without all the strife of war. Yes, to a much better life. So why was he still trying to find out all he could about Captain Soledad Scott?

Strangely, even in his official capacity, he wasn't able to access the captain's genetics, although he tried several different queries. Master blocks encrypted her files. Why?

"Boss?" Gabe's com whistled again in Tetra's high Mulanian lyrical tones.

"Tell me good news, Tetra. Please." He ran a hand over his head.

"Captain Scott has a sister. A registered Academy breeder." Tetra's words lisped from her multiple mouths, and Gabe wanted to kiss all three stuttering lips in gratitude. A Space Academy breeder bred with highly ranked officers, mixing the best genes for the best of the best in offspring. Surely Scott's sister would know where she was. And if she didn't fork over what she knew, pressure could be brought to bear for the information, even on one of the protected breeders. In this instance, Gabriel would use his rank to get whatever he wanted. Blood pounded through his pulse, thundering in his ears.

"What's her name and address?"

Tetra's deep face creases deepened further into a darker green. Her multiple wide, frog-like lips pouted. "That information is restricted—Military and Academy protected. The captain's sibling only uses sperm donors; all rights, all genetics, confidential. It is noted that she has produced several highly decorated cadets and has friends in high places. The file is encrypted, sentry posted." The Mulanian hesitated then hastened to add. "But I am still working on it, sir."

Gabe's heavy hand disrupted the slick order of his hair. One loosened section fell over his face, and he longed to rip at it in frustration, but one didn't hurry a Mulanian. If he pushed Tetra any harder, he'd have to listen to an hour long lesson on proper patience etiquette. He didn't have the time for a lecture.

"Thank you, Tetra. Keep me informed." Gabe noted and returned the pleased nod Tetra gave before she signed off. Then he finally hissed the exasperated breath he'd held. His pulse again throbbed in his ears. Rage surged in the blood that pounded through his veins. He closed his eyes and drew in deep, even breaths. He hadn't been this close to losing himself in years. He forced himself to breathe deeper, draw in slower. *Diplomacy.* That's what Gabriel was good at. Perhaps, if—no *when*—he found Captain Scott, he could talk her into . . . what? Exactly what did he want from her?

He didn't want a child. Never a child with his Chakkra blood. Gabe did want that exhausting sex with her again. No, he wanted more than sex from her. He needed to feel that blunting of outside interference, that muting of thousands of distracting, conflicting emotions. And for Soledad Scott— Gabriel wanted to join with her, hold her while she slept so that those painful shadows didn't creep back into her eyes. He wanted to still the restless, hot need she exuded. He wanted to kiss her warm, soft mouths—both her upper mouth and her lower, darker, and juicer one. A shiver swept over Gabe, and he licked his lips. He wanted to taste Sol again, to caress her smooth tight skin, tangle his legs with hers and slide into the delicious slick heat between her legs. He wanted to fight verbal battles with her until morning's light. And he wanted to do this until—well, until he got her out of his system. When would that be? He hadn't a clue. Perhaps he wished that she would want him for always—that she would forever feel a need only he could fill. Never had a female taken so much from him and, without even trying to please him once. The few who knew him distrusted his Chakkra temperament.

Suddenly, an awful thought occurred to Gabe. What if the

captain found out what he was and never wanted him again? She'd said she had gotten what she came for—his sperm. What if she didn't feel the same attachment he felt for her? What, then?

Five

"Gellico, I am telling you the truth. I-Do-Not-Want-Commander-Gabriel-Merriweather." Sol glared at the ebony beauty who just smiled back at her in the mirror's image. Gellico de' Marco, Sol's longtime friend as well as a consummate exotic dancer, applied more red sparkles to her wide lips, air kissed at the mirror and didn't comment.

"Well, I don't," Sol insisted, not liking the sound of her whining voice or her pout. Galactic ship captains never pouted or whined. But, lately, she was doing a lot of things she had never done before—and liking some of them. Liking a lot of them. That thought made her angry enough to focus on the one thing she hated about Gabriel Merriweather. "The only thing I want to do to the commander is slit his throat for costing me my ship. Him and the Guild's damned age edict."

"I hear what you're saying, darlin'. And I see your pretty lips moving. I just don't believe you." Gellico puckered again in the mirror's reflection, then smiled at Sol before she sprayed on more of the potent aroma that wafted around her in a fragrant cloud of hotly-spiced sensuality. A little something extra had been mixed with the normal fragrance. She stood, an exquisite black Amazon dressed in playful, sparkling silk scarves that exposed more than they concealed of her lithe, trim body. As an erotic dancer at Dante's Circus, another pleasure den in the Straits, Gellico topped Soledad's six foot height by another good four inches. The thought came to Sol that Gellico stood nearly as tall as the commander. Her heart rocked at just the thought of him curving over and around her. Prickly sensations ran the gauntlet of her insides. Moisture gathered between her legs. Sol shifted on Gellico's sofa, uncomfortable with the knowledge that just thoughts of Merriweather could make her wet.

The performer took the sting out of her words by placing gentle, long-fingered hands, painted with flashing red lacquered nails, on Sol's shoulders and air-kissing her lightly on both cheeks. Sol knew Gellico refrained from kissing her on the mouth, and that wasn't because the dancer feared messing up her new lip gloss. Genuine love reflected in the dark depths of Gellico's sloe eyes. But throughout the long years of their friendship, she had never done anything to make Sol uncomfortable. Her soft, warm gaze had so steadied Sol that she had never felt off center with Gellico, even though she knew Gelli wanted more than friendship.

Early in Sol's military career, they had met on the prison planet of Hydra, where, fighting back-to-back during a rescue of stranded playmates, they had saved each other's lives. Sol quickly shoved the dark nightmare of Hydra back under cover. She owed Gellico more than she could ever repay—or ever tell.

"What makes you think I want the commander?" Sol asked. She kept her face free of any expression. Again, the thoughts of what had happened that night with Merriweather made her insides dance. That was a night she would never forget. She had done and experienced pleasures she had never experienced before. *Ye gods, on his husky whispered command, she had even licked her sexual fluids from his mouth and face!* Shivers overcame her. Again, she throbbed between her legs. This was becoming a habit—think of Gabriel Merriweather and her ovaries clanged. Thankfully, Gelli didn't notice. Or perhaps she did.

The dancer grinned. "I hear you when you sleep, dear girl. You're restless and—" Gellico's grin widened, showing her brilliant white teeth. "—you moan, Sol. You moan a lot."

"I—Do—Not—Moan." Heat crept up Sol's neck. *Liar.* She knew she moaned; she had even awakened herself with the noise, her body aching, pulsing against a phantom lover. On more than one occasion she had to use her fingers as a poor substitute to slack her raging desire.

"Oh, yes, you do moan. And don't say it's all due to that overload of lusty hormones. Those have worn off—long ago." Gellico waved a graceful hand at Sol. "And ever since you discovered that the commander is looking for you, you've been as pleased as pie and as hot as Chin's volcanoes. I know the signs, girlfriend. You're in love or at the very least, in lust with the man. And why? I don't know. Let's see." Gellico counted off on those long fingers of hers, "Big. Broad. Penis-wielding. Knuckle-dragging Neanderthal." She grunted an unladylike groan then flexed her arms in a he-man pose, but the silk scraps draping from her bare shoulders ruined the effect that her sleekly muscled arms made. "He must have done you up good is all I'm saying. But, yeah, I guess the commander has a body that would please most—if you're into that kind of he-man thing. I'm not, but you give me a soft, sweet female, eweee— wheee!" Gellico expelled a long, exaggerated breath, and batted her enhanced eyelashes furiously, her fingers demurely tucked under her chin.

"Gellico de'Marco!" Sol choked out Gelli's full name. That heated flush rushed over Sol's neck and shoulders again, covering her face before she grabbed for her friend. She had to divert this talk somehow. Wrestling sounded good. They had engaged in the sport many times.

"Ha, got 'cha!" Gellico leaped at her at the same instant. The dancer laughed a deep-throated rumble before she twisted and landed with Sol in a headlock. But not for long, Sol escaped with a wicked twist and grappled Gellico from behind. She spun and they danced until Gelli tripped her, then the two rolled on the floor, squealing and tickling each other. Neither really used their deadly fighting skills, as they so often had in the past. Both were very aware of Sol's condition.

A crystal lamp fell from a kicked table with a crash, and Sol grimaced. She had bought that lamp for Gellico on Rigel Three, and it had cost a small fortune. More furniture scraped the costly fake wooden floor before Gellico's door slammed open and bounced off the wall with a thud. Sol yelped as they were suddenly jerked apart. She couldn't see who twisted hands in their clothing and hoisted them off the floor and into the air. She barely heard the door crash open over the sounds of their laughter. In the dancers' private quarters, rooms weren't soundproofed, more for protection of the playmates than for employee privacy. Sometimes, though not often, overzealous customers found their way backstage to private living spaces.

Bouncers were always on alert to disturbances. Even though she couldn't see him from this angle, Sol knew who held them. She also assumed that Punch, the Circus's Rigelian bouncer wasn't happy.

"Put us down, Punch." Gellico swatted ineffectively at the gigantic fist that gripped behind her neck. She still laughed, but the sound was restricted by one of her scarves that threatened to cut off her air. Sol didn't even try to speak.

Punch wrinkled his single bushy brow on his low forehead. He turned the girls to face him at eye level, their bodies hanging loose in his grip. His beady eyes searched their faces with puzzled intent. "No fighting allowed," he grunted first at Gellico, then at Sol.

His massive fists eased his grip and dropped them so that they were on tiptoe, but he kept his hands tight on the backs of their necks. His touch was dry, rock solid and somehow reassuring to Sol. She sent a quick look at Gellico, swallowed her laugh and dipped her head. Gellico hid her grin with her hand. Punch frowned deeper, hunched in closer and glared nearly nose to nose from one female to the other, clearly upset by their laughter. Normally, his services were needed for violence not levity. Punch was clearly at a loss as to what was expected of him. Sol knew his distress was because he loved Gellico and was torn between the duty of keeping the peace and pleasing her.

"No more fighting, Punch." Gellico swallowed her next laugh and swatted his massive shoulder heartily. He wouldn't have felt a lighter touch. "I promise."

Punch nodded, although his thick uni-brow remained knit. He was still confused, but he stepped back. "No like fighting," he commented in grunted syllables before he lumbered out, closing Gellico's door softly behind him. Clearly, he was a gentle giant who loved peace and quiet.

Sol couldn't help it. When she looked at Gelli, they both dissolved into laughing fits, hiding the sounds with pillows over their mouths.

Gellico was the first to recover and said, "Now that I think of it, your Commander Merriweather reminds me a lot of

Punch." Her perfectly shaped brows arched, and she tapped her chin, a lacquered nail under pursed lips as if seriously thinking.

"He does not!" At the thought, Sol snorted before a deep, cleansing laugh started from her toes and rolled up and out her mouth. Commander Merriweather was nothing at all like Punch except for maybe his size, but somehow the comparison was funny. Sol glanced at Gellico, sputtered and continued laughing until tears surprisingly flowed.

Laughter had never come easy to Sol. Amusement had been even scarcer since her retirement. Now she laughed and cried . . . all the time. *Damned hormones.* They were surely to blame for her mood swings and her indecision regarding the commander. Did she want him or not? Alive or dead? Only one way to find out. Sol would have to see Merriweather again just to satisfy her curiosity. Right? She had to make sure the commander wanted her for reasons other than filing against her child. Just let him try to force her to give up this baby.

Soledad sobered. She hadn't realized the depth of her commitment until that moment. She'd fight him to keep her baby. She'd fight the whole damned galaxy.

Gellico, always so attuned to her mood changes, gave her an intense look and a gentle shoulder pat. Sol dredged up a smile. "That's better." Gellico hugged her, then pushed her toward the door. "Now, go on out and get a good seat in the shadows so no one sees you. It won't do for someone to recognize you. They'd try to collect that reward your caveman is offering in a microsecond."

Sol sobered further, her spine stiffening in defensive military fashion. "What reward?"

"Haven't you read the latest postings?" Gellico's dark eyes rounded, as if widening those large orbs was possible. "Now Merriweather's offering a reward for information about your whereabouts. It seems that the poor dear can't find you." She snorted a delicate sound that was in direct opposition to her Amazon stature.

"Maybe I shouldn't go out tonight." Sol frowned, torn between being thrilled and angered by the fact that the commander was still looking for her after all these weeks. She ignored the way her heart raced. That it did so made her anger dominate her emotions.

"But you always watch my show when you stay with me," Gellico protested, taking Sol by the arm. "Really, honey, you'll be fine in the dark. I can even have Punch keep an eye out, if you like."

Sol hesitated, and then she nodded. If the commander got wind of her, she'd just find a new hideout until she was sure what she was going to do about him. *And about how she felt about him.* When she'd first learned her lover's identity, all she'd done was fume in a hot rage. Then, for days, she had read everything she could find on the "noble" Gabriel Merriweather, Commander of the Diplomatic Corps, the rat bastard who had indirectly cost her the command of the *Icarus*. Sol was impressed with his resourcefulness—among other things. But she still couldn't believe that there were no drugs in the wine they'd shared. She had discovered that the Dome only told customers that so they'd have an excuse for their loosened inhibitions and their lovemaking would be more natural. The commander's technique had been as raw and as natural as they come—and as healthy. Perhaps their attraction was their shared Chakkra blood. That thought made Soledad laugh, although she had felt a strange stirring inside—almost a draw to Merriweather. Was the attraction only because he was Chakkra? And what, exactly, did that mean? The Chakkra.

There was so little intel about the reclusive warriors. They hired out to warring worlds as mercenaries, but over time, fewer and fewer such incidents were recorded. Perhaps their culture was dying out due to more worlds reaching peaceful settlements. That thought brought her back to Merriweather and his damned Diplomatic Corps. Him and his message of peace. His records showed that he had an eighty-eight per cent success rate. Well, bully for him.

At the moment, Sol was more interested in their combined genes. She rarely gave her weak Chakkra bloodlines a second thought. No one in her family ever showed any talents or special attributes—at least none that she knew of. Most of the time,

Sol forgot she was anything but Terran. Human to the core. Maybe she was a little taller than the average female, but that was it. A little taller and now getting a little wider perhaps. She touched her still flat abdomen; six more months to go. She smiled and wondered at her tender feelings. Tenderness was never one of her frequent emotions, and Gelli gaped in mock amazement at her. Sol made no comment, pointedly ignoring Gellico's open-mouthed expression and returning to her inner thoughts.

Despite losing the *Icarus*, life was creating new experiences for Sol, and with a Chakkra, no less. No one had seen or heard about the ancient warring race in years. They kept to their own world, almost religiously so. Few outcasts roamed the universe. She wondered if it was true about Merriweather being a half-breed. How had he escaped their confines? He hadn't acted any differently than any other arrogant male she'd had sex with. *Liar.*

Her internal jab startled her. She was doing that a lot lately, self analyzing. But who was she kidding? She had never had sex like that in her entire life. What happened between her and the commander was more than sex. It was…ummm…well, it was just more. Besides, taking an innocent life, even one that she hadn't bargained for, wasn't in Sol's makeup. Without conscious thought, her hand smoothed over her belly again. She had been right in keeping the baby, even if it wasn't the one she was supposed to have. She'd take a chance on it having Chakkra genes. She'd never be able to live with herself if she did anything to harm this child. She'd seen enough lost lives.

As if in agreement, a tiny flutter tickled her inside; a bubble like that of laughter roiled through her. Sol gasped and lost her breath in wonder.

"He moved?" Gellico's round eyes got bigger still. She reached a tentative hand out to touch Sol's stomach.

"You can't feel him yet." Sol said, but she took Gellico's hand and rubbed a gentle circle. "He's here."

"When will you let me feel him move?" Gellico turned her palm and gripped Sol's hand in hers. Sol squeezed her long fingers.

"You'll be the first."

"Don't make promises like that, sweet thing. By then, your man will have found you."

"He's not my man."

"We'll see. Now go get your seat and watch the show."

Six

Gabe watched the sensuous, drum-pounding, writhing dance of the long-limbed black vision with a distracted gaze. His Chakkra blood roared, and his body responded to the dancer's gleaming movements that stripped the teasing scarves from her curves. How could he not respond physically to the female's beauty and the aromatic sexual pheromones drifting down from the ceiling? The drug-laced sexual scent added to nature's call from all the enthralled watchers. One didn't have to be an empath or even a half-breed Chakkra to feel the sexual tension in the place.

Dante's Circus would certainly be a busy pleasure palace tonight, but the owners wouldn't be getting any of Gabe's money. He had discovered in the past few months that he didn't want anyone but Soledad Scott. No one else would do. The captain haunted him day and night. None of the universe's other beauties would satisfy him. Dear gods, but he had tried. He hadn't gotten any farther than the initial meeting to know he didn't want any woman but the captain. All paled in comparison. He couldn't stand their touch, and he longed for the captain's.

Dammit. What was wrong with him? Scott had made it more than plain that she didn't want to be found by him. And his damned empathic talents were no help at all in locating her. Damned tranq that she was, she neutralized his sensing abilities. Gabriel's human Marine sergeant was the one who'd spotted her. Gabe gulped the last of the heady drink he didn't want and slammed his glass down on the table. In the darkened room's throbbing noise, no one paid any attention to his muttered curses. No one spoke Chakkra outside the home world, so he was safe in spewing a few choice oaths. In fact, he was sure no one heard anything above the increasing pounding rhythm of the drums. The pulsating beat rose, gathering toward a crescendo. On the floating stage that drifted above the customers' heads, lights gleamed off graceful curves that flexed and swayed in the shadowed lighting. Firm breasts jiggled enticingly; belly and hips undulated in a blatant invitation to enjoy forbidden female fruit. Silken scarves loosened, exposed their favors and wavered with their enticing smell above the crowd. The tempo reached its peak then the pulsing throb abruptly ended. A brief glimpse of sleek female nudity flashed. Darkness fell. The crowd gasped and thunderous applause filled the air.

Subdued table lighting came on. The stage was bare. End of the show. Too bad. Gabe sighed. He had failed to pay enough attention to the performance to even get more than a token hard-on. His fickle cock was back to being under his control. Despite the swamp of sexual emotions swirling around him, the swirl of lusty pheromones, his body rested now that the show was over. Customers disappeared into the shadows.

"Commander Merriweather?"

A tingle went down his spine, and Gabe looked up through a slight drunken haze and met the black dancer's intense stare. His empathy senses buzzed a warning. That direct gaze stared too deeply into his. Gabe felt the threat that this woman presented a danger to him, and he drew his warrior senses over him like a shroud. His muscles bunched. His nerves sparked. Blood throbbed. But the dancer only pulled a sheer, glittering robe over wide shoulders that shone like glossy satin from her exertion. Her slight, white-toothed smile didn't quite reach her sloe eyes. Her cool, dark gaze flicked over him with such disdain that Gabriel flushed. He forced down his responding anger. This was a dangerous female but nonetheless a female. And he'd learned to always exercise caution around females. He could do such damage to them without meaning to. Moments passed, but he still picked up violence from the dancer's mind. Gabe pretended indifference.

"May I help you, Ms.—?" He rose, purposely stumbled on a chair leg and waited for the dancer to supply her name. Most people didn't consider a clumsy man a threat. Gabe knew the dancer's name of course. He had heard the announcer proudly announce her act. He also knew from gossip that she was Captain Scott's best friend.

"de' Marco. Gellico de'Marco." She added her first name almost as an afterthought. Her elegant brows knit together, and her dark eyes shone in the shadows as if she assessed Gabe and still found him wanting.

He again flushed. And again he controlled his heated response. Then he firmly held a chair and motioned for her to sit. de'Marco ignored him for a moment, a brow raised and her jaw tight. Gabe jiggled the chair, thumping the legs on the floor. His best patient grin was finally rewarded when she snorted, shook her head and sat. Gabe glimpsed a quick flash of mocking white teeth in the dim light. He leaned in over her chair, as if to push her closer to the table, but instead, drew in the heady scent of her exotic jungle flower perfume. It was designed to entice, but although his blood surged, all Gabe felt was a stirring of appreciation, a token rise in his pants. He sat down across from her and waited for her to speak.

As if she realized his near lack of sexual response, she gave him an annoyed frown, drew away from him and settled back in her own chair. She pulled out a smoke from somewhere and stared at the tip. In those few moments of closeness, Gabe felt her relax, her deep calm stilling her roiling thoughts. Perhaps he had passed whatever test she had just given him.

"You don't come here often." de'Marco squinted her dark eyes at him and lit the long, brown reefer. She took a drag, held it, then puffed fragrant blue smoke in his face. Gabe didn't need a kit to identify the heavy tang of sweet contraband in the air. He ignored it. He wasn't on any kind of drug duty. Besides, he was a diplomat not an agent for the drug enforcers. They didn't frequent the Straits where contraband flourished. Pay off credits flourished here.

"I've never been here," he replied, wondering at the game she played. Even with his enhanced talent for reading people, he felt like a mouse under a cat's gaze, especially in his near drunken state. Gabriel knew better than to drink like this. Empaths never drank, even socially, unless they had backup. Chakkra never drank at all. The warriors were violent enough without the haze of alcohol.

"Did you enjoy the dance?" de'Marco's even, mysterious

gaze disconcerted him. What lay behind it? Gabe couldn't resist the temptation, and he reached out with a tentative mind touch. Pain roared back at him. His chair rocked forward from his lazy, tipped-back position. His teeth clicked together from the jolt of his seat connecting with the floor. The dancer's violent past shot out from her and gripped him by the throat, and Gabe shuddered under flashes of violent, bloody impressions of death and destruction. He swallowed hard and shook his head clear. An awful truth filled him. de'Marco hid a tormented past, almost as tortured as his, but he didn't try to understand the images that nearly made him gasp aloud. Sometimes his empathy talent twisted his visions and couldn't be trusted.

He cleared his suddenly dry throat and wished for more of the nasty tasting drink before he spoke. "Yes. I enjoyed your dance very muchhh. You are extmly . . . extremely talented." His purposely slurred words sounded strange to the roar still echoing in his ears. Perhaps if she thought him drunker than he was, she'd let something slip about Scott.

"I know." Her strong chin lifted. Her defiant eyes assessed him in a narrowed glare. "Don't you feel the need for a room, Commander? A private room like the one you stayed in at the Pleasure Dome?"

The dancer leaned closer to the table, and more of her sleek flesh escaped through the costume's flimsy, loose top. The rouged tips of her nipples poked through the gossamer fabric. Sweat popped out on his brow, and Gabe looked around, noting that they were the only two people left in the place. He gave an exhale that puffed his cheeks. Evidently the others had found rooms to their liking. The Circus's pleasure business was really good tonight.

"I don't make a habit of staying in the palaces. And I'm afraid that I can't do justice to your dance, Miss de'Marco. I'm here because I'm looking for someone." Gabriel ruined the seriousness of his statement with a hiccup. It was feigned. He no longer felt that drunk. His thoughts were focused arrow straight. He was here for a purpose, and she—that purpose— stood in the shadows. This close he could even feel each soft exhale of the captain's breathing. All his senses died under her influence. All except his damned cock. Gabriel stretched first one leg then the other under the table. It didn't help.

"Oh?" The dancer's perfectly arched brows rose. She seemed amused as if she read right through his pretense of indifference. "You're here looking for someone who, perhaps, means a lot to you?"

Again, Gabe felt like he was being tested. Ms. de'Marco was reading him as if she were an empath. He knew she wasn't one. There had been no tingling of minds when he met her, only that prickling of threat that had gone up his spine. The dancer was dangerously astute just the same. He cleared his tight throat again before speaking, "Yes, someone I care about. But, evidently, I mean nothing to her, so I'm giving up." Gabe lifted his palms in a defeated gesture and stood. Thankfully, his cock cooperated and rested.

After fumbling in his pocket a sufficient amount of time for both the captain and the dancer to think, Gabe threw enough credits on the table to cover his drink plus a healthy tip.

"She must not be worth your time." Again, the dancer's elegant brows lifted in a mocking arch. She rested her elbows on the table and placed her chin on her joined hands, as if praying.

Before she spoke again, Gabriel said, "Look Ms. de'Marco, let's cut to the slip stream. We both know who we're talking about. I know you are a friend of Captain Scott's. Just tell her that I give up. If she wants to talk to me, she knows where to find me. I'll be waiting." Gabe hurried for the exit, but turned at de'Marco's call. Her words stopped him dead in his tracks.

"What about the child, Merriweather? Can she have it? No trouble from you?"

Gabe's breath left his lungs in a whoosh. So the captain *was* pregnant. *Damned fertile Chakkra blood.* It always came through with its driving need to procreate. There were only a few true Chakkra left, thank the gods.

Gabriel had been hoping for a sterile ending from their one night at the Pleasure Dome,but she was pregnant. And what did he want? Gabe rubbed the back of his neck. He tilted his head back and closed his tired eyes. Only an honest answer would satisfy de'Marco—and the captain. "I don't honestly know about the kid. I need time. I . . . I don't think I want a child, but . . ."

"Then leave Soledad alone." The dancer snapped to her feet so suddenly her chair crashed to the floor. The heat of her angry glare surprised Gabe. He didn't need his talent to feel the venom that emanated from her. It radiated in waves.

For a moment, Gabe lost his diplomatic composure. Blood pounded in his throbbing temples. He fiercely whispered. "I can't give her up. I wish I could, but I can't."

"I'll fight you for her." de'Marco strode toward him, magnificent in her rage. Her robe fluttered from her long, bare legs, but Gabe could tell that she didn't care. She glared up at him, even thrust out her chin, her features hard and fierce in the dim light. "Commander or no, I won't let you hurt her."

"I won't hurt her." Gabe backed away from the truth of her edgy anger. The dancer was like a raging warrior bent on breaking his neck. It was hard to believe that she had been a lithe and tender seductress just moments before. In his checkered past, Gabe had honored his mother by never striking a female. A single blow from a Chakkra warrior would kill a delicate-boned female. But this one looked like she could split his spleen without blinking and laugh while doing it. Gabriel used his best asset, his diplomacy, to convince her of his sincerity. "I mean it, de'Marco. I have no intention of ever hurting the captain."

"Oh, you men never do. But you will hurt her, Commander, just the same." For a moment, de'Marco's dark gaze looked sad then her features hardened. She glared at him. "You have before." Somehow Gabe knew she meant his involvement in Sol's forced retirement.

"That's the Guild's doing. Not mine. I just told you the truth. I give up. Tell the captain to do whatever she wants. Have my . . . my child. Raise it to fly the wonders of space." He waved his hands expressively in the air. "Or whatever. I don't care. I'm too tired to fight anymore. She knows where to find me if she wants me."

With those parting words, Gabe stormed out of the

establishment's forced darkness, forgetting to stumble. He stopped and blinked in the dome's light of the recycled new day. He hoped Captain Scott had enjoyed his performance. At the end, Gabe had sensed Sol edging ever closer to him. Even before he felt her muting of his tormented emotions, her troubled thoughts had come from the shadows, so vivid that he'd known her exact location.

It had taken every bit of his will power to walk out of Dante's Circus. For once, he thanked his damned half-breed bloodlines.

He'd given the captain the bait. Now all he could do was wait to see if she took it.

Seven

"What do you mean? An hour ago you said you wanted nothing to do with the commander. Now, you *want* him?"

Sol shrugged. "I don't know. I guess I do, Gelli." Now that she knew that Merriweather wasn't pursuing her to take her child, Sol was curious about the rat bastard. She'd already devoured all the information she could find on him, which wasn't much. Hacking into sealed records, she'd discovered that he'd grown up on Chakkra with the warring race before going to Academy on Rigel Three, where he was an excellent student. Figures. Sol had also researched the mystic Chakkra people and learned nothing new. But she and the commander could share traits in their offspring. What might those mysterious traits be? Sol shivered at the thought.

"I don't know my own mind anymore, Gelli. Maybe I just want to talk to him again. Maybe find out if what I remember is right or if it was just wishful thinking." Sol sighed deeply. "He made me feel so good with all the giving—made me feel as if he meant it." Her words trailed off. She felt her cheeks heat. Never in her life had she blushed as much or as often as she did now.

Gelli snorted. "Oh, sweetie, I don't know what to do with you." She sat down next to Sol with a tired flounce that sent her flimsy garb to dancing in the air. The thickly padded, zebra-striped sofa cushions sighed with her sudden weight. Looking at her friend's deep scowl, Sol thought that the room's jungle theme, with its prowling tigers and angry lions depicted on the grassy plains' straw-wall coverings, suited Gellico. Only fake animal fur covered the floor and furniture. Gellico would never hurt an animal—humans, however, were a different story. The sharp swords, the lethal knives, the spears and the decorated shields that adorned the walls had been used for more than superficial art in her friend's lifetime. Some carried brown stains.

"First you don't want this man, and now you do." Gellico continued to frown at Sol. "What made you change your mind?"

"He looked so lost in the theater the other night." Sol couldn't keep the slight tremor from her voice. She sounded a far cry from the hard captain she once was. What the hell was happening to her? Too many years sterile or too many hormones all at once? Or had she discovered her femininity after all these years? Who knew? Sol sure as hell didn't, and she wasn't sure she liked the changes.

"Lost?" Gellico laughed and shook her head. "Him? The Great Gabriel Merriweather? Bloody hell! More likely he was drunk."

"No." Sol bristled, surprised at her defense of the commander. "I don't think he was drunk. I think he was making a last ditch attempt at getting my attention—and it worked."

"Yeah." Gellico snorted then muttered, "Perhaps, it worked too damned well." It was evident that she didn't believe a word she'd said. She swirled the contraband whiskey drink in her hand. "Well, he sure has been quiet ever since."

"Yeah, you're right." Sol sighed. "Maybe he meant it when he said he was giving up."

"Meant it, my ass. Gabriel Merriweather will give up on something he wants when Drakian pigs fly." Gellico grunted and rose from the comfortable sofa that Sol was using as a bed while hiding out from Merriweather. She gulped the last of her drink and wheezed, "Well, sweetie, if you're serious, perhaps we can change his fickle mind."

"What do you mean? How?" Even Sol heard the pathetic sound of hope dancing in her voice. She frowned it away. Gellico grinned wickedly.

"We'll dazzle him with a little com-link sex," She wagged her pencil-arched brows up and down.

"With what?" Sol felt her own brows go up to her hairline.

"Oh, come on, dear. Let me dress you as something besides a galactic warship's captain and fix your makeup. Then you can send a sexy little looove message to your commander."

"Dress me how?" Sol looked down at her stretched uniform. All she ever wore was the one piece spacer jumpsuit. The dark captain's red was beginning to look a little worn in places, but she refused to give them up. Even as a child, all she had ever wanted to do was command her own ship. But now the Spacing Guild leathers drew tight over her swelling belly. "I don't want a bunch of frilly things." Sol gestured toward the ever present silk trappings that Gellico wore. "And no makeup."

She frowned at Gellico. The dancer laughed and waved an elegant hand. "Oh, just let me do you up. Follow my instructions, sweetie, and I promise you'll be pleased with the results—and so will Commander Merriweather."

* * * *

Pleased wasn't the word that Gabriel felt when the captain's message arrived—surprised, yes. More than surprised, he was astounded and aroused to the point of blood-pounding pain, but pleased—no.

In the midst of a dull diplomatic meeting, Gabe's wrist link had beeped. He quit tapping his fingers on the table, and without a second thought, pressed the receive button. Scott's sultry recorded message surged forth with the same leap his heart made. Quickly, Gabe stabbed the mute tab. He only grunted at the speculative glances on the assorted, refined faces of the ambassadors.

With a quick "I'm not feeling well," he hastily fled the room, his heart rate rocketing. He really didn't care what the foreign ambassadors thought. The meeting was going nowhere anyway. They were all lying, as usual. Maybe a delay would soften them up. How had the captain managed to not only get his private link, but to block the return trace on it as well?

In the privacy of his room, Gabe jabbed the replay button over and over again, listening to Captain Scott's voice and watching her recorded image move and entice. She hadn't faked anything. Everything about her screamed truth, and Gabriel got just as hard the many times after as he had when he first heard it. How many times ago? He had lost count.

"Hullo, Commander Merriweather. Or should I call you Gabriel? After all we've done with—to—each other, I guess I'll call you Gabe. And you can call me Sol." Her image grinned at him with sincerity, and the captain looked years younger. "Or you can call me Legs, as you seemed so fond of doing. But come to think of it . . ." She pouted, her mouth pursed in a pink-tinted moue of disappointment. ". . . you don't call me at all anymore, do you?

"Don't you miss me?" The captain looked off to the right, gave a slight nod then rolled over onto her stomach. The captain's feelings weren't lies. Too much truth showed in the clearness of her direct gaze.

The camera vision left her face and zoomed in on the valley of ample naked breasts revealed by the low neckline of the flimsy nightshirt she wore. The garment looked like male attire, and a sudden flash of heat swept over him. His pulse leaped. Gabriel recognized it for the jealousy that it was. How dare she wear another male's shirt? He snorted at his useless posturing and stared at her image. The camera zoomed out, then back in.

Gabe knew who skillfully operated the camera, just as he knew who coached Sol in this carefully rehearsed sex tease, but for the life of him, he couldn't help enjoying the show. Why else had he played it over and over all night?

Were Sol's breasts bigger? They looked it, or perhaps his dreams of her were fading, but Gabriel didn't have that worry for long. On the vid, he clearly saw the white mounds of Sol's sweet butt rising behind her while she lay on her stomach. Her feet playfully kicked the air. She wore nothing but the nightshirt and red four-inch stilettos. Gabe's palms itched. His balls drew tight, his cock twitched. He remembered the feel of her smooth skin under his hands. Gabe rubbed his palms over his knees, but he never took his eyes off the terminal screen. He had enhanced the com-vid to screen size. Hell, if he could have, he would have projected the image onto the ten foot wall. Sol's message continued in succulent whispers. Her sultry gaze beckoned.

"I miss you, Gabe." She sat up on the bed on her knees and stretched her arms over her head before settling back down with her bare butt resting on her heels. She moved her knees farther apart, and Gabriel sucked in a much needed breath. The end of her shirt's hem hid what he strained to see. On the camera, Sol gazed out through half-closed eyes with an exaggerated longing reflected in their heated-whiskey depths.

A long lock of silky red hair fell across her strong-boned cheek. The tint of the innocent blush that stained her cheeks was endearing.

Gabe's heart stuttered at the sight. Oh, he knew the captain's act was staged, and that the black witch had staged it, but he responded anyway His cock was rock hard steady and demanding. And he couldn't stop the vid, even though he had played it to death.

Now the captain pouted at him with her rouged lips, and her tilted gaze was lowered through painted lashes while she toyed with the top button on her nightshirt. "I miss the things we did to each other that night, Gabriel. All the many things." The top button came loose under her fumbling fingers, and her hand moved down to the next one. His entranced gaze followed her route. How he remembered those cool fingers trembling over his body. He shivered.

"Remember that night, Gabe?" The next button popped. More of that sweet curve of breast was exposed. Slowly, she reached inside the shirt and cupped both fleshy mounds toward him. Her pert nipples rose and beckoned. Sweat dotted Gabe's brow. Unconsciously, he nodded. Yes, he definitely remembered.

"Remember how you bathed me?" Sol hid the peepshow of her self until the last button was undone. Then she rose up on her knees again, the shirt hanging open on her body.

Gabe saw the slight, sweet roundness of her belly, and an uncomfortable feeling came over him. The desire to nurture and protect? That surely wasn't a feeling that he knew—or understood.

"How good you felt when you rubbed oil all over me after my bath." Sol slowly rubbed her hands over her exposed skin from her belly to her breasts to her throat in imitation of his touch. Gabe's hands tingled again, and he held his breath, his gaze following every slow-circling motion of the captain's fingers. They reached her shoulders and pushed the shirt off all that beautiful skin one shoulder at a time, proving what he'd suspected. She was completely naked except for those damned red heels. Gabe sighed aloud; a ragged sound in the quiet of his room.

The captain turned her head to the side. "Do you remember what I smell like, Gabriel?" Her voice dropped into huskier tones, and she stage whispered, "Do you remember what I taste like?"

The blush that lit her cheeks moved to cover her neck and chest. He saw the rapid pulse jumping under the thin skin of her throat. This farce was affecting her, too. One thing Captain Soledad Scott wasn't was a tease. Then again, she had done one hell of a job so far.

"Remember what you did to me next, Gabriel?" Sol looked up at him, her chin tipped down so her coy glance shone through her lashes. "Remember? You did this." She licked her index finger and slowly traced the wet digit from her chin to her neck to between her breasts. She continued down her middle until she came to the lips of her sex. With two clever fingers, the captain parted the hairless folds so Gabe could watch her roll the nub of her sexual drive between the fingers of her other hand. Her eyes closed and she plunged one long finger inside. She jerked.

Gabe heard the frustrated cry she smothered, and he swallowed—hard. Sol moved her finger in and out. He could see the glistening slickness covering it with her moisture—her sweet moisture. He licked his lips. Gabe thought he could hear the wet slide of that finger delving inside her. He could almost remember that phantom warmth sucking his fingers. His rigid erection pulled on his balls. His pulse thumped in his ears. The captain's sweet butt rose and fell with her rocking rhythm. Gabe breathed in tune to her motion, unconsciously moving his hips to match her movement.

"Remember this?" Sol panted. Her fingers still played between her legs, her breaths becoming shallower and shallower. Her chest was rising and falling faster and faster. Gabe was also breathing that way, still in tune with her. Suddenly the captain moaned, "Come, find me, Gabriel. I miss you. I miss this."

With that, her head fell back, the long red silk of her hair spiraling down her naked back. She spread her knees. Her finger plunged deep inside her swollen lips a final time. She arched up with a cry.

Gabe exploded, just as he had done every time he had watched the vid. The screen went blank. Message over, but unerringly delivered.

He sat there, shaking in the aftermath, before he rose from his chair and wiped off the sticky evidence of just how much he missed her. Missed her, hell. Gabriel Merriweather was an idiot over her, but no, he wasn't going to go chasing after her. Not yet. He'd wait. Perhaps she'd send him another message.

Eight

"He hasn't responded, Gellico." Sol rose, naked, when the timer from the tanning bed that supplied the correct amount of vitamin D, without the harmful UV rays, dinged. Dante's Circus came fully equipped for its dancers' comfort as well as its customers. "It's been nearly a month. He's not interested anymore."

"The hell he's not!" Gellico snapped before handing Sol a sheer black robe with embroidered silver dragons splashed in three strategic spots. "His Marine snoopers are still in the club every day, every night, every godsdamn minute. I had Cheri seduce one last night, and he confessed to her that his orders are to not let you out of his sight."

Sol grinned slightly. "Well, I'm sure I wasn't in his sight while the Marine was in Cheri." Her brows rose and she smiled for the first time in days although, it was just a faint lifting of her lips. "Was I?"

Gellico snorted, "Yeah, right. Fucking men. Always thinking with their dicks." She patted her close-cropped head, and her jet black curls sprang tight under her hand. Sol knew Gelli kept her hair short these days for safety's sake. Never again would her hair be used as a weapon, holding her against her will. It had taken years for the hair Gelli had ripped out to grow back in, but it had. Sol swallowed old nightmares and focused on Gelli's words.

"He knows where you are. If he wants, he'll send for you. Come on, let's get some juice." She slapped Sol playfully on the shoulder as they entered the sonic showers. "Perhaps, we need to remind dear ol' Commander Merriweather again. Jar his memory. Tweak his dick, so to speak."

"Gelli, don't you think I'm a little too round to be sexy at the moment?" Sol curved her hand over the smooth, tight mound that barely arched her middle. Gellico's eyes narrowed.

"No, you're just perfect," she answered and reached out her broad palm, laying it on Sol's sweet rise. "I think you are the sexiest thing I've ever seen." The contrast between the darkness of her hand and Sol's paleness was apparent. Gelli murmured, "Sol, you know that I'll do anything to make you happy, don't you? Anything. I'll even take you to see the Commander. And if you want Merriweather, even as pregnant as you are, I think he'll take one look at the evidence of his love and yours and capitulate."

Sol caught the implied "if he doesn't, I'll kill him" and shook her head. She knew how Gellico felt about her but neither spoke of it. She thought it safer discussing Gabriel. "Love?" Sol snorted. "I don't think the commander will think of my stealing his sperm as love. I also don't think he will capitulate. Besides, I don't want him that way." She shook her head again. "And I don't think he wants me at all. So maybe all I want is a little revenge."

"We'll see." Gellico snorted. "Perhaps we can have fun and a little revenge at the same time."

* * * *

Gabriel wanted Sol so badly even his eyelids hurt. Her second message had caught him as off guard as her first, coming as unexpectedly. His empathy senses failed when it came to Sol. He had just lifted his wine glass in a toast to the prime minister of Alsakasse for making the new treaty with the Doranians happen when his link went off. Just as before, he had responded without thinking. The embarrassment wasn't the same. Thankfully, after his first message from the captain, he had set his vid for mute while he held meetings. So no one knew why Gabe choked. His face reddened, and he had made some ridiculous excuse about "early to bed, early to rise" while leaving the dinner party.

Oh, yeah, early to bed to watch the vid again, and Gabriel sure was rising. How could he think when all his blood supply seemed to be throbbing in his lower extremities? And he didn't mean his legs. *Jesu*. Both those women were witches—the one on screen as well as the one running the camera.

"Gabriel, I haven't heard from you, so I thought I'd better remind you of what I look like, just in case you've forgotten. You haven't forgotten me, have you?" The captain gazed at him from solemn, soulful eyes that had been heavily outlined with black while her eyelids were dusted a sparkling silvery green that enhanced the gold of her gaze. She blinked, and Gabe blinked in reply. Surely the captain's lashes were never that long or that black. And why was she dressed like some ancient Egyptian queen?

Some sort of gauzy, gold material floated from her shoulders, and a thick metal jewelry piece gleamed around her neck. A red stone hung from the center and dangled between her breasts—breasts that were naked again except for the red rouge that decorated her nipples. A filigreed chain hung from the tip of one enticing nipple. Was it pierced?

He swallowed—hard. They were larger again, her nipples and her breasts, and for a moment, Gabe could have sworn he remembered the taste and feel of those puckered nipples rolling in his mouth. His empathy talents were backfiring. Tremors shook him, but Gabriel skillfully delayed his release. He dared not touch himself, although he ached to do so.

"Do you like my outfit?" The captain twirled on the screen, and the see-through material she wore parted from her hips, further displaying her lower body. Gabe mutely nodded. He was so lost that it never occurred to him that Sol couldn't see him. He drew in her image. He thought he smelled her enticing fragrance and sucked in a deep breath. His vision narrowed on her. A wide belt encrusted with twinkling jewels rested so low on the captain's hips that it barely covered the beginning crease of her thighs. If she had pubic hair, it would have shown. Unexpectedly, Gabriel felt disappointed at the lack of those curls he knew would have been fiery red. He would have liked to part them with his tongue—slip that tongue deep between those fragrant lips, thrust inside her until she shook with release. Another shiver shot through him. The captain's remembered taste haunted him.

She moved, undulating her dance on the screen. More flimsy material flowed from the sparkling belt and fell from it to the tops of her jewel-accented feet. Tiny metal bells tinkled from the glittering bands on her anklets. The captain wiggled her naked toes and dipped her head. She smiled up at him, her eyes peering from under her lashes. Someone had taught her that coy look, but Soledad made it look natural and unrehearsed. She was clearly enjoying a sexual freedom she probably had never experienced before. In that outrageous outfit, her golden, whiskey-colored glance should have been the dark of night Egyptian eyes of ancient Earth legend. Gabriel didn't care, her intense gaze entranced him. Her eyes glowed like jungle cat's eyes—lion eyes or were they lying eyes?

"Want to paint my nails?" The captain held out one elegant narrow foot then shook it slightly with her toes pointed. The nails were already painted. They glittered with some kind of sparkle paint. The bells on her ankle tinkled again. A faint smile tugged the corners of her enticing red mouth. Gabe felt his mouth spreading in answer. *Gods.* Even her lips appeared wider, wetter, and more kissable. He caught his breath. His tongue stuck to the roof of his mouth. His hands twitched in his lap. Gabriel held them together, refusing to touch his aching member.

Rhythmic, sultry music continued playing, and Sol thrust her pelvic area, in tune to the beat, toward the camera. "Do you have something better than painting my nails in mind, Gabriel? You seemed very good at innovative ideas. Remember? I sure do." She swayed and raised her slender arms. They waved gracefully with one hand sliding up from the wrist to her shoulder on the opposite arm, then the other hand repeated the motion on the other side. Gabe's gaze followed her actions, lingering on her quivering breasts. Her hips gyrated back and forth to the haunting music, and her limbs gleamed with some sort of body oil that caught the eye and boggled the mind. The thin material covering her long legs parted and concealed, opened and closed, time and again, giving just a glimpse of what lay between her legs. Gabe caught a shallow breath. Behind her, shadows deepened in the room. Firelight, a fake or real campfire, flickered across her limbs. The music quickened along with her movements. The captain pirouetted on her toes, a graceful swirling circle that hid what he wanted so badly. She tilted her chin up, her head tossed back. Her fiery hair flew out behind her. Gabriel remembered the silken slide of it across his body. The captain bent farther back at a staggering angle, but her garments fell between her bent knees effectively hiding her secret. Gabe swallowed his dry disappointment, a noise so loud that he heard himself make the sound above the drums' throbbing rhythm.

He couldn't say which affected him more, the remembrance of those swollen, nether lips under his tongue or the new roundness that stretched Sol's middle, emphasizing her sexuality. Sol's changing beauty suddenly reminded him of an ancient archeological model for fertility, a heavy-breasted stone mother figure that lured and compelled men to fall at her feet and do her bidding in continuing their race. He'd volunteer. The captain was certainly made to be a mother. Her long torso carried a child so well that even in what Gabe calculated as her sixth month, she still looked as sexy and as beguiling as ever. She continued her dance. He couldn't stand much more. Sol moved closer to the camera. He groaned. Gabe swore he could smell her enticing scent, taste her sweetness. She held her shimmering skirts closed.

"I'm waiting, Gabriel," she panted. Her gleaming breasts heaved. The sight encouraged him to reach for her although he knew she wasn't within his grasp . . . yet.

"But I won't wait much longer." She snapped and flicked her costume open, her riches exposed. Her upper thighs glistened. Wet.

The first time he came, Gabe nearly fainted from his delayed release. He shook in the aftermath. Before midnight, he had reached a decision. His vision narrowed. He would have what he desired. And he wanted the captain. Gabriel only hoped he could wait her out. He wasn't a Chakkra barbarian who just took what he wanted, and he wouldn't become one. Not even for her.

* * * *

The captain lay across his bed with one arm tucked under her head. Her bare underarm beckoned him, as if the soft, smooth skin there was the sexiest of female organs. How could something so ordinary be so compelling? She moved, settled her hips deeper into the softness of his mattress. Gabriel groaned. He moved toward her with only one thing in mind—he had to touch her, smooth his fingers over that soft, glowing skin; put his lips in the bend of her arm that lay so exposed. He still, after all this time, remembered her unique flavor.

Gabriel's mouth dried. He felt lightheaded from the loss of blood to his brain. He wanted nothing more than to swoop down on the captain and lap her up like cream. He wanted to lick and kiss every inch of her until she screamed that she was his. His balls swelled, hardened into rock, and his bobbing cock throbbed. She watched him and waited, her lips rising in a faint, knowing upturn. Her hair glistened in the moonlight. Those silken locks spread across his pillow like spilled blood. And she knew what she did to him. Deliberately, she lay naked, her body revealed to him with one knee bent far to the side, exposing her riches. The vulva lips between her legs were deep red and swollen, either from wanting him to fuck them or perhaps because he already had. If he had, he was ready again. Gabriel felt as if he was going to burst from wanting to feel her sliding over him, sucking him dry.

Her eyes were half closed, heavy with sexual invitation. "Come and get me, Gabriel," she whispered in husky invitation, and he couldn't resist. Gabriel reached for her . . . .

And awoke. He was still swearing Chakkra oaths when he finished jerking himself to a finish. By the gods, he was done waiting. The captain would be his before the day was out.

* * * *

"They're coming!" Cheri burst into Gellico's room without knocking. The little dancer rocked to a halt and bent over, her hands braced on her knees. She gulped rapid breaths, and Sol felt sorry for her. As Gellico's understudy, the petite Cheri was in top shape, so she must have run nonstop all the way through the ever present crowds from the space docks. Gellico had posted Cheri there for the past few days. After their last vid, they were certain that Gabriel's ship would be docking soon.

Gellico said he'd never be able to resist their last message, but Sol wasn't so sure. She had her suspicions about Cheri's announcement.

"Who's coming?" Sol calmly pulled pins from her mouth. Material that was to be a new gown draped forgotten in her hands. She could no longer wear her favorite regimentals. Her breasts might never fit them again. Gellico grabbed the pins out of her own mouth and threw them into the sewing case.

"Commander—Merriweather—and his men." Cheri gasped before a deep breath restored her breathing. "His ship just landed—without the proper protocol, and his troops have disembarked and are marching here. Damien said they are going to take Soledad. Just to make sure, he's standing guard outside the club so no one can leave." She sucked in another quick breath. "But don't worry, Punch is there, too. He won't let anyone in either."

"Punch won't have a choice. He's outnumbered." Gellico grumbled. "And I won't have him hurt on our account." She grabbed a short sword from the wall and strode toward the door. Her eyes sparkled with anger that came off her in heated waves. "I thought the asshole would at least call for you like a gentleman, but oh no, not him. Well, he'd better not hurt anyone if he knows what's good for him."

"Please, mistress, please don't hurt Damien." Cheri pleaded. It took both her hands to cover Gellico's thick wrists. "He's only following orders."

"No, Gelli, she right," Sol echoed the little dancer. "Don't fight the sergeant. It's not his fault. He really is just following orders. We started this."

Sol gently tugged on the weapon's hilt. She didn't want anyone hurt over what she had set in motion, and she gave a relieved breath when Gelli nodded. The dancer's grip on the sword loosened, but her dark gaze still glittered hard as she watched Sol replace it back on the wall.

"Well, what do you want to do, then? I thought you'd get an invitation from Merriweather, like a civilized person in his position would offer. But instead the great Commander has got to charge in with guns blazin'." Gellico shrugged. "Diplomat, my ass."

Sol sucked in a breath and pursed her lips. "You're right, Gelli. He could have asked me." Unexpected anger flared, and heat flushed over Sol in a wave. She didn't know which irritated her more, her angry reaction to the Commander's methods or his rash action that made her heart pound. Was she really delighted that he'd come for her, or was her response just raging hormones?

"Damned straight, I'm right." Gellico emphatically nodded. "If not, why send in the guards and troops like he means to arrest you?"

The idea that the Marines were being used so frivolously made Sol furious. Marines had better things to do than corner some sex captive for the Commander of the Diplomatic Corps. Sol held a lot more respect for fighting men than that. She'd never abuse her crew that way, at least if she still commanded a crew.

The reminder of why she didn't command one made her angrier. "That sonofabitch! How dare he? He doesn't own me." Sol glared and snatched down the same sword she had replaced just moments ago from the wall of ancient weapons. Gellico stopped her and laughed wickedly.

Her dark eyes glittered. "No, dear. If he wants it this way, with no rules, two—or three—can play that game."

Gelli pulled Cheri close to her, towering over the diminutive blond dancer. "Calm down, Cheri. I just want you to tell Dante that I'm taking my vacation now and that you'll be headlining for me for the next few nights."

"You mean it? About me headlining for you?" Cheri's mouth hung open in a perfect O.

Gellico smiled and kissed her on the forehead. "Yes, dear, I know you can do it. Now run along. Don't stop to tease with your big, bad Damien along the way."

"No, mistress." Cheri shook her head. "He won't talk to me now anyway. He's on duty." Cheri nearly skipped out the door

Gellico muttered after her, "That asshole sergeant was on duty the other night when he fucked her, but it didn't matter then." She grabbed Sol and said, "Quick, down the delivery entrance. We'll catch the supply freighter to Faro's Hump. I have a friend there who'll hide us."

"I'm still taking this with me." Sol clung to the short sword.

"Great idea," Gellico snatched another lethal-looking, foot-long knife from the wall for herself. "But we'll need to hide them from the supply traders. We don't want to make our rescuers nervous, the poor dears." She gave that twisted grin that showed her teeth to perfection, a fierce gesture that was ever the Amazon savage.

Sol grabbed her in a quick hug.

"What?" Gellico gave her a puzzled frown.

"Thanks for being my friend, even when I don't know what I want."

"Sword sisters." Gellico lifted her weapon and nodded in all seriousness. Sol knew that neither of them would forget the day they had fought back to back against overwhelming odds on Hydra; the day they had forged a bond that would last a lifetime—a ship captain and a courtesan, but what a pair of warriors. A Diplomatic Corps commander with his team of Marine regulars didn't stand a chance!

* * * *

"What?" Gabriel growled at the jarring live feed on his com vid. "This had better be fucking good." He stormed around the dancehall, kicking offending chairs out of his way. Futile rage simmered inside him. His Chakkra blood slammed in the red tint of his vision. He had to kick or punch something. The chairs worked off a little steam, but not enough. The bar was not where he wanted to be at the moment. He had expected to have his cock buried deep in the captain by now, and he couldn't believe Sol had slipped through his fingers again. *Damn!* He had been so close this time. Just where the hell had she gone?

His com-link beeped, and when he glanced down at it, his snarl froze. Over the link, a red-haired vision snapped back at him. He had a flashback to his last dream and became rock hard in an instant.

"It is fucking *bad*, Gabriel. Just what the hell do you think you're doing?" Sol's angry bronze stare glared at him, but she didn't wait for his response. "Most sensible people would have just invited me for a visit, but you? Oh, no, not the great Commander of the Diplomatic Corps. You had to storm a peaceful business establishment with military guards bent on my capture. Whatever *were* you thinking?" She huffed pink, flushed cheeks. "Diplomat, my ass. Dante would be within his rights to file for censure judgment against you."

"I don't give a flying fuck about Dante," Gabriel interrupted before she could continue, and he could tell that the captain had a lot more to say. Her kissable mouth, for once free of paint, hung open. She was right. Gabe hadn't been able to think like a diplomat since he had first met Captain Soledad Scott. She drove him to distraction, and apparently, he must do the same to her. He could almost see the steam rolling out her lovely ears. "Where are you?" he snapped.

"I don't think I'll tell you." Sol raised her chin and gave him a speculative look. "And don't waste your time tracing this call, Commander. It's blocked."

"That figures," Gabe snorted.

"I just wanted to warn you about hurting anyone at Dante's. They are my friends, and I protect my friends." The fierce look she gave would have wilted a lesser man. Gabriel read the truth without his empathy senses.

"I wouldn't expect any less of you, Captain." Gabe did his best to keep his injured pride that she would think he would harm her friends from showing in his words. They knew so little about each other to be so involved, and he was more involved with her than he'd ever been with anyone. Empaths were never allowed the luxury of sharing thoughts so completely. Chakkra warriors enjoyed even less sexual freedom. Their mates were chosen from birth—nothing more than a way to procreate and rut. Thankfully, his father had shunned his chosen mate and became a defiant outlaw in love with a gentle Terran ambassador. The captain was the first woman Gabriel had ,known, outside of his human mother, who was so truthful. He read her without using his talents. The captain's thoughts lacked painful hidden agendas. Her every move told him exactly how she felt. And Gabe didn't like what she was thinking about him at the moment.

"What makes you think I'd hurt anyone here?"

"From the way you stormed in with your troops. Using Marines—" She shook her head. Light bounced off her tousled hair and touched her flushed cheeks. Had she been running or was she just angry with him? "I thought you, of all people, were diplomatic enough to ask me to come see you."

"I am diplomatic . . . most of the time," he replied. "And I have waited for you to come to me. But some people—" Gabriel gave the captain his best narrow-eyed stare. "—some people push me too far, and I don't like being pushed. I push back."

"People like me?" Sol shook her head again and extended that stubborn jaw. Gabe could almost imagine someone taking a punch at such blatant defiance and flinched at the thought of anyone marring that beautiful face. He'd kill any sonofabitch that ever hurt her.

Surprise shattered Gabriel's ordered life with the depth of his violent, proprietary reaction. For the captain, he would release his Chakkra rage and shred any enemy.

Gabriel felt his eyes widen. One thought filled his head: he had to find her—now. *Oh, god, there was that protective streak again.*

"I want you, Captain." Gabe lowered his voice and put his heart into his words. He hunched over his link as if closing off the world. "I want you so badly I can't think straight. I can't eat, I can't sleep, and as you said, I'm a piss-poor diplomat at the moment. Don't torture me anymore. Please, tell me where you are, Sol. I'll come to you. I just want to see you, to talk with you, be with you."

After a long moment, Sol softly said, "No." She shook her head again, but Gabriel read real regret in her voice. "But I promise I won't send anymore vids." Her voice dropped, matching his tone. "And I'll . . . I'll think about coming to you." She straightened. Her gaze and her voice hardened. "Now, go home and leave my friends alone."

"Did you really think that I'd harm your friends, Captain?"

Her head dipped. She sighed then raised her chin; her eyes glittered with unreadable emotion. "No."

"Thank you."

"Good night, Gabriel," she whispered, and he closed his eyes, wanting to capture the sound of his name on her lips. With a click, she signed off. The dead screen mocked him with its blankness. Gabe knew without checking that he wouldn't be able to trace the call.

* * * *

"Let's go home, men," Gabriel told his tired Marines. They were exhausted from their failed mission to Tantra, but Gabe hadn't been thinking of them when he had ordered this unscheduled stop on Dante's Circus. He should have known that Sol would take his unauthorized visit as an insult. He would have known better, too, if he hadn't been thinking with his *other* head. But sleep was in short supply these days. His wet dreams of the captain hadn't helped. What a blunder.

"Commander?" Damien, the Marine sergeant that he'd stationed on Dante's Circus, vied for his attention. In the flood of outside emotions, Gabe's focus was wandering again, just as it had since the day—or rather the night—he had met Captain Soledad Scott. He knew from the riot of feelings that swamped him that Sol wasn't here. But his Marines were randy with the lousy pheromones of Dante's.

"Yeah, Sergeant," Gabe ran a hand through his hair. "What now?"

Damien shuffled uneasily from one foot to the other, "Well—the men—you know, haven't had leave in a long while, and they . . . uh—"

"Oh, for the gods' sake, Damien, just spill it."

The sergeant snapped to attention, gulped and said quickly, "Since we're already here—at the Circus—the men would like a bit of R&R, sir." He hurried to add. "If it's all right with you, I mean—Commander—sir."

"Oh, by all means, take some time off. Get laid. Why not? I haven't slept in the gods know how long, but who cares?" Gabriel snapped then looked hard at the Marine who bore the brunt of his misguided anger. His empathic skills surged to the forefront of his mind, and he inwardly cursed. The sergeant actually felt pity for him, and Gabe didn't want anyone's sympathy. He was *not* a lovesick idiot. "Tell the men that we leave at dawn," he muttered. "We leave, with or without them. They can all go AWOL for all I care." When Gabe realized what he'd just said, he was glad that the sturdy sergeant was long out of sight and hearing.

Gabriel suddenly wished that he was just a military crew member on liberty, not a half-breed Chakkra warrior, and certainly not the diplomat who was panting after a retired Guild captain who taunted him with sex one minute and denied him the next.

Gabriel gave a disgusted shake of his head, deciding that he was either in love or in lust. Either way, he was in deep shit with the captain. Oh, yeah. Really, really deep shit.

Nine

"I really don't think we should be doing this, Soledad." Gellico's whisper floated in the night air, just loud enough to reach Sol's ear. Gelli only called her by her full name when Sol was making her do something she didn't like to do. And on her hands and knees, following Sol, Gelli obviously didn't like crawling around in the dark.

Back again at Dante's Circus, they crept through a corridor that was nearly the pitch dark of midnight. Their pinpoint light gave poor illumination, showing only the three foot circle they moved in. The stiff woven-grass carpet they crawled over rustled a little too loudly for Sol's liking. And the floor smelled not only of the dried straw but of the hundreds of varied species who had passed this way. In other words, it wasn't the most pleasant thing she had ever smelled. By the way her stomach heaved, the baby didn't particularly like the odor either, so Sol refrained from breathing too deeply. She swallowed the thickness that rose in her throat. After all, this was her idea. She had again changed her mind about meeting the commander in a one-on-one. She snickered at the unintended pun.

Thankfully, no sounds came through the proofed and fully occupied pleasure rooms; rooms filled with Merriweather's Marines. Sol kept her voice low anyway. "I know we shouldn't do this. At least, I think I know that. Anyway, the Marines are busy, Gelli. You heard Cheri's message. They're only here until dawn. I'm sure they'll be occupied all night, revved up by her dance and the Circus' pheromones." Sol slunk along the wall, feeling her way to the room Punch had said was Gabriel's. The bouncer had made Gelli promise that they meant the commander no harm before giving them the old fashioned master keys and the pen laser. Only Gellico could have gotten them from Punch.

In the shadowed circle of light, crawling along on their knees, they wouldn't be easy to spot if anyone did happen to look down the long, dark hall. Sol didn't want to be captured by

Gabriel's crew. If spotted and confronted, Gelli would certainly fight, and Sol wouldn't let that happen. Someone would get hurt, and Sol wasn't sure it would be Gelli. That would mean charges being filed and a whole mess of trouble. Trouble Gelli and Sol didn't need. No one needed to poke into their pasts. And she wasn't wasting any time. Even the trip back from Faro's Hump had taken longer than she had expected. Lumbering cargo ships weren't big on speed or comfort. She was glad that Gelli had come along without too many complaints about idiots who couldn't make up their minds. But she wished that for just this once her friend would shut the hell up. Her long, muttered, profane litany was becoming annoying.

"Help me with the key," Sol whispered in hopes of distracting her grumbling friend. The master keys felt all the same, or perhaps it was just her numb fingers that refused to move. Surely she wasn't scared of meeting the man in the room. Months ago, she had spent a whole night with him, sharing raunchy sex under the Pleasure Dome. This wasn't that different.

Oh, hell, who was she kidding? On the Dome, she hadn't been Captain Scott, and he hadn't been Commander Gabriel Merriweather. They had been strangers who fucked without inhibitions. The slippery keys slid through Sol's grasp. It was her turn to curse the antiquated means of entry. The Dome was big on faking reality, and their keys were shaped to their rooms' themes.

"Here, give them to me." Gellico took the keys with an exasperated sigh. "Once you're in there, what do you expect to do?"

"What do you think?" Sol snapped.

"I mean, besides fucking him silly," Gellico snapped back. Then she gripped Sol's shoulder in the darkness. "I'm sorry. I didn't mean that."

"Yeah, you did, Gelli." Sol sighed. "But it doesn't matter. I know how you worry. I'll be fine. I'll meet you here before dawn. I promise."

"You're not going back to Delta Three with him?"

Sol shook her head, then realized that Gellico couldn't see

her in the darkness. "No. I don't think that's a good idea. The baby's due soon and my friends are here. And right now, I want my friends with me."

"Thank you, dear. I want to be with you, too." Gellico rested her forehead against Sol's. Sol felt her breath puff on her face. "Okay, this is the right one. Here." She thrust the appropriate shaped key into Sol's hand.

The shape of a snarling lion's head took form under Sol's numb fingers—the key to Gabriel Merriweather's room. Each key to the pleasure rooms of Dante's Circus was formed in the shape of a circus animal. How appropriate that Gabriel's key was her image of the man himself. How like a jungle cat he was. "Okay. I'm going in. Wish me luck."

Gellico mumbled, "Luck."

Sol barely heard her above her rioting emotions. She swallowed hard, and a shudder passed over her. She felt as if she were losing her old life by bits and pieces. "Are you all right?" Gelli asked out of the darkness. Sol felt her light squeeze on her shoulder. As close as sisters, it seemed as if Gelli knew Sol's distress. Sol's gaze misted. Gelli was always so protective, even when she thought Sol wouldn't know.

"Yes," Sol whispered. "I'm fine. I'll just go on in and get this over with. I'll be out here at dawn."

"Okay." Gelli's hushed whisper sounded like a commando's on a raid, and Sol felt just as jumpy.

The turn of the key inside the lock made a soft click in the dark. Both waited with baited breath, but only the sound of soft snoring came back through the shadows.

Gelli squeezed Sol's hand and pushed her forward. As the door closed behind her, Sol barely heard Gelli's profane curse. She also couldn't see a thing.

* * * *

Sol started rising from her crouch. From out of nowhere, a rough hand covered her mouth and finished jerking her upright. *Damn it!* She hadn't heard the snoring stop over the clink of the door latching or her heart's heavy thumping. A strong arm held her tightly against a definitely male body. Her teeth pinched her lips under a hardened palm. She didn't panic, she knew that scent.

Sol blinked in the sudden light of a flipped switc as Gabriel said, "Well, well, Captain Soledad Scott. Fancy this. You certainly have kept me waiting long enough," Gabe released her and stepped back so quickly he tripped over the tall woven basket that acted as a table near the door. His toe cracked against the fake marble vase next to it, and he danced around on one foot, swearing.

Sol laughed aloud, her anger fading along with the pain in her lips. Merriweather looked so silly, jumping about in his blue and white striped shorts. Only a diplomat would wear such atrocious underwear. Suddenly her laughter died, and she stood gaping at the room's splendor. In all the years Sol had visited Gellico, she had never seen this room, or any of the Circus' pleasure rooms, for that matter. She'd never used Dante's professional services.

Under golden beams that blazed from a seemingly limitless blue sky, sun-drenched, sandy plains surrounded Sol while snow-capped mountains loomed high over her head. From one jungle-leafed, green-splashed wall, a noisy waterfall with a fountain spouting real water ended its fall in an inviting pool filled with fragrant, floating water lilies. Their smell wafted on the gentle, warm breeze that came from hidden ventilators. Mesmerizing 3-D murals adorned each wall, the holograms so lifelike that Sol felt as if she were surely on a desert safari. She even smelled the heated tinge of sage in the desert air, felt the humid moisture of the cooling water of the falls. A soft hypnotic drum beat, coinciding with the lights, only added to the out of place feeling.

"Like it?" Gabriel smiled at her, evidently recovered from his toe-tripping accident. Sol suddenly wondered if the whole incident had been faked, a distraction to give them time to reacquaint themselves. He hovered at her side and acted as if he'd chosen the room especially for her. The thought that he might have presumed that she would come to him irritated her. He wore that irritating crooked-tooth grin and didn't wait for an answer about the room before he strode to the bamboo bar and lifted a glass in Sol's direction. "Drink?" He moved with the hurried movements of a nervous man; a big, nervous man wearing only ridiculous underwear. Sol couldn't miss the unease that darkened the blue of his stare.

Despite her flush of sympathy, she still glared. "You know I can't have liquor in my condition, Commander." She curved her arm over her swollen middle, then turned her back and marched across the room, only to turn back with another glare. She still hadn't forgotten about the *Icarus* or his involvement. Perhaps she did hate Commander Merriweather after all.

Gabe frowned, the gesture matching the hurt in his eyes. He held up the glass of pinkish-orange liquid. "It's organic, vitamin-filled fruit juice, Sol. Contrary to what you think, I'm not an idiot."

"That remains to be seen," Sol mumbled ,and strolled further into the room. He had ordered a special health drink for her. He *had* thought she would come running to him. She was an idiot for sure. But somehow the idea that Gabe took such measures for her comfort pleased Sol. She moved the draped netting from the side of the four-poster bed before sitting down. Yeah, like any mosquito would dare disturb the tranquility of this place, much less get past the pristine filtering system. "Come over here." She patted the bed. "So we can talk."

"Talk?" His normally deep voice sounded strangled. His high cheekbones flushed deeper, and he coughed into his fist. Strange to see such discomposure on such a large man. Even stranger to think that she could cause it.

Sol grinned. Her commander had lost that polished diplomatic veneer that she disliked so much. "Yeah, talk. I told you we had a lot to talk about." He walked toward her slowly. And she warmed at the natural way Gabriel moved, so graceful yet so dangerous, just like she remembered him, a jungle cat padding its cautious way toward her . . . a very nervous cat.

"Uh huh. Yeah, we can talk." He eyed her with his head tilted, his pale eyes speculative. "But right now I'm feeling a bit tongue-tied." His intense gaze moved over her. The hot look in it left her trembling. His eyes revealed such naked longing.

For the first time, Sol read real emotion on his face—hunger.

Her heart thumped furiously at her planned seduction. She tried for a light tone but her voice sounded husky to her own ears. "Awww, poor baby. And here I was hoping you'd make better use of that tongue." She smiled her best wicked enigmatic smile, a gesture that Gellico had taught her, abd that Sol had perfected. Gabriel's eyes widened. Sudden redness covered his neck. Sol curled her fingers and motioned him closer "I remember the feel of your tongue, Gabriel." Her whisper sounded loud in the room. Sol told herself that she was just seducing the commander to make up for sending him those seductive vids. Surely, she wasn't doing this for herself.

Gabriel couldn't think of a speedy come back to the captain's suggestive remarks. He knew the honesty of what she wasn't saying, felt it through his system, and for the life of him, he couldn't help responding to it. His knees buckled near the bed, and he fell heavily down next to her. He laid his head in Sol's lap and let her fresh, spring-like scent surround him. Her calm muting of his raging empathy senses came like a warm blanket's covering. He had felt the dampening effect when the captain neared his room. He had prepared himself for this meeting, but knowing and experiencing were two different things. Now in her presence, Gabe closed his eyes and snuggled his face into her softness, drowning in the intensity of the sensations that flooded him and those that no longer bothered him. He breathed a deep cleansing breath and drew in her scent as he tightened his arms around her hips. No one smelled like Sol, felt like her or sounded like her. *Springtime.* He had missed the captain so much. The vids paled in comparison to the real thing. Since Gabriel had come into his powers at puberty, he had never had this experience, had never allowed this closeness. He could have cried at the sweetness of it, but his tears had died a hard death long ago. An empath, especially a child with empathic abilities, could only cry so often before the useless grief killed him.

Her hand touched his bare shoulder. It trembled but gave such warmth. As if from a great distance, Gabe heard her ask, "Are you all right, Gabriel?" Real concern reflected in her voice and in her sudden, easily read emotions. They seemed so attuned to each other.

"Yeah." Gabe curved himself tighter around her hips. Without conscious thought, he pulled her closer in his arms. His needy desire for her overwhelmed him. Sol felt like a shelter from all of his storms, but her loose, silky gown hindered his efforts to lose himself in her heat. Gabe pulled the front apart with a rip to the fabric. Without stopping, he mumbled an apology and laid his head on her bare, rounded abdomen. "I'm all right. I'm fine, just a little worn out from chasing you, Captain. Gods, I still can't believe you're here—in the flesh, so to speak." He rubbed his hot cheek against her stomach, nuzzled his lips across her skin. She shivered.

"Well, I am here, Gabriel. Believe it." She bent to him, placed her palms along his jaws and raised his mouth for a quick kiss. She whispered against his lips, "You don't have to chase me anymore, Commander. I'm really here."

"For how long?" Gabe growled as he rose to her and claimed her lips again without giving her a chance to answer. No teasing this time. He cupped a hand behind Sol's head and prevented her from moving back. They held the kiss for so long that when they pulled apart, Gabe didn't know who was more shaken by the intensity. The look in her eyes was dazed, shattered gold. He wondered if his eyes looked the same. He certainly felt unfocused, breathless. Sol caught a heaving breath. Gabe enjoyed the push of her breasts against his chest.

"I'll be here at least until morning." Sol's gaze dropped first, and she straightened her back, moving her too far away for Gabe's liking.

"Then where will you be?" He gripped her upper arms and tugged her all the way to his chest. He craved her skin's touch. She felt warm and soft in all the right places. They lay back on the bed with their lips a mere fraction apart. Gabe drew in her breath. Her heavy breasts strained against the gaping silk, and he swallowed a groan at the sight of the points of dark nipples showing through the thin fabric.

The captain's desire slammed through her thoughts and into him. Her arousal mixed with his raging needs and clouded his thinking. That husky voice of hers finally broke through the sexual fog that threatened him. Sol's logic was like a douse of cold water.

"You know that what we have won't last, Commander. We come from two different worlds. A peacemaking diplomat and a warring space captain—how ludicrous can you get?"

"Bullshit." Gabe thrust her away only for a moment before snuggling her back to his chest, his legs thrown over her thighs, careful of the mound of her middle. "What makes you think we're not suited?" He kissed the hollow indent in her throat. *Go slow—slow*, he warned himself. A rapid pulse beat under his tongue. Her scent surrounded him again, filled his nose, his head with her strength. He felt her trembling or was it his?

"Really, Gabriel, think about it. You come in after a crew like mine has risked their lives, some losing their lives, and you make nice-nice with the same people who have killed us. You make concessions with the bastards, bowing and scraping, all in the name of peace. I don't get it. It's as if our loss of life means nothing to anyone." She drew away from him, turned a cold shoulder to him, but didn't get up. Yet, she was still too far away.

Gabe smothered a disappointed sigh before he leaned forward on one elbow next to her, so close he could still smell her subtle perfume, enticingly clean, not the heavy spice scent he'd expected after her last vid. He took his time answering. Somehow he knew that their entire future depended on his response. In his mind, he heard his mother's last words. *"Hate and violence is not the way of a wise man. Learn, grow and bring peace, my son."* Her words had haunted Gabriel all his life—as did her violent death. He had to make Sol understand his life's work—his atonement for his violent past.

"You don't see the urgent need for peace, Sol?" She turned back to him and he hurried on before she could answer. "Yes, you're right. I do go in after you or other military have finished a battle, when the region is still hot with the bloody stench of the dead and the cries of the dying. That very thing drives me to make peace. Any loss of life affects me. Useless grief chokes every breath I take. In the aftermath of war, I see firsthand, the innocent—the children, the wives, the loved ones left behind without fathers, brothers, sisters and mothers. I feel the need for peace in the very marrow of my bones. And, yes . . ." He nodded again, looking deep into Sol's eyes. He reached out and gripped her by the shoulders. Despite his control, his voice cracked and broke. He nearly growled, "I do make concessions. I would sell my very soul to stop the wars and bring peace. I do whatever the job takes, and sometimes it works." He drew her down next to him and sighed, deeply. "Sometimes it doesn't."

Gabe really didn't mean for Sol to hear his next murmured thought. "And sometimes, I wish to all gods' hell that I had never heard of the Diplomatic Corps." Past failures haunted him with taunting remembrances. Ghosts of victims he had been unable to save remained as vivid reminders of his weaknesses. An empath's talent is at best a curse.

"Then why do you do it?" Her soft question was followed by a light-fingered caress on his chest. She wasn't afraid to touch him. Her honest concern lay open to Gabe. The captain had listened to him, more importantly she had heard him. His skin tingled under the path of her trembling fingers. Chills followed her touch all the way to his groin. His balls swelled, tightened. His cock lengthened until it hurt. This was better than any dream.

"It's my job. It's what I do—who I am. Who will do it if I don't?" The need for her to understand and agree with him overcame Gabe in soul-shattering waves. "Without diplomats, without peacemakers, Captain, where will it all end? With the death of us all?" Anguish was awash in his words.

"Oh, my god!" Comprehension dawned in Sol's widened eyes. He felt the exact moment that truth struck her and hid his wince. She traced the tattoos on his side and up his arm, stared at them so hard her eyes bugged. "You're a Guild registered empath, aren't you? I—I saw the tats that night on the Pleasure Dome, but their meaning didn't register in my mind." She smacked the heel of one hand to her forehead. Gabe refused to look her in the eye, afraid he'd read pity there, even if he didn't hear any in her voice.

"How stupid of me." A pink flush crept up her neck and flooded her cheeks. "Oh, Commander, I don't think we're suited at all." Sol rose to his position, her elbow supporting her head and her face level with his. Her gaze lowered, and she visually traced his tattoos again through lash-shadowed eyes.

Gabe noted a small scar on the side of her temple, a battle scar no doubt. This close he could see the soft hair surrounding her face. He wished for a lifetime to memorize every line, every curve and every mark on her body. He longed to kiss each one and smooth any remembrance of hurt away. "If we are so doomed as lovers, Captain, why did you come here tonight?" Gabriel's breathing became a hurtful thing that lodged in his tight chest. He feared her answer.

She pushed up, but came no closer to him. "I couldn't stand to see you hurting and know that I am the cause." Her gaze dropped down to the bed. "I didn't know about your empathic ability. I didn't know that you felt everything we shared so deeply. I shouldn't have sent those messages. I wasn't thinking straight, and—" Sol raised one brow and looked him in the eye again, sincerity shown in the golden warm depths of her gaze even if he couldn't read her emotions. "Perhaps, I took bad advice. Believe me, Gabriel, I didn't mean to hurt you."

He relished the sound of his name on her lips. She couldn't know what that closeness meant to him. He had to go slowly with her or he would scare her with the depth of his caring. He kept his tone even and light. "I know, Captain. But you did hurt me, so what are you going to do about it?" Gabe held his breath, living in the moment. He couldn't tell the captain that he knew she was a tranq. She would think that was the only reason he wanted her and that would spoil the mood. Besides, she acted as if she didn't know. The fact was, Sol was here and she wanted him. Despite her being a tranq, Gabriel felt her intense need crying out to him. The scent of her arousal still wafted thick in the air. He breathed her in. He'd worry about tomorrow later. She took her cue from him. Her voice was just as teasing, although her tone grew husky, just like in her vids to him.

"You don't have to hurt anymore. I can kiss it and make it better." Faint tugging lifted the corner of her sweet mouth. She rubbed her hand over the tent that rose in his shorts. Gabe froze in place, raised on his elbows. With no assistance from him, the captain found the slit in the front of his shorts and smoothed the fabric down over his jutting cock. She stared at him. He lengthened further under her gaze.

Gabe gritted his teeth at the pull of his balls. *Damn it.* Just being with Sol was bad enough, but having her touch him after all this time and then eye him so hungrily just about pushed him over the edge. Remembered images of her from the vids swamped him. The captain had danced for him, enticed him with her eyes, her body. Now she touched him in reality. He couldn't remember ever being this close to ejaculating and denying the urge. But if he came, she might leave, and that action he wanted to delay for as long as possible.

Help me, please, Gabe prayed to the stars and tried to ignore the light fingertip caress she gave to his cock's rounded head. Then . . . *oh gods* . . . she leaned over . . . her soft lips closed on him.

He wanted to scream but could only groan. Wet heat surrounded him. Her silken tongue caressed. She licked up his entire length, and Gabe felt the sensation inside and out. His head fell back, but he remained upright on his elbows, his hands clutching the bedclothes in his fists. But he had to see this, memorize her loving him like this so he looked back down and watched her through narrowed eyes. Exquisite torture continued. The captain slid her tongue around him with the velvet touch of a master seducer . . . around and around then up and down. To know that she wanted to do this, that it excited her, warred with the extreme pleasure her touch brought him. After excruciating moments of more blissful agony, Sol pulled up, sucking, licking, only to begin again. Massive shudders shook Gabe. He swallowed hard.

"Stop it. Oh, gods—" He grabbed the captain's shoulders, bringing her up to his face. He kissed her temple, nuzzled her hair then slid his lips down the length of her throat. "If you don't stop touching me, Sol, I swear, I'll come. Our pleasure will be over far too soon."

"You mean to tell me that you're only good for once a night, Gabriel?" She laughed, the throaty sound washing over him with pleasure almost as intense as her touch. He loved to hear her speak his name with such sexual intent. "I seem to remember things being different a few months ago under the Pleasure Dome."

"Damn you," he sputtered. "Of course I'm good for more than once a night . . . for all night, if you can take it in your condition."

Sol paused and lifted an eyebrow. "My condition isn't a problem for me, Commander. Is it for you?" She hurried on, her voice breathy. She was moving her hands again, trembling over his skin. "I've heard that some men don't like pregnant women. They're afraid of them or something."

"I'm not afraid of you. I'm . . . enchanted with you." Gabe felt the heat that crept up the back of his neck from his spine. He wasn't thinking clearly, almost slipped there and confessed that he loved her. He hid the surprise of that admission to himself. He would analyze it later. "Besides, this is mine, too." He placed his hand gently over her swollen abdomen. He rubbed a circle in an unconscious caress. A sudden kick came against his palm.

By the holy stars! Gabe lost his smile. He pressed his hand more firmly against her flesh and reached for that mental connection again, felt infinite love for him flow up his arm. His heart strangled on the response. By the stars, his son was an empath!

"Oh, good gods—he—he moved," Gabe breathed. He dared not tell Sol that their child was like him, imperfect, burdened with a gift that she might not appreciate.

"Yes, he does that quite frequently." Sol smiled gently, first at her stomach then at him. Her indulgent smile was such that Gabe was further lost in the beauty of the gesture, such awesome strength hiding such tenderness. He didn't know which affected him the most, his son or Sol. Gabe wandered in sensory overload. His son was an empath; he had touched Gabe with such love, such understanding for one so young.

For a moment, Gabe couldn't swallow. Words wouldn't form on his tongue. He laid his head against the silk covering Sol's lap, but the baby didn't move, didn't connect again. Lost in thoughts of possibilities, Gabriel kissed Sol's belly and wrapped his arms loosely around her hips. Her whiskey-heated eyes glowed down at him. Honest need reflected there in the golden depths and in her thoughts.

"My condition doesn't stop me from making love, Gabriel." She flicked his still rigid cock with a playful finger. "Does yours?"

With a growled response, Gabe grabbed her and ripped at the flimsy blouse, baring her completely to his hungry sight. He meant to go slow, but he felt driven. Those wonderful breasts *were* bigger, the circles of her nipples wider, darker, more enticing. Gabriel rubbed his face against them then pulled her heated skin against his naked chest. Satiny smooth, her skin felt so much like the silk he tore from her.

"I'll get you new clothes tomorrow, sweetheart, I promise." He barely restrained himself, kissing her mouth, her neck, all the way down to her nipples. Hastily, he pushed the pieces of clothing past her waist. He hurried, urged on by her moans, tantalized by her unspoken feelings. Her fingers tangled in his hair. With a trembling grip, he raised her, slipped the tattered garments off her hips. At the sight of her naked, Gabriel slowed, lingered, sliding his palms over her, feeling her gentle curves from breasts to thighs, remembering her heat, knowing her body inside and out as surely as he knew his own. But dreams were never as good as the real thing, especially when he held her trembling in his arms. He reacted like a hasty, untried boy again, shaking as badly as she. Gods, she was so pretty, and she smelled so good, like spring and like new life.

"Gabriel, hurry. Please," Sol tugged at his waistband, trying to rid him of the shorts that snagged on his erection. With a grunt, Gabe wiggled them to his knees then used his right foot to take them to his ankles where he finally kicked them off. Stars, he hadn't been this clumsy since he was that untried boy.

"Slow down, Captain." He gulped a shaky breath, wondering if he warned her or himself. "We don't have to rush."

"I don't want to give you time to change your mind."

"I won't change my mind, sweetheart. Not after all this." *Not on your life*, Gabe moaned to himself, swallowing the words in the heat of her mouth. Her lips tugged at his, nearly undoing him with their demand. She scraped her teeth over his bottom lip, but Gabe refused to be hurried. He began at Sol's top and worked his way leisurely down her body until he straddled her thighs, careful of her stomach, but wanting to taste her again.

She put her hands over her bare pelvic area, barred his view. "No. I—" She shook her head.

"You let me before." Gabe watched her familiar blush creep up her chest to her throat. He envied its path. Thank the gods, she hadn't pierced those perfect nipples with jewelry. He reached up and fanned the tip of one to a puckering point.

"I wasn't myself that night." Her golden eyes gave no hint as to what she was thinking, but her smoldering gaze reflected the fire within. Perhaps the captain didn't really comprehend that in the full joy of their mating she had flooded his awareness. Gabe had felt everything she did. He wouldn't tell her. Knowing the little he knew of Sol, she'd take it as an invasion of her privacy.

"Oh, I think you were yourself, Sol. Maybe for the first time in a long time, but you were yourself, a passionate, demanding woman instead of a cold, calculating captain. Be her again. Be the passionate one again . . . for me." Gabe blinked an irritating mist from his eyes.

Slowly, her hands fell away. Sol turned her head to the side and avoided his gaze.

Gabe refused to let her off so easy. "Look at me, Captain, while I pleasure you again, like that night under the Dome."

He bent to her and kissed the warmth of her bare vulva. She shivered. The heat and the salty taste of her moist sex filled his nostrils, hardened his balls. He gently raised her hips, his words of love lost in the kiss he crushed against her flesh. She moaned, tossed her head. And again Gabe thrilled at the sound of his name whispered on her lips. Lost, he was so very lost in all of her; all of her emotions lay so bare to him.

Sol rolled and thrashed beneath his mouth until, finally, Gabe gave in to her wishes . . . and to his own. She wanted him inside her, filling her, and he was only too happy to oblige. He lay on his side and, with his hands on her hips he gently drew Sol over his erection. The long, slow slide into her silken heat was an agony Gabe relished. Each second, each movement, became a sensation to last a lifetime. Time grew still and yet moved too fast. All too soon Sol's cry of release echoed his groan. Never had he waited so long, and never had it felt so good, so right so—*permanent?*

Gabe's mind thankfully blanked for the first time in weeks. Deprived rest caught up with him. The commander's last coherent thought was that he would never let Sol go. He wanted her and their child. And he knew the captain wanted him. He could read that much in her veiled, drowsy thoughts.

Gabriel Merriweather cursed himself royally, then he cursed Sol to perdition, when he later awakened to an empty bed.

Ten

"Think he'll find us here?" Sol stretched her arms above her head and yawned in the midday light. A long nap in the wealthy plunder of Dante's hidden smuggler's den was just what she'd needed after a heavy night of lovemaking with Gabriel Merriweather. After said night, she arose like a thief, hastily dressed in the torn rags of her clothing, already missing Gabe's warmth before she slipped out of the room. But she had watched the commander for a long time as he slept so innocently, his low breaths raising his naked chest up and down. His long lashes spread over his strong cheeks like dark fans. Asleep, the man didn't present such a looming presence, but he still exuded a quiet sense of strength and protection. Just why did she feel so secure and comforted lying closely snuggled against his side? It couldn't be love. Sol didn't like or want the responsibility of caring for someone so deeply—but, damn it, she was no closer to knowing how she felt about the commander or what she was going to do about him. To say she was confused was a colossal understatement.

Just before dawn, Gellico had whisked Sol away to this sanctuary with only a few choice words about lovesick idiots. Sol had slept like the dead for hours. Now, she moved down gingerly from the bales of illegal imports—the gold and silver tissue-thin fabrics and the rolls of micro-fiber that so much of the galaxy used for its armor-like durability. The fortune of plunder made the softest of beds, but Sol groaned, feeling the sweet soreness from Gabriel Merriweather's slow-ride loving. She didn't know whether to smile or frown. Just like she didn't know what she wanted anymore. The commander was an enigma—strong and powerful but sensitive and giving—an empath and a damned Chakkra half-breed, for gods' sake. Sol knew about his tainted bloodlines and didn't care. Hell, she too carried Chakkra blood from some obscure ancestor. So what? But the empathy talent wasn't noted in his public files. It should have shown up and probably did in his guarded military listing which would show his Guild registration. How had she missed that? She should have known why he knew just where to touch her to bring the most joy. The rat bastard must surely feel everything she did.

For a moment Sol's temper flared at the thought of the commander being inside her head, but she dispelled the useless anger. It was too late to worry about an invasion of her privacy. After all they had done to each other, Gabriel Merriweather knew her better than anyone, and he certainly hadn't hidden the markings on his arm or his chest. Not once. Any idiot knew what they meant. Idiot-with-hopped–up-hormones Sol just hadn't paid attention. And no wonder the commander gave so much of himself to his job. He had to take the loss of life personally when a treaty failed. And as for meeting the survivors of a war—Sol shuddered at what torment he must feel. Perhaps she should forgive him for costing her *Icarus's* command— then again, perhaps not. The loss of her ship still caused a hollow ache inside her. With a start, she realized that Gelli had been speaking and was waiting for an answer, looking at Sol with a puzzled frown.

"I'm sorry Gelli. What did you just say?"

Gellico answered with a soft "I said, no, they won't find us here." She lost her frown and went back to whittling on a piece of brazor wood. In her skillful hands, the razor sharp knife flickered back and forth with the delicacy of a hummingbird on a flower, a very large, sharp hummingbird on very soft wood. Long shaving curls fell to the floor. "No one knows about this place except me, Dante, and Punch. I won't talk, and neither of them had better." A faint, wicked expression lifted the corner of Gelli's full lips.

Sol shuddered, suddenly struck by how much her friend looked like a lusty pirate, especially with the long blade in her hand coupled with her current wild style of dressing in loose, silken shirts and tight leather pants. Even one shell-like, curved ear glowed with a large diamond while the other sported a thick round hoop of gold, just like the pirates from ancient legends. Gelli's smooth ebony jaw flashed with a flexed muscle bunching the smooth planes of her face. Sol frowned at her.

"Gelli, I know that Dante probably won't talk since he'd lose a
fortune in your shared profits, but how can you be sure Punch
won't spill his guts?"

"Because he loves me. And I told him not to tell." Gellico
looked up and gave that sideways grin that dimpled her cheek.
The look softened the chiseled sharpness of her features. The
tight muscle relaxed. "He likes keeping our little secrets. It's
something we share. Punch likes secrets and sharing."

Sol wasn't sure about that relationship but decided not to
ask about it further. Rigelians were rumored to have special
sexual abilities, too, but Sol had never dealt with gossip. Instead
she said, "Why do you call him Punch? Most Rigelians I know
carry familial names."

Gellico opened her mouth, but only silent laughter came
out. Her broad shoulders shook with the suppressed emotion.
She tried again, then waved her stick and said, "Just a minute.
I'll tell you, dear, but give me a minute." After a few moments,
she sucked in a deep breath and stood, brushing the thin shavings
from her lap. "Ever offer a Rigelian fruit juice? No?" She
shook her head at Sol's shrug. "Well, don't. They can't handle
the stuff, at least the ones from Rigel Two can't. The first time
I met Punch, he was flat out wasted. Some S.O.B.s had rolled
him in the back alleys of Faro's. Big guy like him and he was
totally blitzed. I had to drag him all the way to the meds, and
whenever I asked him what he'd been drinking, he'd just say
'Punch' over and over." Her dark eyes narrowed with an angry
gleam in their depths. "The guys who rolled him knew what
the juice would do to him. They got a whole night's receipts,
and the asshole that runs Faro's fired Punch." She gave a one-
shouldered shrug, and on Gellico, the gesture became an elegant
dancer's movement. "I got him work here at Dante's Circus.
End of story."

Not quite. Sol bet the muggers didn't live to tell the tale.
Gellico was ever protective of the needy. She cleared her throat
then nodded toward the ceiling. "Think they've left yet?"

"No." Gellico frowned sourly. The wrinkle lay heavy
between her shapely brows. "That damned man has torn
Dante's apart looking for you. Now, he's starting over. What

did you do to him? No." She raised her hand, long fingers spread in a stop sign. "Don't answer that. It's bad enough that you're sporting sucker marks like some juvie, I don't need all the gory details." She contorted her face, wrinkled her nose and gave an exaggerated shudder that shook her long frame.

"Ah, come on, Gelli, I've seen you wear worse," Sol sputtered. Her face felt hot, and her hand stole up to self-consciously cover her neck. Her abraded skin burned under her blush. In their heightened sexual coupling Sol couldn't remember when Gabe sucked the hickey there, but she vaguely thought that she had returned the favor.

"Yeah, well, at the time, I happened to be in love with the *female* I let bite me." Gelli's gaze still drilled Sol. Suspicion lingered there in the liquid darkness. "Are you in love with the commander, Sol?" One elegant brow arched.

"Hell, no!" Sol snorted. "Believe me, Gelli; I don't even know what real love is." Her heart skipped a beat. Didn't she? She touched her stomach. The touch became a lingering, circling motion. She couldn't help the smile that curved her mouth. "At least, I never knew before now." Her blurred gaze met Gellico's. "Oh, Gelli, this is the most special thing that's ever happened to me. For so many years, I've fought so many battles and watched so many good friends die.

"Until Te' talked to me about having my own child, I didn't see a reason for going on after they forced me to retire and I lost my command." Her hand made more soothing paths over the mound of her middle. Sol's gaze widened. With a start, she realized that she not only glad to be carrying a child—she was also glad that the child was Gabriel Merriweather's. Glad? Hell, she was ecstatic. Wonder of wonders.

Sol lifted her head. "Now I know things aren't so bad. I'm beginning to understand the real meaning of love. Maybe I do love the Commander . . . at least for what he's given me." When Gellico's features became stark and hurt creased her face, Sol gave her a quick hug and said, "I didn't mean that I don't love you, Gelli. You know you've had my friendship and my love from the beginning, but this is different."

Gellico nodded a bit stiffl,but genuine warmth echoed in

her voice when she said, "I'm glad you're happy, Sol. If you are, then I am, too." Gelli cleared her throat, dread obvious in her gaze.

"What?" Sol couldn't help her exasperated sigh when he friend glanced guiltiliy away. "What is it, Gelli?"

"I . . . uh . . . heard some of the commander's men talking last night while I was having a drink in the bar." Gellico looked at her, reluctance obvious in her expression. "I hate talking about this. I even considered not telling you, but we've never, in all the years we've known each other, kept secrets." Sol was glad Gelli didn't notice her flinch. Her friend continued speaking, her gaze on the floor. "I decided that you'd find out soon enough, anyway." She raised her head and looked Sol in the eye. "The Diplomatic Corps is being sent to Hydra," Gellico stated flatly.

Sol felt the blood leave her face. Blackness threatened with the loss of her breath. She folded at the waist like a child's paper doll, but Gelli caught her easily. She laid Sol back against the plundered cloth bales. "Damn it! Listen, Sol." She patted Sol's cheeks and grinned when Sol finally slapped her hand away. "It's not as bad as it seems. Talk is that the convicts want a peaceful settlement. They say, after the . . . uh . . . rescue on Hydra, the main killers were eliminated, and a new leader elected who has united most of the men. They've colonized Hydra . . . formed something other than a prison planet. I guess they want to establish Colony Rights with the Guild. You know that sending new prisoners there ceased long ago."

Sol felt a tingling in her face and realized that her thinking was improving. She was making sense out of Gelli's words. With an exasperated puff, she pulled her self up and noted how Gellico drew in a relieved breath. Despite her near faint, Sol's voice was steely. "Colonize hell. Talk like that is cheap, Gelli, and you know it. We've both heard those lies before. Who told you this?" Sol stood with her legs braced wide apart. She knew her mounded belly was at odds with her fierce determination. She'd get to the bottom of this.

Gelli finally answered. "I told you, Sol. Last night, I

overheard some of Merriweather's Marines talking at the bar. They didn't know who I was, and were just gabbing about being sent to the prison planet, like it was some big adventure. *"Yep, gonna kick us some convict ass."* She mimicked in a deepened voice then she shrugged. "Dumb shits deserve everything they get if they go there."

Sol brushed past Gellico, muttering. "I've got to warn the commander. Gabriel can't go to Hydra. He can't possibly do anything with those animals."

Gellico grabbed her arm. "You're too late, Sol. Listen. The commander's ship is leaving."

Both felt the deep vibrations of a ship's liftoff through the wooden boards of the hidden shelter. Dust rained down from the overhead rafters. They were close enough to the docks to feel the afterburners' rumblings of starships' liftoffs and landing activities.

"I've got to go after him." Sol started for the stairs only to have Gellico grab her arm and spin her back.

"You can't go in your condition, Sol! Short flights out here in the Straits are one thing, but you know you can't go to Delta Three. It's too dangerous to you now." Gellico lowered her voice. "Think of the baby. You can't risk it, Sol."

Sol's eyes filled with moisture. She blinked it away before she gripped Gellico's forearms. "Then you go to Delta Three and convince Gabriel that he can't go to Hydra. Tell him whatever you have to, Gelli. Please. Keep the commander away from there—keep him safe—for me."

Gellico's face turned a muddy brown, her eyes dulled.

Long seconds ticked by. Sol's heartbeat counted each one. Sweat dripped down her back. Nausea threatened again. She knew what she asked of Gellico, but she couldn't let Gabriel go to Hydra. He'd be killed by those animals. And the thought of that place made her blood run cold. Prison, my ass, it was hell. Healthy color finally came back to Gelli's dark skin. Sol sighed with relief.

"All right, Sol, I'll go." Gellico's strained gaze reflected such desolation that Sol nearly reached out to her. Instead, Gelli moved back out of her reach and nodded. "You lost your commission and the lives of your crew on Hydra for me. This is the least I can do for you." Her words ran bitter, cold and flat, her lips so tight that not a hint of her teeth showed.

"Oh, Gelli, forget that I asked it of you." Sol crossed the room and hugged Gellico as close as her expanded girth would allow. "I'm sorry. There's got to be another way. I'll find it somehow. We'll use the vid again. The commander will have to listen if we send a message." She patted Gelli's stiff shoulder. "I know you don't want to talk about Hydra. I don't either, but I can't let Gabriel walk in there cold."

For some reason she didn't tell Gelli that the commander was a Guild empath. "I know only a little of his job—his work but I wouldn't want it." She stepped back and searched Gellico's face. "I don't mean to hurt you, but he's important to me, Gelli. He's the father of my child."

"My sweet dear, I think he's a lot more important than just that." Gellico grasped her shoulder. "I'll do this for you, not for him."

Sol knew that tonight they'd both relive the nightmare memories of Hydra.

Eleven

In the Star Year 1251, the newly launched Guild battleship, the Icarus, neared the prison planet of Hydra on the outskirts of the Straits of Tralarie. So far, their routine patrol had been uneventful. The seasoned Captain Soledad Scott knew the quiet wouldn't last, it never did. Patrols were never uneventful for long so far out in the Straits.

"Captain to the bridge. Captain to the bridge," the com's command blared, and Sol hurried to comply. When she stepped on deck, a downed ship's SOS was sounding loud and clear over the com. Set on automatic, the unmanned signal appeared to be coming from the planet's surface.

"No response to our hail, Captain." At Sol's nod, the com-operator switched off the sound and tried to establish communications again. But Sol didn't expect an answer from Hydra. There was no technology on the prison world. Or there hadn't been before now. No telling what the prisoners would or could do with a downed ship. And may the gods help the crew or passengers. Sol shuddered. She knew this was a trap at best. Most likely, the ship's survivors were all dead by now and the convicts were using the radio beacon.

"You can't mean to land there, Captain." Sol's first officer raised his brows at her order for a landing party. His clear-eyed gaze searched her face, but he kept his voice pitched low for her ears only. And she heard him clearly, perhaps too clearly.

Sol bristled. *"Are you questioning my authority, Lieutenant Jones?"* Sol tried to still the thundering beat of her heart at what she planned. She risked her command as well as the lives of her crew. And she counted Asher as one of her few friends as well as her first officer.

"No, sir," the gray-eyed first lieutenant jerked to

attention, his back ramrod straight. He only came up to her chin with his average height, but his broad shoulders hinted of hidden strength.

"Good," Sol spoke aloud, lifting her voice so all in the vicinity heard. "Because—I'm not giving a command. I'm asking for volunteers on this one. I won't order my Marines to go against Guild law. It says we don't land on Hydra for any reason. Therefore we don't land—we'll shuttle down." At the wry expressions reflected on her crew members' faces, Sol couldn't help the answering tug at the corner of her mouth. "For humanity's sake, I can't ignore a distress call even from a civilian craft." She sobered at the thought of what might be happening on the surface. A sick feeling roiled in her stomach.

"Sir," the com-officer said, interrupting her thoughts. The distraction calmed Sol's rising gore. "I've traced the signal's signature to a pleasure dancers' vessel that has gone missing, overdue in the Straits for over a month now."

"How the hell would one of them end up on a prison planet way out here in the Rim?" Sol muttered to no one in particular. The ship was way off course from the Straits of Tralarie. The Rim was the edge of explored space; beyond that was undiscovered mystery. There was no reason for a bunch of pleasure mates to be anywhere near the Rim. Maybe they had made an emergency landing—though it would take one hell of an emergency for any intelligent being to put down on Hydra. A chill stole up Sol's spine at the thought. But then, perhaps one of the dancers was trying to rescue a convicted lover. Too many questions crowded to waste time speculating. Sol turned to her first officer. The lieutenant waited stoically for her orders. "Tell whoever volunteers that their military ass is on the line, but I'll take full responsibility. Now, jump, Lieutenant. I want to land within the hour. You'll have the helm."

"No, sir." His steady gaze with his cool gray eyes calmed her flare of anger. His lips barely moved when he voiced the low negative. The rest of the crew didn't hear him. Or did they?

"No?" Sol couldn't believe Jonesy had refused a direct order. All other crew personnel kept their heads down, busy at their stations. "Are you questioning my orders—again, Lieutenant?" she hissed under her breath.

"With the Captain's permission, I wish to volunteer." Bright spots of color decorated his cheeks, lightening the freckles on his broad bones into vivid display. Sol knew that the lieutenant personally hated his inherited ivory skin, so she hid her grin and the relief she felt at his obedience or, rather, lack thereof.

"Why?" She folded her arms across her chest. Did he think she couldn't handle the operation? He had to know better. Was he pushing one night of drunken mutual sexual relief between them into something more than what it was? That immature mistake had happened months ago, and Sol thought she had established her command better than this. Despite her youth, Sol was a seasoned warship captain.

"Why volunteer, sir?" His brows rose, "Maybe temporary insanity." He shrugged one sturdy shoulder.

"Yeah, there's a lot of that going around," Sol muttered. "I don't think the Guild is going to buy that defense though." She raised her chin, "But I will." She unfolded her arms. "Go on, get your volunteers and full war gear, and I mean that, Lieutenant. Volunteers only. Meet me on the flight deck. Michaels can take the helm." Sol strode stiffly towards the ship's arsenal for her own fighting gear. She couldn't believe that after all she had worked for, all the years of fighting and rising in the ranks, that she'd risk it all for an SOS from some idiot that had landed on Hydra. Didn't they know the whole planet was a prison of the worst kind?

* * * *

Sol watched from the jungle's safety as the scantily clad woman picking berries edged closer to the wreck only to be jerked roughly to her knees by the cutting vine wrapped around her ankle. She caught most of her fall on her palms but still grunted from the ground's impact. She didn't react further to pain; she just got back up and gave her captor a heated glare that promised future retaliation. The man holding the other end of the vine chuckled and shook his dirty finger at her without getting up from where he lay in the shade.

"Don't get any funny ideas about getting away, bitch. I'm watching your black ass. And I'm wise to your devilish tricks. Harris wasn't, and look how he wound up—dead as dirt." The man holding the rope leered at her with his broken, brown teeth. "Well, I'm not a pussy like Harris. I'll kill you first." He pointed a jagged piece of metal from the ship's wreckage shaped into a knife at her and shook the vine. "Now get back to work."

Gellico de'Marco, a dancer in an earlier life, picked more of the big red berries that gave the prisoners the needed nutrients in their meager diets. She ignored the blood dripping down her ankle from the cutting vine. Gellico ignored the scraps of clothing that barely covered her as much as she ignored the groans of her hungry belly. She had lived through worse. In the time she had been on Hydra, she had lived a lifetime of worse torment. Only one thought kept her alive—vengeance. She wanted to live long enough for payback. Harris was lucky she had only bit through his carotid artery and he had bled to death. This asshole wouldn't be as lucky. No, she wanted this one to suffer a longer, more painful, slower death. If she could reach the remnants of the Scheherazade, the ship that had crash-landed her here she'd make her own weapons. And nothing would stop her except her death.

The dancer gritted her teeth and bided her time. Surely, a Guild ship had to answer the SOS soon. All she had to do was remain alive long enough.

It was all a waiting game. The convicts knew of the distress signal. They'd discovered it that first awful day of the crash, but they had left it going. Nothing of value remained of the wreck's scavenged hull except the signal. The convicts planned to steal the rescue ship that answered the call. That's why they posted their spy here every day as lookout. Picking berries was just an excuse, as if the

*convicts needed any reason for anything they did. But
someone had heard a strange, mechanical humming last
night. Or at least, someone had said that he did.*

*Another thing that Gelli learned a long time ago was
that some prisoners would lie just for attention, for the
favor of the leaders. Some of that favor ended in death,
and Gellico didn't want a useless death. She wanted hers
to count for something. It was better to wait and see, not
get your hopes up—not waste energy.*

*"You've picked enough damned berries." The man
jerked the vine again, but this time Gelli had made sure to
keep the rope slack. The thorns didn't cut her. She glared
at the man holding the rope's end. He grinned at her with
his yellow-brown teeth and wagged his tongue at her. From
the crazed shine in her captor's eyes, he had other things
on his mind than eating berries. Gelli swallowed against a
bruised, swollen throat. He'd have to hold his knife to her
again, but he'd get what he wanted just the same. Hold
on, Gellico told herself. Just hold on. Surely, someone
would come soon. For a moment, she couldn't see through
the haze in her eyes, and she stumbled, cutting her ankle
on the vine's thorns all on her own. But the pain centered
Gellico, focused her thoughts. Her gaze cleared. She
tightened her jaws and clenched her teeth for what would
come next.*

* * * *

*Lieutenant Jones won the coin toss and led the small
scouting recon, but Sol wasn't surprised at what he had
reported. From her hidden spot on the hill, she was a little
surprised at how she reacted to watching the convict
torment the female prisoner he kept tied to a line. Only
strict military training kept her from giving away their
position. But the training didn't keep Sol's stomach from
revolting at the inhumanity of the rape. She knew that her
failure to act right then and there would haunt her for the
rest of her days. She vowed to never forget that she owed
the tortured woman.*

Sol wiped the last trace of bile from her lips onto her

sleeve and refused to look away. If the woman could endure the pain, how could Sol be any less brave? The black female was as thin as a rail. Her sharp ribs jutted out from sunken flesh. Her knee and elbow joints looked like knobs sticking through her skin. One side of her head oozed blood from a raw, bloody scalp where her hair was missing. Long braids filled the other side with a messy collection of leaves, twigs, and dirt. She needed medical attention badly. Her stoic bravery humbled Sol.

"How many?" Sol muttered to her lieutenant when Asher knelt next to her without disturbing the brush surrounding them. She wiped her mouth again. She'd made certain none of the Marines saw her empty the contents of her stomach.

"In the camp? I can't tell for sure, a hundred or more. Records show that over two hundred prisoners have been sent here. How many left alive now? I can't tell without further investigation." The lieutenant's grim features were hard and as gray as stone. His pale eyes looked haunted. Although outnumbered two to one, he didn't say there were too many convicts to fight. "There are several more females in their main camp, but they won't be of much use in the rescue. They're in worse shape than that one." He pointed toward the berry thicket near the ship's ruins. Asher grimaced, and Sol noted the long shudder that ran through him. It was evident that her lieutenant, too, had witnessed the brutal rape.

He whispered in a harsh voice, "They've hamstringed some of them, Captain. Crippled them so they can't run, and the men could use them over and over. What kind of animal would do that to a woman?"

Sol pretended that she didn't notice her lieutenant's distress. She had enough of her own to deal with. "Sick animals, Lieutenant, real sick ones. That's why they're here on Hydra." She gave a soft sigh, her mind made up. "I don't think we can risk any more time. The shuttle's bound to be discovered sooner or later. Even landing at night, someone had to have heard us."

He nodded. "I agree. Tonight, when it's dark again, is our best chance."

"Our only chance." Sol checked her ammo and her laser pistol again. "Explain the situation to the men, Lieutenant. Leave any who aren't fully committed to the operation with the shuttle. And whatever you do, don't leave it unguarded. We may need to leave in a hurry." Sol repressed a shudder. Dear gods, she didn't want to be stranded here.

"Yes, sir," Asher flicked Sol a respectful salute and slipped into the brush with hardly a leaf disturbed. The man blended with the forest. One second here, the next gone. Asher Jones was too good a man to risk on an operation that could cost him his career as well as his life. Sol regretted their one and only time of sexual gratification. She liked him as an officer and as a friend. And she knew he felt the same for her. But now was not the time for woolgathering. Sol drew a deep breath. She would do everything in her power to keep all her Marines and their careers safe. She'd never ask them to do something she wouldn't do herself. If they followed tonight, every one of them would be committed fully to the cause.

Sol need not worry. All her crew followed her. In fact, Asher had to order the two left with the shuttle to stay behind. Only the importance of their protecting the vessel for escape kept them from arguing about joining the rescue team. Sol had never felt so proud of them. And someday, she was going to check that damn coin of her lieutenant's. He had won the toss again—he got to lead the assault with his group. Sol and the others would lay down covering fire.

Despite their superior technology over the prison's primitive condition, confusion reigned that night. Mortar shells exploded. Dirt and smoke roiled. Short range cannon from the Marines blasted again and again from the shelter of the thick trees. The shooter deflected his shots, missing the known areas where the female captives were being held. But as in most wars, some innocents got in the way.

Hamstrung cripples couldn't run. The Marines who carried some of them came under heavy attack from the prisoners' deadly accurate arrows and spears. Some Marines never made it to cover. Others fought against overwhelming odds. Some won. Some lost—as in any war. But some of the captives fought, too.

* * * *

"*Come on!*" *Gellico pulled the thick tree branch that she had plunged into her tormentor's stomach free, but she didn't take time to watch the man die. Too much mayhem existed for gloating delays. But the dancer would savor the sight of the convict rolling on the ground, holding his gray and pink guts inside with his hands, at a later time.*

Another mortar shell exploded nearby. Dirt showers pelted Gellico. Sharp pebbles cut her skin. Hell of another kind had come to Hydra. At long last. Escape was Gellico's only thought other than to help the solders rescue as many of her fellow dancers as she could—if she could kill convicts on the way, so much the better. "Fight, damn you," she yelled at the straggling dancers who, stumbled in her wake.

"*Come on! Help yourselves. Help them." She dragged one of the dazed dancers to her feet and shoved a cooking stone into her hand. "Use this. We're being rescued, you dumb bitch, fight." The stunned woman struggled after Gellico, and more were added along the way, their eyes cloudy with dull confusion but willing to follow her. A few were lost to the fighting convicts, and more died under the shelling but those cripples had longed for death. Gellico finally reached a stand of sheltering trees and nearly ran into the camouflaged chest of a Guild uniformed woman with a long rifle who rose up in front of her.*

"*Here." The woman shoved a long laser rifle into her hand. "Know how to use this?"*

"*Hell, yes." Gellico pressed the kill switch and swung the barrel. From the corner of her eye, she noted the gold officers' bars on the red and black uniform. "Thanks, Captain."*

"My pleasure. You've earned it. Just don't hit any of my men." The captain drew her pistol and laid down covering fire for the Marines that Gellico saw searching the camp.

"Call them off, Captain." Gellico pulled on the woman's arm. *"There aren't any more left alive."*

"You sure about that?" The officer frowned, and with a start, Gellico realized how young the captain was. Her big bronze eyes were wide, and her intense gaze searched the camp.

"Yeah, I'm sure. I know them all, and I've helped all the ones who were left alive. There are too many convicts for you to fight." Gellico paused to catch her breath, and an awful thought came to her. *"Others may be attacking your ship, wherever it's hidden. They've been waiting for you to come out."*

Sol nodded to the rape victim and clicked on her mike. She yelled, *"Abort operation. Repeat. Abort operation. Return to ship,"* into her mouthpiece. She hoped her Marines heard her command above the firing. Determined to attempt an extraction of her men, Sol set the command to auto and stepped from cover only to hear Asher's breathy voice rasp in her earpiece. He must be running; his words jumped high and low.

"All clear, Captain. Head for the shuttle. We're right behind. Will cover you."

"Roger that." She closed the link. Jonesy still overstepped himself. She would lay down covering fire in relays.

"You conniving bitches!" A convict, screaming and firing a Marine's stolen laser, rushed Sol's location. In seconds, the man and his followers overran their position. So close that she smelled the awful sour stench of sweat and grime, the convicts reached Sol just before she shot the leader between the eyes. Hot blood and loose brains sprayed her face, but Sol didn't take more than a moment to wipe her eyes free of the gore. More raging convicts followed behind the first. Sol vowed to go down fighting

before she'd allow herself to be captured and tortured like the dancers had endured. With the black female fighting at her back, Sol bullied their way through the forest from tree to tree until they reached the shuttle. Twice she saved the dancer from sure death only to have the dancer return the favor in the next second. Sol's Marines were hardpressed to protect them in the hidden jungle.

Covering fire zipped past them and cut leaves. Bark splintered from the trees. There seemed no end to their nightmare struggle. As one convict went down, another took his place. Once Sol felt a sudden jolt to her companion, knew the dancer was hit, but in one breath, the bony shoulders straightened. The woman screamed her defiance.

"Come on, you bastards. Come and get me now, why don't you?" The dancer fired her laser, and a rocket fired from the shuttle at the same time. A whole section of forest went up in smoke and debris. The men who were hiding inside flung themselves forward, only to die under another blast. Dazed by the blast and unable to hear, Sol shook the woman by the arm. Dull, glazed, red eyes stared blankly back at her. Sol doubted the woman could hear, but she mouthed the words at her as loudly as she could.

"Follow me. Come on." Sol pulled on the dancer's arm that seemed the less wounded of the two. Both were streaked with blood. In fact, the woman's whole body seemed covered in sticky red. The Marines were laying down heavy cover for them from the shelter of the shuttle. Sol's hearing was still muffled, but she heard the continuing battle clear enough. Bullets still zipped past and zinged through the trees. Men screamed in the night.

"I hope every last one of them dies as slowly, as painfully as that bastard did with his guts hanging out." Sol's hearing had returned enough to hear the dancer's muttered words.

She turned at the shuttle's entrance, numbed by the sight of the feral grin on the female's face. More blood dripped from a shoulder wound and flowed down from the woman's wounded scalp to her heels.

"Thank you," the woman whispered just before she collapsed. *Asher caught her before she hit the ground.*

Sol gave the command to lift off, a distinct, "Get us the hell outta' here." Her lieutenant still stood with the dancer in his arms, stark horror reflected in his gaze and in the grim lines of his face. He cradled her as gingerly as a babe.

"Take her to sickbay with the rest," Sol ordered while looking around at the few Marines that were left of her brave volunteers. "And, Lieutenant—" She waited for his slight nod. "All the medical team is to be female, got that? All of them."

He nodded again and Sol felt his gaze on her as she uncovered the bodies of her Marine dead on the shuttle's deck. No one had been left behind. Before the night ended, Sol would write the parents and relatives of the crew she had lost. They had died heroes, but, when she reached Delta Three, she would face charges and possibly a dishonorable discharge. Soledad would be lucky if she didn't get prison time. She hoped it wasn't here on Hydra.

* * * *

With a jerk, Sol awoke from the lingering nightmare of her memories. Her night clothes stuck to her from the shaking sweats that she hadn't felt in a long time. "Gelli?" she called toward the room where Gellico slept. An ominous quiet rested in the hazy light of dawn. Oddly, there was no sound of breathing coming from there either; no soft snoring, no gentle moaning. "Oh, Gelli, you didn't do this for me, did you?"

Sol picked up the red *churvet* flower that lay over a note on the table.

Sweetie, Went to see your commander about that vacation trip he plans. Stay healthy and do what Punch says. Don't worry.

Love, Gelli

P.S. Eat your vegetables.

Sol snorted and crumpled the note, then gripped the blossom. Thorns cut her palm. Yeah, like she wasn't going to worry whether or not either Gabe or Gelli would survive their confrontation, let alone a trip to Hydra.

* * * *

Gabriel tossed and turned, twisting the sheets and reliving the nightmare of his birth—his lifelong nightmare.

His first awareness, still the unborn child in his mother's womb, was filled with love and the blissful loving desires of his mother and father. Their hovering presence surrounded him with the most joyful comfort, but in the background, Gabe sensed the sharp bite of their fear, the taint of flight and the sourness of frustration. He remembered hours and days of frantic travel across light years and star systems. He knew his father was a great figure of unsurpassed bravery, a warrior prince to the Chakkra throne. But he was also a warrior who defied his race and took a mate from another world—a woman ambassador from Terra. This was forbidden. Only the Chakkra outcasts were free from death for polluting the Chakkra blood. A blood prince was never allowed that freedom. Gabriel's Terran born mother was light years too different from the Chakkra. Perhaps it was those very differences that attracted the prince. He—born of a warring nature and she of gentle disposition. Their love defied centuries of tradition.

Yes, Gabriel's blessed mother was different from the warring Chakkra, so wonderfully different, so intelligently different. She filled her unborn child, her Gabriel, with gentleness and peace—and such fear. Wisely, his father fled his kin who were intent on killing him and his mate. After months of searching, their only place of refuge became a barren and near lifeless world far out in the Rim of explored space. No one would ever find them there.

How wrong the thought. How fickle the fates.

Not long after Gabriel's mother bloomed fully with the evidence of their doomed love, a lost Rigelian starship landed, badly in need of repair. Over Gabriel's sire's vehement protests, his mate made the crew welcome with hot meals and shelter until their ship was repaired. Even as he ordered the men to secrecy, he knew they would boast of their adventure. The Chakkra prince longed to cut off their heads even knowing that his little mate would plead for their lives. Against his better judgment, he let them go.

Not a month later, Chakkra forces landed. Warriors ran them to ground.

With his great heart heaving, Gabriel's father fell to the rocks under the pounding marstriss' hooves of the Chakkra king's mounted forces. He could no longer run, but he cradled his mate from the worst of their fall. She lay sheltered beneath his chest, her face hidden in his warmth. Not one hoof scarred her flesh, but she cried out at each jerk his body gave though not a sound escaped his lips. But inside his mate, surrounded and protected by thick amino fluids, Gabriel cried out at the searing pain that wrecked his father. Although yet unborn, Gabriel was still aware of each painful strike against his sire. Along with that, grief and fear from his mother burned and tormented him. He twisted and rolled against her sheltering muscles.

Finally, at a hurled command, the fighters reined back. Gabriel's sire rose and pulled his mate upright, curved over her without loosening his hold. Fierce warriors surrounded them. They jeered and taunted them with their sharpened spears.

Gabriel's father ignored them. He held his mate to him tenderly, knowing this was the last time he'd touch her. Her hot tears flowed onto his chest. His skin burned with her grief. He reached his arms around her swollen girth and laid a hand over where his son spilled his trembling awareness.

"Never forget me, my son. I would have given all to have seen you and held you—for at least one time. Feel me and know my heart." Love, pride, joy and a fierce sorrow flowed to Gabriel in that one link. He saw in his infant mind the towering warrior figure of his sire. His great stature, his fierce pride was a thing never to be forgotten.

Even the death warriors who circled them remained in awe—for a few moments. Their immobility broke when Gabe's sire bent to his mate and kissed her lips. Defying the warriors surrounding them, she gripped her lover's head and pressed her tear-salty lips to his until the fighters pulled them apart. She sobbed and reached out to him. One warrior sneered at her. She spit full in his face. He made to strike her.

"Do not dare," Gabe's father commanded in a bellow that rang over the crowd. "She carries my heir. A king's grand prince." He struggled in the grip of the many warriors who held him. Ropes snagged his strong legs apart. More around his wrists jerked his arms level to his shoulders. He couldn't get away.

"She carries filth." A warrior jeered back. Another warrior stepped forward and stayed the arm that again rose to strike her. He whispered, and Gabriel understood his words to Gabe's mother. She would live only until his birth. The warriors then struck his father in her stead. His mother staggered but willed her legs to hold. She would live to give her son life. Her frantic glance sought her mate's and held his even as the first spear entered his chest. She screamed. Gabe's father made no sound. He absorbed the pain and straightened back to his full seven foot height. Another spear entered and another moan escaped her. Now tears flowed unchecked down her face. Gabriel twisted in her belly. She cradled her arms about him and gave herself up to grief, never once looking away from his father's eyes. It took seven spears to bring Gabriel's father, a royal prince of Chakkra, to the ground. Only then did the ones who held her release their hold. She fell next to her mate in time to see the light flee his pale vision. She kissed his still warm lips; breathed in his last breath.

Gabriel felt the depth of his parents' love when their lips met, but his mother's terrible grief swamped him. Her abhorrence of bloodshed and death took a backseat to her desolation. She longed for her own death, but she was torn between that and giving Gabriel life. Her deep reverence for life forbade her from taking his life. From his first stirring in her womb, she had named him Gabriel for a winged religious figure of her faith. The Chakkra had no religion. Warriors needed none. They made their own way. No one but the king governed them.

The warriors kicked Gabriel's mother in the head when she prayed over her mate's body. Gabe's father meant nothing to them. He was a traitor to them, mated outside their race. The king had ordered his son's death but he wanted an heir. Even a half breed grandson was better than none. Gabe's mother would die soon, too. She welcomed the black oblivion of unconsciousness.

Only a month later, in the king's cold stone prison, Gabriel's mother lay in the painful throes of childbirth with only one birthing woman present to attend her. No medicines were given her, no comfort of any kind. After all, she was to die soon. Sweaty and fatigued, weak from loss of blood, Gabriel's mother, nonetheless, sent words of love and assurance to her child. Gabe sent back as much as he could. Her human senses could not read him, and she was much too frail to survive his birth even if she wasn't under the king's death decree. She didn't care how death came, only that it came after Gabriel's birth. Since his father's death, she had only eaten the barest minimum for life. She drank even less.

After a day and a night of pain, Gabriel wriggled free of his mother's warmth. He cried loud in the cold air. He struggled and longed for her. Finally, someone roughly wrapped him and placed him in his mother's fragrant warmth. She hugged him. Her wet face rubbed his hot cheek. Her voice whispered to him like that of the softest breeze. She tasted of the sweetest mother's milk. Somehow Gabriel knew it was the only time he would be so blessed.

"Do not forget me or your father, my son, my angel. Remember we loved you with all our hearts. Hate and violence is not the way of a wise man, my son. Learn, grow and bring peace."

Suddenly, Gabriel was ripped from her arms. A great

pain entered her chest. Metal pierced her heart, but she gave a joyous cry on her last breath. A beauteous smile remained on her lips. The Chakkra who saw it averted their eyes and never looked at her again. Her body was dumped outside on the midden heap with the other rotten waste.

"Ahhhgh!" The baby Gabriel cried long and loud. No one answered. He quickly learned that crying availed you nothing, and so he quit. He also learned about kicks, slaps and pain as he grew. Bruises faded, broken limbs knit, but memories still lingered. He never spoke of his parents in the cold, stone halls of the Chakkra. In his growing years, he learned quickness and stealth, along with cunning and reasoning. He never revealed that he was able to read the warriors' thoughts and intentions. He grew adept at staying clear of trouble. Only the old king's hidden grief consoled him. Better the old warrior suffer in solitude than Gabriel breaking his mother's wishes. He longed to kill the bastard despite her whispered admonitions. The king slowly went mad. The old beast never got over the execution of his oldest son. Gabe thought that was poetic justice.

Years later, after escaping to schooling on another world and entering the Diplomatic Corps, Gabe learned of his grand sire's final death. The warrior king had been dying inside for years. A lesser princely offspring took the Chakkra throne, but the old king had sent word to Gabriel. He longed for Gabriel to return to Chakkra and take his rightful place, half breed or no. Fat chance of that. Gabe snorted aloud—

—and awoke.

Gabe jumped from his bed and paced the floor. Why? For a long time, he swayed in place, lost in his past, in the violent memories. Why, after all these years, did he dream that awful nightmare again? As if he gave a good damn about the Chakkra. He had left them and their warrior philosophy long ago. He would never be like them.

Later, he would remember his vow.

Twelve

"Commander?" Tetra chirped on Gabriel's com. He pushed the button and noted that her multiple frog-mouths opened and closed several times but no further words croaked forth. Anyone who knew Mulanians would know Tetra was perturbed. She had been that way since thwarted from discovering Sol's sister's identity. Mulanians prided themselves on their ferreting abilities. No secret was safe. Gabe knew that well enough. Tetra was the only one who knew his true princely identity and nature. But he didn't worry about her revealing anything; Mulanians were noted for their fierce loyalty and secretive natures. They were also notoriously nosey.

"Yes, what is it now?" Gabe growled. If he had one more interruption, he'd shoot the insolent bastard that dared. He had very little time to prepare for this meeting. Before an operation, he'd usually spend days going over topographic maps and intelligence reports. But there were next to none of those for Hydra. It was almost as if someone was hiding something.

"There is a Gellico de' Marco here." Tetra spoke the sentence as if she didn't know what species a *"Gellico de' Marco"* was.

"Send her in." Gabe's irritation vanished in shock. Several times in the past week, he had considered sending a message to Sol, but he still smarted over the way she had run off and hid from him again. Perhaps she was sending the dancer with a message—one that said stay lost. He ran a hand over his head and snorted. He'd never understand females—any of them. Gabe drew a deep breath, smoothed his straggling hair. He was tranquility itself when the black beauty entered, her scowling stare daring to dismiss him as she idly gazed around his modest office. But she wasn't as disinterested as her outward appearance let on. Her distress was easy to read. Something that had to do with bloody horrors and nightmares troubled her. Black waves of dread poured out from her mind, and Gabe fought against their pull. The strength of them threatened to tow him under in a miasma of terror. He still felt the remnants of his own nightmare. Silent, he waited the dancer out, fidgeting in his chair. The wait was an effort.

"Nice decor," she finally quipped with a wrinkled-nose snort at the room's nondescript but orderly arrangement of desk, chair, cabinet and visitor's chair. No window, no art work, no statues, just a benign beige place to work; a shielded and protected place where leaking emotions couldn't get in to bother him. Unlike the spewing fount in front of him who destroyed his sanctuary.

"Yeah, and I like your outfit, too. What is it, a bandana and a belt?" Gabe didn't wait for an answer. "I don't have time for idle chitchat, Miss de'Marco. What do you want?"

"Soledad sent me." A white-toothed grin creased the dancer's elegant, strong features, and she smoothed a graceful hand over her thigh-high black leather skirt whose hem ended just a little south of the border. A scrap of white silk bandana did drape around her neck and down her breasts. And it didn't meet in the middle. The ends were tucked in her waistband, and a broad band of ebony skin shone all the way from neck to belly button. Gabe was sure her back was bare, too. Pointed nipples poked the thin fabric covering them. Did she wear anything under her skirt? She couldn't miss the look of real appreciation that Gabe gave her or the speculative gleam in his eye. She smiled another flash of white, no doubt, mocking his typical male response.

"Sol, huh? I figured as much," Gabe nodded and sighed. He ignored his cock that rose at the thought of Sol. "Why didn't the captain come herself?"

"B-a-b-y." de'Marco spelled the word, her brows rose as if Gabe was an idiot. And idiot that he was, Gabriel felt the prickly heat of a flush but couldn't think of a quick put-down. Thankfully, the rest of him quickly deflated as well.

"What does she want?" He kept his tone neutral and was surprised by the burst of heated anger that came from the tense woman in front of him. He didn't need empathy senses to read that.

"How the hell do I know what Soledad wants? She doesn't

even know." The dancer ran a hand over her close-cropped hair and glared at him. "You might think you know her, Commander, but you don't. No one does. The woman you met that night under the Dome was so hopped up on hormones and fertility drugs she'd just as likely have fucked a robot. You were just a convenient dick, at the right place and the right time, so to speak." Her frown deepened. She waited, hotly glaring at him as if daring him to deny it.

He waited a moment, as if really giving the idea some thought, then he cocked his chin. "Nah," he shook his head and grinned. "Contrary to your thinking, Miss de' Marco, I know some things about Sol that you don't." His tone softened, and he lowered his voice. "And, for that . . . I am sorry for your pain." Gabe watched her from the corner of his eye. She struggled mightily to maintain control.

A few moments later, the heated tension faded. He felt the exact moment when the dancer's shoulders relaxed. The stiffness went out of her stance.

"Drink?" he offered and opened a recessed panel next to his desk. The room was full of secrets, not all of them in the walls.

"Sure. Whatever you're having." de' Marco folded herself neatly into the guest chair, moving with such grace that her abbreviated hemline never exposed a thing. The contour chair molded to her curves.

Lucky chair. Gabe stifled the thought and handed her a heavy crystal tumbler filled with ice and an imported golden whiskey.

She sniffed and sipped a quick taste that raised her arched brows. "Wonderful blend, Commander, but illegal here, isn't it?"

"I get a lot of perks with the job." Gabe sank back into his chair, toasted her silently, and gulped a fiery swallow that blurred his vision. *Whew!*

When he could see again, he frowned down at the sketchy Hydra report that taunted him from his desktop. "Sometimes, contraband's the only thanks I get. Now—" He rose on steadier legs and came around his desk to sit on its corner. "—what does Sol want?" He could tell his higher position didn't intimidate de' Marco one bit although she stiffened again and leaned back from him.

"It's what she doesn't want." The dancer took a deep breath. Under the thin silk, her rounded breasts rose, perky nipples poking their outline. Gabe ignored his natural male response to the sight and read the internal struggle in her hesitation. He gleaned some of the hidden nightmares she covered behind her shield, the ones she couldn't quite forget. de'Marco didn't want to talk about whatever was troubling her. Finally, she cleared her throat.

"Soledad doesn't want you to go to Hydra." Her words came on a quickened breath. The prison's name brought a rush of blood and violence to her memories, and again Gabe felt her struggle to compose her internal thoughts.

"How do you know about my mission?" Gabriel just managed to contain his shock. Had she read his mind? Did she have empathic or telepathic abilities? He caught enough of the dancer's memories to know there were violent hidden depths to her that no one, except perhaps Sol, saw.

de' Marco smirked before answering. "Your men talk when they're drinking, Commander."

"Damn it, I knew I shouldn't have given them R&R in the damned Straits." Gabe screwed his fist into his other palm before letting out a breath. He paused, automatically gathered his thoughts like a diplomat then frowned. An awful suspicion lingered in the back of his mind, swirled there like an ominous fog. He frowned at the dancer. "What does Sol know about Hydra?"

"No more than I do." de'Marco's flat inflection gave no hint to her thoughts, but he caught the great whirlwind of darkness that filled her. But no one would guess it to look at her. Her sculptured features didn't change expression. Her cold, black eyes gave a slow blink. Gabe couldn't read a thing beyond the endless black.

"And just what do *you* know?" He leaned forward, almost in her face.

"I . . . was there. Sol rescued me—and the other dancers

who were there with me." Her words bore a hollow ache.

"Oh—my—god." Gabe reeled back and nearly lost his position on the desk. Chills rose on his arms. An awful roil erupted in his stomach, and he nearly spewed his drink. "Sol was the Guild captain who disobeyed standing orders and landed on Hydra in 1251," he breathed, wonder evident in his voice.

"Yeah." de' Marco nodded, her complexion gone to a muddy brown in recall. "I'm alive today because Captain Soledad Scott risked court-martial and death to save a few whores who had the misfortune to crash-land on Hydra." She downed the rest of her whiskey in one gulp. Her haunted eyes filled, and she blinked against moisture several times before continuing with a defiant glare. "I'm only telling you this because she asked me to keep you from going there."

"She was never advanced because of her disobedience," Gabe whispered. He barely saw de' Marco's image beyond his swirling thoughts. Everything about Sol's discharge without advancement upon retirement became clear now.

"Yeah, the Guild let her keep her commission on the condition she never spoke of Hydra. They transferred her crew and rotated new ones every year for the rest of her career. Big of them, huh?" de' Marco rattled the ice in her glass suggestively. "They thought they'd keep her sense of command on a tight rein; new crews would never give her the loyalty of the old ones." She snorted. "Of course, they were wrong. The military grapevine told its own version of the battle. And the tales they told…" The dancer shook her head, a faint smile lifting her thinned lips. "To this day, the honorable Soledad Scott commands loyalty from the minute you meet her." de' Marco sucked a lone ice cube and frowned longingly into her glass.

Gabe finally acted on her not so subtle hints and refilled it. He also refilled his own. He had a feeling he was going to need most of the bottle before they were done. He didn't bother with ice; he just sat down behind his desk. His legs felt weak. "Tell me about Hydra—all of it," he ordered then added, softly, "Please. I need to know."

"Yeah, I suppose you do. That's why I came." Gellico de' Marco pushed back in her chair and uncrossed her legs. She recrossed, then uncrossed them again, and stood. She began pacing the small confines of the room almost in the same pattern that Gabe usually did. Her voice lowered to a feral growl. She had no idea that Gabe felt her pain. And there was a lot of pain. He felt even sicker than before, and several times he swallowed sour whiskey that rose unbidden in his throat. The drink tasted better going down the first time.

"Altogether, there were a hundred and twenty of us, not counting Aladdin and the crew on board the *Scheherazade*. We were a traveling Arabian Nights show and had just finished a tour in the ring of Brittany's Skirt when our turbo drive mysteriously failed. We drifted for days, way off course, out into the Rim. We crash landed on Hydra over the advice of the captain. But we had no choice, what with the damaged drive system and all." She waved her long fingers. "All of us knew that the prison was off limits; that only convicts were there, just waiting to steal a ship with technology so they could escape. But what total dumb asses we were. We should have taken our chances on blowing up in space." Her tirade ran down, and she snorted and gave him a mocking, pathetic grin. "Well, it was too bad for the convicts, too. Our ship didn't have enough tech left after the crash to make a good bonfire." She paused, then muttered to herself. "We all would have been better off to have died in the wreck."

Gabe shuddered at the bleakness that drained the light from Gellico's eyes, leaving them dulled like those of a wounded animal's. He no longer thought of her as an impersonal acquaintance, as the dancer named de' Marco. He felt her pain, lived in her nightmares, but Gabe didn't say a word. After all, what could he say? After a moment of composing herself, Gellico continued.

"The surviving crew set an SOS beacon and fought off the convicts for as long as they could." She paused in her pacing, took a breath, and Gabe gulped too. Luckily, Gellico didn't see and continued her low litany. "The convicts killed all the men first, even the few left who surrendered. Then, afterward, we women became the property of the winners in the battle of ownership." She nodded her thanks at Gabe's refill and drank the entire contents in one noisy swallow. A visible shudder went through her entire body before she lifted her tortured gaze. Gabe hid his own shiver at the reflected nightmare.

"Do you know who the inmates of Hydra are, Commander?"

Gabe shrugged and repeated what he knew from his reports. "Until five or so star years ago, hardened criminals were sent there in lieu of death." His miserly reports stated that monthly supplies were dropped from space, and that no contact whatsoever was ever made with the inmates. The Guild government supplied food, clothing and medicines, but the convicts supplied the rest, the survival skills . . . if they had any.

Gellico snorted and smiled, if you could call the faint twisting of her lips a smile. Her dry voice rasped with wry bitterness. "Hydra is home to the criminally insane, Commander—the psychopaths, the sociopaths, the deviant torturers of children, and the murderers that the government wanted to dispose of *humanely*." Her hollow laugh rang near hysterical before she shook her head. She rolled the heavy, empty tumbler across her brow then she paced some more. "It's possible some political opponents and military personnel have ended up there, too, but not enough of them to matter. Nothing innocent survives there for long. And nothing sane survives Hydra." She glared at him, and Gabe felt his balls draw up closer to his body in search of protection.

He cleared the tightness from his throat. "How long were you there before Soledad came?" Again, he filled both their glasses. This was the last of his contraband whiskey, but it would have never seen better use.

"Forty-three days." Gellico nodded her appreciation and lifted her glass toward him in a mocking toast. "Forty-three glorious days in hell."

"How many survivors were left—after Sol's rescue?" Gabe wanted so very much to comfort the stiff, weaving woman who stood with her feet braced wide apart and hid such awful pain inside. He would probably have drawn back a bloody stump if he so much as offered his hand. Never had he felt such desolation and despair. And never, since his mother's death, had he known such strength and courage in females as in Soledad and Gellico.

"By the time the battle ended, there were five of us women still standing with Soledad and her Marines." She flashed another evil-looking grin. "When the fighting began, and we knew a rescue attempt was being made, we women grabbed whatever we could and began battering our way out of the caves and huts the convicts called quarters. Some of us had fought before, only to be maimed or to die. For gods' sakes, we began as simple dancers; we ended up as crazy as the convicts. After we landed there, death, for some, was the goal, but the convicts were smart. Like the smart of cunning rats, you know? They did everything to keep us available for their needs. Some of the more rebellious women were hamstrung to keep them from running. Some died as used-up cripples in their beds. The strong psychopaths ruled." Her eyes glittered dangerously.

Gabe did know. Some of the alien species he had dealt with in the past showed some of that same deceptive cunning. They even fooled an empath. At times, he had lost good people to the treachery of winning a peaceful settlement only to see it collapse in deceit. But only five women survived Hydra out of a hundred and twenty?

Gabe fought the glimpses of horror emanating from Gellico. "What happened in the rescue?" His harsh voice sounded strange to his hearing.

"Oh—" Gellico laughed that borderline hysterical laugh again. "Sol came in, guns blazing and saved the day." Her mocking smile died. Her features hardened into ebony. "If not for her and her Marine crew, all of us would have died there. And, Commander—" Her eyes blazed. "—I didn't want to end my days without taking some of those bastards with me. Sol lost thirty of her Marines before we were able to fight our way back to her ship, but she never complained about the ratio. To my knowledge, neither did the remaining Marines." She paused, lowered her head, and said in a soft, wondering voice, "Sol took full responsibility—the blame. Her crew just followed her orders. They became military heroes, given medals of valor for duty above and beyond and transferred out of her command. But Sol has never complained about her loss of advancement."

"No. She wouldn't, would she." Gabe's low reply wasn't a question.

Gellico lifted her head. "You do know what it cost her to ask me to come here to you, don't you?"

"Yeah, I know." Gabe nodded and frowned at his empty glass. "Just as I know what it does to you to talk to me about Hydra." He nearly choked on the name—a monster out of legend that sported multiple, treacherous heads. So fitting.

Gellico rested her measuring stare on him before she folded back into her chair with all the grace of her former position. Just as before, the lucky seat hugged her contours. She gave him a steady look then snorted. "You don't know a fucking thing, Commander. I'm sure you don't know shit about the situation. If you did, you wouldn't even consider going."

He held up openhanded palms. "What can I say? The convicts have launched a homemade rocket to a Spacing Guild vessel with a message offering a desire to trade supplies and a plea to put an end to their suffering. They've been through hell for years. They say they've established an honorable governing body. The Guild wants the situation investigated, the planet's violent past closed."

"Trade what?" The dancer jumped to her feet. He read the anger flying from her in ionic waves. Her breasts swayed, dangerously close to escaping the narrow strip of fabric, but she didn't notice, and probably wouldn't have cared if she had. Gabe felt the potent whiskey loosening her inhibitions. Her nostrils flared. "There isn't shit on that place worth trading except rotting bones. They brought on their suffering themselves, the bastards." Her dark eyes blazed.

"Maybe so." He nodded and ignored her mocking snort. "Evidently, they have something worth trading now." Gabe walked back behind his desk and picked up the meager report, complete with aerial photos. "The present group leaders have started vegetable and fruit farming from their recycled food seeds. Hydra offers fertile soil for farming. They want to trade their agricultural success for some livestock. My superiors want it investigated."

"It's a trick." Gellico looked forlornly at the bottom of her glass. Gabe shrugged and pointed to the empty decanter. Gellico pouted and stalked around the room.

She turned as he said, "Perhaps it is a trick, but the Guild colonies need fresh supplies such as these. You know we can never get enough for all the colonies. And my superiors want to close this embarrassment. Make the problem of acknowledging these prisoners and their treatment go away."

"Why now? Why, after all these years?" Gellico still prowled the room, much like a confined feline. Gabe felt the dancer's violence coiled around her like a spring. She glared at him. "Do you know that those in authority didn't even acknowledge the deaths of my dancers? They just didn't care. After all, we were just pleasure toys."

"I'm sorry for that, Gellico." Gabe said her name softly and meant every word he spoke. He willed her to understand. "Maybe they didn't care, not then. Then, again, maybe some did and didn't want to rock the boat. But with the new election coming . . . " He let his words trail off before adding, "They don't tell me the reasons why—most of the time. I just follow orders. I'm only the peace negotiator."

"Just the peacemaker, huh? Yeah, diplomatic ass-kissing sure does suck." She sighed and dropped her chin. She stared at the floor. Gabe felt her renewed strength when her head lifted. She had sent her nightmare curving back into the darkness of her mind. Her hard, ebony glare met his. "Sol told me something of your work." Gellico sat down on the corner of Gabe's desk in the same position he had used earlier. And in a similar manner, she leaned forward so she was near his face and swung one long, boot-clad foot, tantalizingly close to him. In the passing air, he could smell her warm scent, something wild, filled with exotic spices—dangerous to say the least— enticing to be sure. "Well, if you're hell-bent on going, Merriweather, I guess I'd better go too."

"Why?" Gabe, reeling from shock, couldn't think of one reason why the dancer would want to help him. It was evident that she didn't trust or even like him. And the next fearful leap her heart gave nearly undid him.

"Because—" Gellico leaned closer, her breasts again in danger of escaping the scrap of silk that barely covered them. "Sol loves you, you ass, and I love Sol, so I'll be going along to protect your diplomatic butt."

His inner self rejoiced with the news that Sol loved him, but Gabe kept his face impassive. "What makes you such a good protective prospect?"

The words had barely left his mouth before Gellico stood before him with a laser needle in one hand and a butterfly switchblade in the other, both sharp points resting at his jugular. Her smooth, deadly movement had been so swiftly executed that he had scarcely taken a breath. Her inner thoughts had given nothing away. And how had she slipped the weapons past Tetra?

"Well done, madam." Gabe spoke through numb lips. He had trouble stifling the responding roar of his Chakkra blood. Swiftly, he doused the warrior response that longed to snap the neck of the threat in front of him. His hands fisted with the effort. For a moment, he wondered if the glittering in her eyes was something besides amusement. Then she spoke, her voice soft and devoid of any emotion.

"You learn to use whatever weapons are handy in a place like Hydra, Commander. Fingernails, elbows, knees, feet, even teeth." For a moment, her eyes reflected a dull coldness. *The remembered coppery taste of blood filling her mouth and choking her.*

Gabe felt sick again. He was again in danger of losing his best whiskey. He refused to swallow; afraid the muscle action would press his skin against her weapons and slit his throat. With a body-trembling shudder, the dancer made a heroic effort and leaned back. The blades left his neck.

Then she whispered, "You grasp sticks and stones to fight back, but sometimes nothing works but what nature gave you." She clicked her teeth at him. With a tight smile, she sheathed the thin laser back in her boot. The butterfly curved blade she expertly twirled for a moment before giving it the same holster treatment in the other boot. Gabe thought he might have lost at least three fingers if he'd attempted that feat. Warrior training and instinct was no match for nimble fingers or for desperation. He covered his shiver and waited for her to finish.

"I guess I've been training and waiting, without knowing why, for years—for just this chance, Commander. I've got to go back. The pricks can't scare me anymore. There isn't a weapon made that I don't know about. I've learned to use them all, and there is nothing I wouldn't do to deliver payback."

"Ah—Gellico, you do know that this is a peaceful mission, don't you?"

"Peaceful and Hydra make an oxymoron." She laughed; a full-throated sound of real amusement, nothing like her crazy laugh of before. Gabe found himself in danger of really liking the dancer; a situation he had found with few others—male or female. Perhaps loving Sol had given him better insight.

"I can't risk my men or the chance to bring peace to people who want it, Gellico." He stared at her with the fatherly scowl he'd practiced for unruly ambassadors. "I don't think that's what Soledad had in mind when she sent you here."

"No, I'm sure not." A wicked half-grin lifted a corner of her full mouth. She was clearly unaffected by his authority. Gabe doubted that she felt anyone's authority. "Sol just wanted me to convince you to not go to Hydra."

"Now, instead of convincing me not to go, you're going with me." Gabe shook his head. "Great. She isn't going to be pleased."

"Yeah, but she'll get over it." Gellico shrugged one shoulder.

"But only if we both make it back." He offered his hand. "Truce?"

After a moment, Gellico took Gabriel's hand, dueled with the pressure of his restrained grip. "Truce." She smiled with just the right amount of respect and squeezed.

Gabe drew back a hand numb to the wrist. He had held back his own strength, but was surprised at hers. Lost in contemplation, Gabe barely noticed Gellico's flinch when she flexed her fingers.

Thirteen

"What the hell do you mean, Asher?" Gabe scowled at his Marine aide. "If you served under Soledad Scott on the Hydra mission, why didn't you tell me before?" The anger he felt at the major was more than evident in his hot tone—as evident as Gabe's brief glimpse of the major's buried feelings for Sol, buried but not forgotten. Gabe choked back his violent response to what he knew was jealousy—a man's lousy, green envy that Sol knew Asher before him. Rage clouded his vision. He blinked rapidly and reasoned it away. No one would ever see Gabe's violent nature if he could help it. He didn't know which made him angrier, the major's dereliction of duty in suppressing information or his own damned warrior bloodlines that urged him to kill his aide, a possible rival for Sol's affections. Perhaps, Gabe should dig deeper, use his empathy to spy on his aide's feelings for Sol. The lieutenant eyed him, speculation in his calm gaze as if he dared Gabe to try something. His voice was even neutral.

"The Hydra operation is still officially classified a 'Need to Know' order, sir." The major shrugged, seemingly unaware of the violent danger he faced in this man of peace he now served under. "Before this, there wasn't a need for you to know about my previous assignments."

Major Asher Jones remained looking "oh so cool and calm" with his lazy-eyed blink, but Gabe read the turmoil the Marine kept in check. This man was slow to anger, or at least slow to act on his anger, but it wouldn't be wise to make him mad. And Gabe wasn't sure what the major felt about Sol. The memory was more than just respect. Gabriel hesitated to delve deeper. A telepathic empath didn't do that to his friends. And Gabe had always counted Asher Jones as more a friend than an aide. Besides, he might not like what he found and that would destroy their friendship. Some secrets from one's past were best left as secrets. Gabe continued practicing his diplomatic mind exercises, whose reasoning had saved him from himself more than once, and from more dangerous enemies than he remembered.

"We both know that I'm not talking about Hydra," Gabe turned back to his desk and fell into his chair. "Although, I do want to know what happened when you left that hellhole."

The gray-eyed major cocked his head and arched a brow. Gabe felt as if he were being studied under a scope. Finally, Asher took a breath. "Captain Scott's crew, what was left of us, were medaled for heroic action above and beyond, then broken up and reassigned to different ships. I haven't seen or spoken to Captain Scott or anyone from the old crew since."

"Hmmm." Gabe sat back in his chair, steepled his fingertips together, and gave the major his best glare. "But you definitely knew I was looking for Captain Scott." He cocked his chin and gave his practiced glare. "I bet you even knew where she was the whole time, Major. Why didn't you tell me?"

The major gave a slow grin that lit up his face and crinkled the skin around his light eyes. Freckles dusted his nose and cheeks. His pale gaze remained steady on Gabe's. He wasn't the least bit intimidated by authority and wasn't afraid to show it. "Perhaps I wanted to see if Sol wanted to be found by you."

"Ah." Gabe nodded. He stared intently into the man's eyes. Asher didn't blink. "So that's how it is." Gabe understood loyalty to a former officer. He let himself be diverted and softly muttered a curse before he raised his voice. "And now, what do you think?"

"Permission to speak freely?" The major assessed him with cool regard.

"Yeah, off the record."

"I think if you break her heart, Commander, I'll break your head with no regrets." Not an ounce of amusement rested in that icy look. His eyes as well as his expression went flat. The muscles hardened in the smooth planes of his face, and one long one jumped in his cheek.

"Fair enough." Gabe extended his hand, knowing that he could crush Asher's head like a melon before the man got one hand raised. "I promise on my honor that I will love and respect Soledad Scott with every breath I take. I will never force her

to do anything she doesn't want to do. Fair enough?"
In reply, the major jerked a nod and gripped Gabe's hand.
Damn it, the man was just as bad as de' Marco trying to prove
a point by dueling grips. Gabe tightened his palm a fraction.
Asher nodded again but never spoke a word, although Gabe
noted that the major rubbed his knuckles against his leg. Gabe
had not consciously tried to hurt the man. Not really. He knew
now that Asher would fight to the death for Sol. He needed
that same loyalty. Gabe had to cough against a tight throat
before he asked, "Now tell me what you think of Gellico de'
Marco."

* * * *

"Major Jones, show Miss de' Marco how to break down
and reassemble your MK-30." The major responded to
Gabriel's order, but Gellico showed no sign of recognition of
the Major even though he had been on Sol's rescue team to
Hydra so long ago.

Last night, Gabe had discovered, with amazement, that
Asher also knew next to nothing about the dancer other than
she had been one of the rescued. Ash had even carried her to
the infirmary, but Gellico had been unconscious at the time.
For the remainder of the trip to base, Sol had ordered all the
male Marines away from the Hydra survivors. Then, on Delta
Three where the Guild could keep close watch, the women,
Gellico included, were transferred to a waiting medical facility
without ever regaining consciousness. Perhaps Sol had kept
them drugged senseless. Gabe had hoped for more information,
about Hydra as well as de' Marco.

For the length of this mission to Hydra, Major Jones, as
the commander's aide, would be Gabe's shadow, guarding his
every move. Gabe had given Ash orders to do the same for
Gellico, but he didn't tell the dancer. He knew that de' Marco
could be more liability than help on Hydra if she didn't know
proper fighting technique. Oh, Gabe was sure she knew the
gutsy brawling techniques, but he wanted to ensure that she
knew as much about weapons as she thought she did. Gabriel
hated to risk his men. All of his Marines were important to
him. He knew each and every one as well as every member of

their families. As a telepathic empath, even without meaning to, he knew intimate details that he'd never tell. How Asher had hid his past so well was beyond Gabe's knowledge. His aide was showing hidden depths, and Gabe intended to use them.

Traveling on-board the *Treaty*, Gabriel's diplomatic cruiser, they had an arsenal of weapons and fighting men. All Gellico lacked was proper training time. The major, who was Gabe's best weapons man as well as his senior officer, could train Gellico, but they lacked reasonable time for a complete drill basic. But the flight to Hydra planned one stop—at Dante's Circus—before they flew to the prison world. Not enough time to give Gellico more than a cursory training in the rifle's use. The cruiser's armory seemed the best training ground.

"Just give me the damned thing." Gellico held out her hand for the MK-30, an impudent smirk on her face. Major Jones regarded Gellico for a moment with his calm gaze before tossing the lightweight laser rifle to her.

With the efficient speed of any experienced Marine, Gellico caught the weapon, broke it down and snapped it back in place in less then thirty seconds. She flipped it back to the major with a graceful twirl.

A large grin broke the stoic Marine's face. Asher turned to Gabe with a twinkle in his eyes and faint dimples marking his cheeks. "Beat your record, Commander."

"Yeah, well, let's hope we don't have to put her experience to work, Major." Gabe huffed while regarding Gellico with a raised brow, that diplomatic look he practiced to intimidate. "What else have you smuggled besides clothing and jewels, de' Marco?

"Cool your jets, Commander. I have never traded in drugs—or guns. Never." Gellico glared at him. "I just once loved a Marine that liked to teach . . . target practice, mostly, that's all."

"No shit? What happened to him?" Gabe couldn't keep the amazement from his voice; he was still reeling from the speed of her weapon assembly. Gellico frowned at his scrutinizing gaze. She glanced over at Asher who regarded her intently with those cool eyes of his. But Gabe knew Ash was as impressed as he. One corner of his mouth lifted, and the Marine gave Gellico a slow, sly wink that he obviously thought was out of Gabe's line of sight. Gellico jerked in surprise. A flush brought unbelievable freckles to view across the major's average looking nose and cheeks. Gabe snorted at the obvious attraction between the two. He realized that a lot of people might overlook Ash's average appearance. Most people would fall under his comfortable presence without realizing his worth. Bad mistake. Gabe knew Asher Jones was a Marine through and through. He might appear nonthreatening, after all, the major was of that average height, average build, with average features. At present, he stood in military at-ease pose, his stance loose and relaxed waiting on Gellico. Gabe coughed. "Ah, can we get on with it, people?"

Gellico snapped her spine straight, and her gaze shot to Gabe's. "Oh yes. You asked what happened to him. *She* died on Rigel Four."

Gabe closed his eyes, hiding his sympathy for her loss. He, too, knew grief for a loved one. With what he hoped was a neutral expression, he dipped his head to Gelli. He looked at Asher. The Marine didn't seem surprised that Gelli was a lover of women. He didn't even look offended.Just a noncommittal compassion rested in his steady gaze. *Hmmm.* Perhaps there was hope for the obvious attraction between the two. For now, Gabe had more important things to do. "I'm sorry, Miss de'Marco."

"Yeah. Me, too, Commander." Gellico hurried toward the armory's exit as if she wanted to get on to the more important things. "Can I get some sleep now?"

"Sure. Major Jones, show Miss de' Marco her quarters. And Jonesy—" Gabe paused, stared intently at his aide. "—no fraternization. I need everyone focused here."

"Yes, sir!" The major flipped a proper two-fingered salute to his forehead, his face stoic but his cheekbones also carrying a flush.

Gelli snapped at Gabe, "There's no cause for that, Commander. Listen to your own advice. I notice we're stopping at Dante's Circus. I wonder why?" She glared, obviously irritated at Gabe's insinuations.

"Yeah, we are stopping there. I thought maybe you might want to tell Sol why you're going with me." Gabe couldn't keep the hopeful sound from his voice.

"Nah. You get that pleasure all by yourself, big man. But . . . nice try at covering your ass." Gellico winked and left the room with a rich laugh trailing behind her.

"Bitch," Gabe muttered without meaning for her to hear.

Gellico stuck her head back in and blew him a kiss, sweetly saying, "Back at you, bastard." She slammed the door with a bang. Gabe rocked with the truth of her innocent statement.

* * * *

Sol pestered Punch a third time. "Are they here yet?"

Punch lumbered over to her table with a cup of Caladinea green tea. Miraculously the big Rigelian bouncer didn't spill a drop. "No." He gently placed the steaming cup near Sol's hand and tapped his blunt fingers next to it for emphasis. Wrinkles creased his broad forehead, but he didn't speak again before returning to his post by the door, nursemaid and guardian to the last.

Sol sighed. It took entirely too much effort to be mad at the Rigelian. Gellico's Punch was a pussy cat despite his fierce look. For some reason, he had taken to hovering over her in Gelli's absence, doing guard duty as per her instructions, no doubt.

"Where's Cheri?" Sol blew on the steaming tea that she didn't want. Butterflies danced in her hollow stomach at the thought of possibly seeing Gabe again. Why did just the thought of the commander wreck her normal stability?

Punch shook his massive head and looked unhappy. Sol knew the feeling well.

Cheri had rushed in nearly an hour ago and announced, "The Diplomatic Corps aboard the *Treaty* is requesting a landing site. I do hope Damien is on board." The little dancer twirled on her toes, then rushed out again without waiting for Sol to say a word. No doubt, she was going back to the docks to meet her lover, the lusty Sergeant Damien.

Well, Soledad Scott would do no such thing—hanging around the space docks like a lovesick puppy, for gods' sake. Besides, Gabe wasn't her lover. Was he? If not lover, what exactly was he? Sol fumed and paced the confines of the dancehall, waiting and wondering why Gellico hadn't returned from her trip to see Gabriel. And just why was *he* coming here instead?

"Captain Scott?"

Sol looked up into the steady gaze of a Marine major, a sandy-haired, averaged-height man with a solid build and no outstanding features except for serious gray eyes that assessed her without expression. For a moment, she didn't recognize Asher. The years had hardened the gray to steel and had deepened the wrinkles around his eyes and mouth. He was tanned and fit in his black and red officer regimentals. When recognition came, her heart stuttered.

"Asher Jones!" Sol broke into a smile at his broad grin, a grin she remembered so well. She leaped into his arms. Suddenly hugged in his strength, Sol found herself sobbing on his uniformed shoulder, although she had to bend her head to reach it. His remembered familiar scent surrounded her with comfort and such strength. How she had missed him.

"There, there." He patted Sol's back. "What's all this? I thought you'd be glad to see an old buddy." Red stained his cheekbones. Freckles peeked through his skin. "Bit of a change of command for you, isn't it?" He hugged her rounded girth with a gentle tightening of his arms.

Sol pulled back and nodded. "Yeah. I've became my own ship, you might say." She patted her middle with a light hand. "I carry my new crew." Her laugh ended her unexpected storm of tears with a sniff. Sometimes she surely felt as big as a war ship. And tears no longer obeyed her command.

Asher's smile died. "I'm Commander Merriweather's aide now, Sol." His voice lost all hint of teasing. "He wants to see you. Would you come with me, please?" His question was more of an order and they both knew it, although Sol inclined her head politely. The command was from Gabriel, and Sol wanted to see him, too, the rat bastard. But she didn't mind the messenger. Asher was her friend, and it felt right to be with Marines again. She missed her ship and her Marines.

"What happened to the rest of the old crew?" She fell into step with him, hoping Asher knew about the others. For years, she had hoped for word of them, but none ever came.

"I don't know, Captain." Asher's crisp tone said he gave her the title for more than friendship. He smartly marched at Sol's side with the smooth, practiced stride of someone always on the alert. And, just as always, his deadly cadence radiated power and efficiency. He had lost none of his expertise. His intense gaze never stopped searching the shadows. "None of us were ever assigned to the same ship. I've never seen anyone but you and Ms. de' Marco again."

Sol knew the way the Guild worked. If they wanted the incident—such an embarrassment that no one had responded to the SOS sooner—on Hydra to remain quiet, the best way would be to reassign everyone with orders to never speak of the tale. She swallowed hard. They stopped before the door to Gellico's room. The major rapped once with the back of his knuckles.

Inside, Sol heard a break in the deep warble of male and female voices. She couldn't tell if an argument waged between the two.

"Enter. Door's open," commanded a baritone voice Sol knew only too well. In a sudden flashback, she recalled the first time Gabe spoke those words to her. Her stomach's butterflies started dancing harder. What would he think of her new size, and just what was Merriweather doing in Gelli's room?

Sol stepped into the familiar room on strangely trembling legs. She glanced first at Gabe, dressed in his official somber gray with black-trimmed Diplomatic Corps uniform. She dismissed his silent assessing look with one of her own that promised she'd be back to him shortly. Her vision was full of Gellico, who looked so out of place in her safari room wearing the tight-fitting black Marine regimentals. Lethal weapons hung about Gellico's curves instead of her usual silk scarves.

Sol held her dark gaze. Her heart hammered in her chest like a trapped bird. "What in hell are you're doing, Gelli?"

"Protecting something that is precious to you?" Gellico snorted, and flipped a glittering curved knife that, just moments before, had been hidden on her person. Where she'd hidden it was hard to figure since the leather fit her generous curves like a snug glove. Gelli caught the sharp blade in midair with the smoothness of a master assassin. Another spun into view and joined the first to become twin curving death blades. Sol's butterflies grew as frantic as the twirling knives.

"You were supposed to convince *him* not to go on this mission." Sol shook her head and scowled at Gellico with her fiercest frown. "Am I to understand by your new fashion accessories and your weapons' demonstration that *you're* now going with him?"

"You got it in one, sweetie." The blades disappeared back into their secret places, and Gellico reached a hesitant hand out to Sol. A tentative smile flickered over her lips—lips that trembled like Sol had never seen them. Sol shook her head and backed away, her palm raised in a stop position. Tears lay too close to the surface again. Anger came just in front of them. She spun back to Gabriel, the back of her neck on fire and her temples throbbing. "And you—*diplomat,*" Sol pointed a long finger at him and spat his occupation like a curse. "You don't know what you're getting into on Hydra."

"Gellico told me all about Hydra." Gabe used his smooth, peacemaking voice. His calmness irritated her. Well, she was having none of it.

"The hell she did," Sol retorted. "I'm sure she didn't tell you *all*. Did she mention that she weighed only eighty-seven pounds when we pulled her out of that hell? Did she tell you of her repeated rape at the hands of those animals?" Those visions of a tortured Gellico haunted Sol with vivid recall. How her bony rib cage had stuck out like a skeleton's, and how her blood had wetly streamed down her battered body from her head to her heels.

"Did she tell you that half her hair had been ripped out of her scalp? How the bastards stood on her braids while they took turns going at her?"

Sol kept on spitting statements at Gabe, ignoring Gellico's

soft cries of "stop" and "don't." Gabe took hold of her shoulder but she kept shooting questions at him. "Did she tell you that she was barely standing and a bloody mess when we rescued her? How it took years for her to recover?" She shook off Gabe's grip, heedless of the tears that streaked her face. Her throat hurt. Her nose ran. She hated crying, and may the gods help the ignorant fool that had pushed her to this point. Gabe, the ignorant fool, reached for her again, and Sol slapped at his hands, but he ignored her and just held on. She gave up and glared at him. "How can you ask her to go back there?"

"I volunteered." Gellico yelled over Sol's tirade. "Sol . . . I *volunteered*," she repeated softly in the sudden quiet.

Silence ruled. Gabriel's hand slid off Sol's stiffened shoulder. He seemed to know that she didn't want his touch, but he didn't say a word. She couldn't look him in the eyes. Instead her blurred gaze sought Gelli's. Sol suddenly realized the anguish her words had inflicted. Gellico's face reflected a muddy visage, ravished by a bleakness Sol hadn't witnessed since Hydra. The dancer swayed in a widely braced stance. Her graceful neck bowed with the weight of a head too heavy to hold up. Her hands fisted at her rigid sides. Sol swallowed a bitter taste. How could she have been so thoughtless, so caught up in convincing Gabe that she forgot the pain she could cause by exposing a secret not spoken? She would never forget Hydra and what Gellico had suffered.

But gods, Gelli was the one who'd lived the nightmare. "I'm sorry, Gelli. Good gods, forgive me. I am so sorry. Please. I wasn't thinking."

Gellico gave a slight nod to her apology, and Sol's throat tightened further.

Without saying a word, Asher stepped to Gellico's side. He wasn't touching her, but the major hovered, a silent presence next to the tall dancer. Clearly the Marine was attuned to Gellico's distress. His narrowed gaze warned Sol off while he drew Gelli gently out the door. The pair stumbled through the opening, Gellico's graceful strides unusually awkward. Asher shut the door softly behind them.

Silence lingered for only a moment before Gabe snorted.

"Well, Soledad, it's apparent that you aren't thinking clearly. How could you think I wouldn't know her pain or yours?" His words were snapped, but he drew Sol to him, cradled her in his arms. "And you know better than to hurt Gellico." He sighed. "You're worried about her—about me, too, I guess. I understand that, but, you must know that I need all the help I can get. Gellico knows the region better than Asher. She's offered to act as our guide, and I need an edge. All the edge I can get."

Sol shook her head, rubbed her forehead on his shoulder and swallowed hard. Reasoning didn't come easy. Her throat hurt to speak. "And you're only too happy to jump at her offer, aren't you?" She tried to pull out of his grip. She didn't know who she was angrier with; herself or Gabriel Merriweather, the empathic diplomat.

"Sol, please," Gabe pulled her closer, his words smothered into her hair. She felt his lips press a kiss against her hair; his breath blew warmth on her head. "We only have a few minutes. Don't fight me for once. We just came to say goodbye." He touched her forehead and brushed her hair with the tips of his fingers. His soft touch moved down her neck, flicking over her skin and stabbing her in the heart.

"Goodbye?" The stiffness drained out of Sol. Her fluttering heart beat so much it hurt her chest. She couldn't draw a breath. They had decided this without her. They were leaving to do this awful thing. There was nothing she could say or do. The finality left her hollow.

"I'm sorry, Sol. I wish there was another way, but . . . "

"It's not your fault." Sol finally pulled away from him, gently this time. She wrapped her arms across her chest to stop the shivers that threatened to tear her apart. "Gellico was bound to go back there someday. Maybe she needs to put an end to that part of her life."

"What happened to the others? There were five women who made it out." Gabe followed her and pulled her back into his embrace. He was such a persistent soul. Sol rested against his solid chest, breathed in his familiar warm scent. She could see a small, dark mole just under his jaw line, hidden, teasing, out of sight most of the time. Such an endearing mark, special, there just for her. Gods, how she needed this—his touch, his smell, his strength. Damn it, how had he gotten under her skin so thoroughly?

Sol forced her thick throat to form words to answer his question about the battered women she would never forget. "One woman completely disappeared after her release. One committed suicide, and the other two are still in mental hospitals. Gellico pays for their treatments. The meds say one of them may make it back outside—someday. The other—who knows? Sol snuggled against him and tried to curl even closer into his wonderful heat. She felt so cold. Gabe was leaving. Her heart was breaking. How like a foolish woman she felt, not at all like a star ship captain. He hugged her tightly.

"I really am sorry, Sol." His words vibrated in his throat, tickling her ear.

"Shhh." She put her fingers over his lips then pulled him to her mouth. Hungry, she was so hungry for his warmth. Maybe his kiss would melt the coldness that enveloped her. "Give me a proper goodbye, Commander."

"Are you sure, Captain?" He lifted his head, his pale gaze gone uncertain. He stroked her hair back from her cheek with such tenderness that Sol swallowed a sob.

She tugged Gabe's hand and led him toward Gellico's bedroom. "I'm sure."

They began before they reached the silk-draped bed. Gabe ravished her with his hot mouth, leaving her shaking with raging hunger to get ever nearer, to crawl inside his body. His clever hands roved over her sensitive skin, exploring openings in clothing and ripping ones that failed to cooperate. Finally bare, skin to skin, they lay so close they breathed each others breath. In one instant, their eyes met. Their storm of passion quieted. Both knew this might be their last meeting. The sexual fire banked but didn't die. It only waited for more fuel.

"I don't want to ever leave you, Sol," Gabe murmured against her neck and hid his face against her flesh. His breath tickled her skin, raised goose bumps.

Sol nodded and hugged him tighter. Tears threatened. "I

know. I don't want you to go either, but . . . " She leaned back with a sigh. "You will go, you damned diplomat." She punched him in the chest harder than she meant. "Just make damned sure you come back."

Gabe raised his head after flinching at her punch, a hint of humor in his shadowed gaze. "If you care so much, Captain, stop hitting me." The teasing fled, and his hand smoothed over the round rise of her body. His gaze grew serious. "I want this—our child, too, Soledad. I love the fact that we are joined into this innocent. I want you both in my life—for the rest of my days. Please, don't run from me anymore. You can't deny that you love me as much as I love you." He stared at her so intently it was as if he could see clear into her soul.

Sol couldn't speak past the thickness in her throat. A mist clouded her vision. She raised her hand to cover his, guiding their palms over her mounded pregnancy. Appropriately, at that moment, their child kicked under their joined hands. Startled wonder washed over Gabe's face. His eyes grew brilliant, and he claimed her mouth in a long, tender kiss that sealed her fate. And Sol accepted what she had fought so hard to deny. She accepted but couldn't say the words. The truth stared her in the face.

Yes, the captain would join with the commander if and when he asked. Sol wouldn't speak of love now, she couldn't. She pulled him closer, wrapped both arms around Gabe's neck, her bulk stopping them from touching as closely as she wanted. He chuckled when the baby kicked against him. She lifted her brows, "Any idea of how we'll be able to do this, Commander?"

"Yeah, I've read up on pregnant women." A rosy flush crept over Gabe's face, neck and ears. It was so deep in color that Sol thought she felt the burning heat of it.

"You did?" Sol gazed at him, trying to fit herself closer into the curve of him. "Oh, you would." She laughed, loving the way his color deepened even further. How very like a scholar he was, to read up on pregnancy. Merriweather had to study every thing. "And how many pregnant women do you know?"

A shadow flickered over his face then he smiled a little sadly. "Just one that counts." Gabriel pulled on her arm. "Turn over." He positioned Sol on her left side, her back to his front. "Now, just relax." His hand roved over her hip and nestled near her waist. She relished the feel of his hard palm.

"This won't hurt the baby?" she breathed in an unsteady breath.

"No. I promise. And if you don't like it, we'll stop. Okay? Now bend your leg." He helped bend her knee to a right angle from her waist. His hand glided up and down her thighs, her stomach, rounding to her breasts while he kissed the back of her neck. Sol closed her eyes and gave herself up to the sensation of just feeling Gabe and his marvelous touch.

All those times they'd made love, Gabe had been giving to her, always. He gave again. With gentle lips, he trailed heated kisses down her neck, across her shoulders, lingering to pay special attention to the ridge of her backbone. After nipping little bites, he licked a circle around the joint of her neck, down the center of her back. At her front, his hands were also busy driving her crazy. His clever fingers delighted in plucking at her sensitive nipples until she wanted to scream. And he didn't wait or hesitate when he reached her spine's joint at the end of her back. He dipped his tongue into her butt's crevice. Sol arched, nearly coming off the bed at the erotic touch. Shivers shot through her, followed by a slow rush of pulsing heat.

"Easy, sweetness." Gabe pulled her back into position. "Trust me, I won't hurt you." He kissed the bend in her waist that was still a gentle curve despite her girth. His hair brushed her skin with a silken touch. Sol couldn't relax. Tremors shook her. This might be the last time she would ever love him this way. She didn't want to admit it, but this great love made her vulnerable, not at all like the strong captain she wanted to be.

But she couldn't lie about her feelings. "I want you, Gabriel." And she spoke the truth. Never had she wanted anything so much. She nearly ached with the need. Denying further delay, she searched behind until she held the throbbing length of him in her palm. He curved closer around her.

"I know you want me, Sol." Gabe breathed hot puffs of air on her back, resting his forehead against her waist. "I want you, too. And gods, how glad I am that you want me in return."

He moved back up against her, her long back to his chest, her butt to his front. His thick erection poked against her. Sol remembered the tight fit of him inside her; the long length that touched her inner walls. She couldn't stop her moan.

"I'll give you what you want soon, honey. I just want to make sure you're ready." Gabe reached his arms around her. Such powerful strength given so carefully. His presence covered Sol like a blanket, a warm, sheltering sanctuary. It wasn't what she wanted. She wanted him as wild with need as she. Sol grabbed Gabe's hand and pushed it between her legs. His fingers slipped on her wet lips. "I am ready for you, moron." She felt frustrated tears and thrust harder against his hand. "Feel."

Finally, he pushed one blessedly thick finger into Sol then shoved another into her slick heat. He rubbed against the hard kernel of her pleasure. Yeah, she was ready. Both of them moaned when his fingers sunk deeper, slid in and out. Both heard the slickness of her desire.

"Give it to me." Sol arched into his hand and reached behind her to grasp him again. She pulled up and down on his length in rhythm to his fingers sliding in and out of her.

"*Jesu,*" he breathed.

"Give this to me. Now, Gabriel." Sol panted.

"Aye, my captain, anything you want."

With that, Gabe eased his way between her legs from behind, slipping inside her slowly, an inch at a time. *Such exquisite torture.* Sol was startled by the wonderful thickness of him. Gabe felt so different entering from behind her. She hesitated only a moment before she found his rhythm, moving back against him and then away. He placed one hand over her mound while the other held her hip and guided them both carefully in a dance as old as time. Faster and faster they moved. All the while Gabe's wonderful heat warmed her back, and his hands guided her front, careful of their child. He kissed the nape of her neck then bit the skin. She moaned. He breathed in her ear, whispered naughty things that a diplomat had no right to speak, and then he nipped her shoulder—hard. Sol cried out, but with pleasure not pain. She surged back against him. Suddenly, Gabe cursed a foreign oath under his breath, and she felt his hot spurt the same instant her muscles clenched and released. She held herself against his solid length, and he pumped the last of his seed into her. In an unexpected finish, he rolled the hard nub of her sex then pinched. She cried aloud. Her trembling release went on and on.

For a time, only the sound of their slowing breaths broke the silence of the room.

"I'm sorry that was so quick, Sol, but I've got to go," Gabe murmured. He rested his chin on her shoulder, his arms loose around her waist.

"I know." Sol turned to face him, flushed at what she wanted to say. His penis lay wet and spent on her thigh. "Gabe, I . . . I . . . " She still couldn't get the words out. She hugged him instead.

"That's okay, my captain." He patted her back gently. "Tell me when I get back." He kissed her lightly on the mouth and quickly slipped into his gray diplomatic uniform. Sol felt just as somber. He didn't bother to wash her from his body, and Sol didn't ask why. She couldn't speak. Her voice refused to budge from where it had lodged in the rock at the base of her throat. Her muscles refused to move, and she couldn't get up. She could only watch him.

"Be here when I get back." He waited at the door, his dark hair mussed and his expressive brow lifted. His pale eyes pleaded with her.

Sol could only nod. Her heartbeat was a heavy, dead thing in her chest.

Gellico's voice boomed from the outer room before Gabe closed the door. "You better not have stained my sheets, Commander."

Both were gone by the time Sol roused and dressed.

And the waiting began.

Fourteen

The first week dragged by. The next went even slower, but Sol knew that it would be several turns before the *Treaty* even reached the Straits region beyond Brittany's Skirt, the remotest populated area near Hydra and closest to the Rim. She would not be hearing from Gabriel any time soon, but that didn't stop her worrying. The recorded message from the *Treaty* the first day out still haunted her, although she had almost given up playing the recording since she could quote it word for word. Almost but not quite. Sol watched it now to see Gabriel's impressive image, an image that swept her with heart-rending longings. His rich voice was like a balm to her soul.

He stood tall and large in his gray and black, and he had never looked more foreign. His dark hair was groomed severely flat to his skull and tied with a narrow leather strip at the base of his neck. The sleek style actuated his slanted eyes and high cheekbones. Pale eyes assessed the world with cool regard. The smooth cloth of his uniform hugged his broad shoulders and slim waist while colorful ribbons and medals decorated his wide chest. Even Gabe's demeanor reflected a seriousness that she had never witnessed.

"By the time you see this, Sol, we will be out of transmission range. Coward that I am, I wanted it that way. You see, Captain, I have to ask you an important question." He paused to drink from a tumbler that Sol was sure contained some form of alcohol. After a quick gulp, his breath hissed on the intake, and he gave a slight shudder before continuing. His watery gaze shimmered. Sol couldn't remember ever seeing Merriweather so unsettled, his voice even rasped strangely.

"I know we met under odd circumstances. For the first time in my life, I was at the Domes seeking something that showed me life was worth living when you came through the door. You were like a breath of fresh air, and I knew I had found affirmation. Yeah, I knew, too, after those first few moments with you, that you thought I was someone else, an anonymous sex toy. But, Sol, I felt that you needed the same reaffirmation of life that I needed. Your eyes looked so very sad. You hurt deep inside. I felt it." Gabe shrugged his shoulders and dipped his head, looking up through his thick lashes. She wondered fleetingly if he mocked her practiced coy look, but his was unrehearsed.

His stubborn chin lifted. "When we first met, I was obligated to inform you that I was a master empath duly registered with the Guild. I apologize for not doing so. I just thought you knew when you saw the tats." He touched his arm that carried the strange tattoos that Sol remembered seeing that night at the Pleasure Dome. One corner of his mouth lifted. "And, Sol—you've got to admit that we were a little too busy for small talk."

His eyes twinkled, but not a drop of amusement leaked into his voice. "I want you to know that I've never used my talents to spy on you. I value your friendship beyond all others, so your deep, dark secrets are safe with me. Besides my respect for you, Sol, you're what is know as a tranq. I've learned of your Chakkra blood; it gives you a special defense mechanism that protects you from rats like me." He gave a twisted grin. "By accident, I read only your strongest emotions—things that are too large to keep inside and hidden. These are things meant to be shared with someone."

Sol could no longer see the pain in his eyes, but she knew it was there. She heard it in his voice. "Even burdens and guilt become lighter when shared with someone who cares. Try it sometime. You'll see that I'm right. You've helped me by just being yourself, Captain. With you, I don't have to be a diplomat. And when I am in your presence, you give me rest. I feel peacefulness, a quiet I've never found with anyone. You grant me shelter, serenity from the thousands of emotions that bombard me from all sides. Not only have I felt your love—" Gabe stopped for a moment, his lip quirked up again at the corner and those crooked bottom teeth showed their tops. Sol's heart thudded at the endearing sight. "—yes, love, which you have been unable to speak of to me, but I know it's there as surely as I'm breathing. I was drawn to your need for love when I met you. The depth of your loneliness called to me. Oh, I know you are a strong woman—ah, pardon me—captain. But, Sol, I did feel your sorrow that night. I thought if I could just give you pleasure, the sadness in you would go away. I didn't know you wanted a child, and at first, I was angry when I found out. You see, I've never wanted offspring. I have a past . . ." He hesitated then hurried on, "And I guess you deserve to know it."

He took a deep breath and said, "I'm sure you've heard the rumors that I'm a half-breed Chakkra. They are true. I was born in pain but also in a great love. My father was a Chakkra of royal blood who had the misfortune to fall for a Terran ambassador sent to seal a treaty with my father's world." Gabriel gave a hollow laugh. "As if peace was ever possible with those savages. They killed my father for his offense, then as soon as I was born, they murdered my mother." He looked straight in the com's lens, and Sol saw the hard glitter in his eyes. "Captain, I assure you, I'm not like the Chakkra. I've denied any connection to them my whole life." He paused for another deep breath, and it was as if he swept his past back into the shadows of his mind, because even his tense shoulders relaxed.

"Anyway, that's the main reason I've never wanted offspring. The worlds we live in are harsh, cruel, dangerous places that no child should ever see." He ran a hand through his hair, dislodging the slick order. Those unruly dark curls were how Sol remembered Gabe when he left this last time—his silken hair mussed from her fingertips. She could still feel the softness of it under her touch. Her heart felt squeezed. Her lungs labored for breath.

"I'm trying to fix those worlds, Sol, and, after all these years, I suddenly realize that a child with you is the second most important thing in my life. You and your happiness are the most important. For me, now, the Guild with its orders comes last. I'll do my best to make you happy. I'll protect you and our child until my dying breath." He looked straight into the vid lenses. "I love you, Sol. Will you link with me as life companion when I come home? At least, think about it."

He bent, as if to shut off the transmission then stopped. The thin skin around his eyes and mouth crinkled. Sol could swear she felt his wry humor, taste his kiss. "Oh, I almost forgot. In Gellico's woven crap that she calls a desk, I left some things for you to consider in the top drawer. One is a ring bearing my family's crest—my mother's crest. Wear it if you accept my proposal." He inclined his head, his smile a faint curving of his mouth. Sol touched her fingers to her lips, remembering the touch of that mouth against hers.

His voice continued on, making her heart ache with loss. "I would like to see the ring on your finger when I come home. That way, I don't have to ask you for your answer."

Sol couldn't help smiling. Gabe was never a coward. But he certainly grinned like the cat that ate the canary. When he continued, feathers nearly dripped from his lips. "The other thing in Gellico's desk is a Corps enlistment with your rank as first commander, along with an induction commission for the Diplomatic Corps—if and when you want it. In other words, Captain—ah, Commander, I want you to lead my Marines. I despair of letting you out of my sight." He shook his head and smiled sadly. "What I really mean is that I need you, Sol. And I love you. For always—even if you don't want a commitment. But think about it." His pale eyes glowed with his promise. The screen went blank.

Sol realized that she ached for his touch—felt as empty as he must have after her vids to him. What a shit she had been for sending them. But then, those vids had brought them together. Gabe never would have continued looking for her without them.

In a wondering daze, Sol searched Gelli's desk drawer. She found the things just as he had said. The heavy gold ring was engraved with a fierce, wide-winged, black eagle holding shafts of wheat in his sharp beak, proclaiming peace, no doubt. Sol thought for a moment that she had seen that emblem somewhere before, but couldn't remember where. Perhaps Gabe came from a long line of peacemakers on his mother's side. Sol realized she knew little of his background, his family— the royal Chakkra link. He had never spoken of it before. How did he become a Guild empath? Were Chakkra born with empathic talents? Well, it didn't matter. Sol didn't care. She knew Merriweather—and she wanted him no matter what his bloodlines were.

For days that slowly faded into weeks after the transmission, Sol considered Gabriel's proposal, both about being life companions and about the commission. Did she really want to love someone so much that she gave them power over her with a connubial contract? Did loving Merriweather mean giving up her independence? And, what about a return to service? Would that work with Gabe as her superior? Thoughts swirled and contradicted in her head.

Peaceful missions would take some adjustment. Life on a diplomatic ship would certainly be different from what she was used to onboard a warship. And with a child. What would that be like? Sol wasn't sure she could handle those adjustments. But she'd never leave her son behind. This child had become the most important thing in her life next to Gabe. She would give her life for either of them.

The thought startled her. Warmth spread throughout her body and soul. She was definitely in love. She never wanted to be parted from Gabe again, and adrenaline pumped anew at the thought of being back in the thick of things. Surely, the two of them could protect their child. She had no doubt that Gabe would be savage in his protectiveness. From him, Sol had learned that a life as a diplomat, especially an empathic one, was not free from danger even on a peaceful ship. He needed her. In fact, his career was perhaps even more threatening than hers had ever been.

At least aboard a war ship, Sol could see danger coming at her. For Gabriel it hid behind intrigue and lies that were only hinted at with their hidden meanings. Well, she would let Gabe think he was in charge since he was the diplomatic commander, and she would be military commander in charge of the troops, but may the gods help anyone who threatened what was hers. And Gabriel Merriweather belonged to her. That statement brought release to the tight band that wound around Sol's chest. It was as if her soul sang with the knowledge.

Without further hesitation, Sol slipped Gabriel's wide ring over her thumb. It clung around her joint with a cold, heavy ache. She missed him so much. With sudden insight, Sol realized that she wasn't giving up anything to love him. Truly, Gabriel completed her, fulfilled her life. Soledad Scott didn't need to command a ship to be of worth. Love completed her. Love of herself, her friends, her family and most of all, Gabriel Merriweather and their child gave her an identity, a reason for living. Soledad Scott was a person of value, and she realized that this insight was all due to the damned commander of the Diplomatic Corps. She would thank him when he returned. And, by the gods, Gabriel had better return safe if he knew what was good for him. And he'd better return soon. She grew tired from waiting.

The papers that Merriweather had left regarding a commission, Sol finally signed at the bottom with a quick flourish. Afterwards, she felt radiant with the realization that she loved Gabe, really loved him, heart and soul. But missing him was wearing on her. Her spirits felt so low that she called her sister on her com link even though she knew it cost more credits then a visit. But when you're as big as a galactic warship, you don't mind the expense. Still bubbling over her discovery of being in love with Gabriel, Sol shared the news with Te'. She was shocked at her sister's angry response.

"Bloody hell, Sol, everyone in the Guild knows Merriweather's a master empath," Te snarled. She ran a hand over her messy braid. Her thick hair that glittered more golden brown than red had escaped the careful weaving that Te' always wore when she worked around the house. She appeared tired and distracted, and Sol wondered what she had interrupted. Then what Te' had said finally registered in Sol's brain. What did Te' mean—in the Guild? Sol wasn't prepared for her sister's next words. "Merriweather will never rise higher in rank since he carries so much Chakkra blood. As a bastard half-breed, he'll always rank as second class in the Guild."

A long silence followed. It seemed to stretch on forever before Sol got over her shocked confusion. "What?" The word exploded from her numb lips. "How do you know so much about the Guild?"

A light suddenly turned on in Sol. "You're in the Guild, aren't you, Te'? *You're in the bloody Guild!"*

Sol's head whirled with conflicting thoughts. A deep weight settled in Sol's stomach, sickened her. She stomped back and forth across Gelli's beautiful wood floors. She wasn't worried about Gabe's damned bloodlines or even her own. She had listed them only for the genetics lab that did the evaluations on her birthing request. *Te'angel was in the fucking Guild.* Sol thought for a moment that she was still in bed dreaming another awful nightmare.

Te' gave a tight laugh. "Don't tell me that you haven't guessed after all these years, Sol. By the gods, where is your head?" Te' shook her own head as if in disbelief and hurried on, passing over Sol's anguish. Sol had the feeling that her sister had revealed more in those first few sentences than she had ever meant to.

Te' drew in a deep breath as red bloomed on her wide cheekbones. Her words ran together without another breath between them. "I've been the Guild's registered master empath for the past ten years, Sol. Do you really think they only want my offspring for simple ship pilots?"

Sol's knees buckled. *Te' was an empath? In the Guild?* She collapsed into one of Gellico's soft chair, even though she knew it would be hell rising back up from the comforting soft depths. Her mind swirled with thoughts of things she had never considered. Te's countless trips to Nabet, Delta Three's capital city, where most of the Guild's business was conducted—her unbelievable success with her children's problems—the many hints of things the kids would say that had sailed over Sol's head with just a thread of puzzlement. Sol had always been so wrapped up in the war effort and battle strikes, she had never delved too deeply into her sister's affairs. She had always used Te's noisy home as a refuge, a place where nothing and no one outside of family intruded. Damn, she should have noticed the way Te' had always, *always*, understood Sol's problems with the Guild—to say nothing of the wealth Te' had accumulated over the years which, now that she thought about it, was more than an Academy breeder grossed in a lifetime.

Te's soft words broke through Sol's musings. Her sister still appeared as a stranger—familiar but somehow wrong. "I really am sorry, honey. I know I should have told you long ago." Te's image in Sol's small com link stared at her with genuinely sad eyes. "I'm sorry for not telling you of the Guild and my part in it. Blame me for being selfish of your affection, Sis. I just relished the comfort you always brought when you visited. I never wanted to disrupt the peace I enjoyed in your company. I know how you feel about the Guild's meddling."

"You found my visits peaceful?" Sol blinked at the thought of the many times she had yelled and dumped her problems at her sister's doorstep. How much had Te' known about her problems with the Guild and never revealed? Te frowned before she spoke. "You didn't even know you're a tranq, did you?"

"Not until Gabriel told me." Sol tried to follow Te's thoughts, remembering what Merriweather had said in his message. She tried to make sense out of the bits and pieces, but admittedly without success. Te's Guild involvement still bothered Sol more than her thoughts of being a tranq.

"You were in your teens before I knew. That, as well as empathy talent, runs in our family. Chakkra and Terran mixed blood breeds all sorts of talents." Te' grinned a little shakily. Then her lips twisted ruefully. "You being a tranq is only one of many reasons that I've always loved to see you."

She again brushed the loose tendrils of her hair back from her forehead in what Sol was beginning to think was a nervous habit. For the first time, Sol noted Te's deep weariness, the stress lines around her mouth, a mouth that gave a tight lifting of the corners, "When you came to visit, even for just a few days, I had some quiet time, some peace. No matter how many buffers I have installed, this place is still swamped with all the kids' rioting emotions. And gods, their hormones when they matured and came into their own talents—wheeeh! Even your problems, Sol, were an enjoyment over the outside emotions that get past my home's filters."

Sol again noted the worry lines around her sister's eyes, the way her eyes narrowed. How much political crap did her sister deal with? Sol's thoughts jumped back to the Guild, and her emotions whirled. *Her sister and the dammed Guild. For how many years?*

Te' interrupted her thoughts before Sol reached the boiling point. "What were you thinking of when you seduced Merriweather?" She scowled. "*The* Gabriel Merriweather, head of the Diplomatic Corps, a Chakkra half-breed, for the stars' sake! You can't really want a life partnership with him. You can't be serious." Te' shook her head like a mother speaking to a lack-witted child. "Don't you know he's a one-sided visionary? Always questioning instead of doing as he's told. I should have fired him years ago for being so weak an enforcer. A gods-damned diplomat." Te's eyes narrowed and another blush painted her cheeks. "Good gods, tell me he isn't the father of your child."

"How could *you* have fired him, Te'?" Sol didn't miss the way Te' stiffened after her slip of the tongue. She, too, could read her sibling well. She wasn't diverted that easily.

Te took a deep breath before using her soft *mother* voice on Sol. "Honey, to tell you the whole truth, I'm—well, in addition to the Guild's master empath, I'm also the acting governor of the Guild. At least, I am temporary governor until the next election."

Sol absorbed the information with a blank stare, and Te' hastily continued, "You see, darling, we are supposed to operate in obscurity. Even our families aren't supposed to know who heads the committee. Our present governor is ill, has been for a long time, and I've been in charge until the election." Te' drew her shoulders erect and lifted her chin. "But I will be in the running for permanent governor this time." Te' sighed. "Do you understand, darling?"

Te's words echoed like a thunder clap in Sol's ears, and she felt as if she wanted to vomit. "You're what?"

Te' ignored Sol's question. "I know I should have told you years ago about my—my talent and my career, but you, in your capacity as captain of a Guild ship, had no need to know. It's against the rules. And, face it. You were so busy with your own life that I didn't want to involve you in all my dirty laundry."

"Dirty laundry? That's what you call being on the board that wrecked my life?" Sol felt as if she was splintering into pieces.

Te' snorted and her placating tone irritated Sol when she said, "The Guild didn't wreck your life, Soledad. You're still living comfortably, aren't you?"

Sol was so angry she choked. After the loss of her ship, Te' had even been the one to suggest she find a new career as a mother! Talk about diversion. How could she choose the Guild over Sol?

Te' took advantage of Sol's shocked pause to continue. "Of course, this thing with Merriweather—of all the stupid ideas you've ever had, Sis."

Sol took umbrage at the rest of her sister's words, and she disconnected her com link. She sat there, stunned, breathing heavily and her heart rate rocketing while she ignored the continual beeping of her link. She thought seriously about never answering the damned thing again.

Finally, Sol drew a shaky breath and blew her nose. Her ragged throat ached and her raw first words as she punched the link were, "I can't believe you never told me about you being on the Guild's council. A Guild master empath, for heaven's sakes. You're on the board making all the decisions about where we went, who we fought—and all this time, I thought you were a career mother."

"And I can't believe you got involved with Gabriel Merriweather," Te' fired back. "Of all the fucking male idiots in the world, why him?" Te' was breathing just as hard as Sol. But Sol didn't want to defend Gabe or her involvement with him.

She also didn't want to fight with her sister anymore. Sol tilted her chin at her com. "You've said hateful things, Te'. You've never talked to me like that before."

Her sister again ran a trembling hand over her forehead, smoothing her escaping curls back into her severe braided style. "Yeah, and I apologize. I'm under a bit of a strain right now," Te' paused and looked through the screen at Sol with an anguished depth to her gaze. She blew out a breath. "I know you think that I'm the one ordering all the Guild ships around, but I'm not. I'm just one voting committee member." Her voice lowered, "Recently, someone has been working behind the scenes, trying to sabotage and discredit me. I'm afraid I've gotten myself into something—something bad. It may cost me a dear friend—and perhaps you one or two friends yourself, Sol."

Te' looked up, her gaze so tormented that all of Sol's anger drained away. Even Te's normally strong voice shook as she said, "I wish you were here, Sol, with your calming influence. You caught me by surprise just now. This Hydra thing has popped up again, with all sorts of repercussions." Te' shook her head and gave a thin smile. "I can't believe this. I thought you had opted for procreation the way I do—without the entanglement of a male. I should have known that you, with your soft heart, would go the old fashioned route. Still, why him? Shit, Sis." Te' shook her head incredulously and muttered, "Why Gabriel Merriweather?"

She stared at Sol so intently that Sol couldn't help cringing under her gaze although she had done nothing wrong. Sol wanted Te's approval. She had always been more of a mother than a sister to Sol. Still, Te' didn't have the right to judge Sol after all the secrets she had hidden all these years.

Sol straightened her spine and realized that her newly discovered love of self gave her courage she hadn't known she had. "I honestly don't know why him, Te'. At least I didn't when all this started out. Now, all I know is that I—I care about Gabriel Merriweather enough to want to spend the rest of my life with him, even if he did indirectly cost me my commission. That should tell you something."

"Yeah, well, about that." Te looked at the ceiling and pursed her lips before blowing out a breath and saying, "Merriweather didn't cost you your commission any more than I did, Sol. Circumstances dictate early retirement for captains, that's it. Merriweather issued his findings years ago, before your career, and I have upheld that ruling for the consequent years."

Sol choked and sputtered again. "You did that, too? How many more things in my life have you twisted?"

"Well—" Te's face tightened into stubborn, hard lines that Sol had never seen before. Her voice rasped strangely, too. "—just be glad I was on the council when that Hydra debacle blew up in 1251. I was able to keep you as captain even though you lost your crew in an illegal rescue. And—" She pointed a finger at Sol. "Before you yell at me, Sis, I've been meaning to tell you about that *and* my other life, despite the Guild's edict, but you've always been so busy. Then when you got so angry over your forced retirement, I just couldn't make you any unhappier. Just remember, if I hadn't moved heaven and earth, you never would have captained a ship again after Hydra."

Te' paused, then hurried on in a harsher voice, her finger still jabbing at Sol over the transmission. "I've been the assistant governor for years now. That's why, my dear, you've held onto your commission as long as you did. But I couldn't prevent your retirement. It's Guild law, and a good one, too. Just look at your decision to rescue those people shipwrecked on Hydra. Any younger captain would have left them to their fate for breaking the law and landing there. But you? You took it into your head to rescue them without consulting the Guild. You were beginning to think too much on your own even then."

Sol saw red. She longed to punch something hard. Control was such an effort, her words gritted through clenched teeth. "If I had waited for Guild sanctions, Te', they all would have died there—even Gelli." Sol's hands fisted so tightly that her nails cut into her palms. The thought of what Gellico had suffered—almost died from—sickened her. And Te'angel had known about the shipwreck. *The fucking Guild.* Sol felt empty, betrayed by someone she had always trusted. It seemed as if she had never known her sister. Even her voice sounded as remote and as uncaring as a stranger's.

"Better they had all died there than all this trouble we've had since. That's why we've had to shut down the prison. It's also why we've had to send your precious Merriweather there for a peaceable treaty with the bloody prisoners. I've risked a very good friend there, too, so don't think you're alone in your concern."

Sol couldn't believe her ears. All these years she had

thought Te's was the voice of reason in her chaotic world. To find that her thinking was just as convoluted as any politician's shocked Sol. Her words rolled from her gut. "If Merriweather has trouble with this treaty, with—with anything on Hydra, I'm holding you responsible, Te'." She pointed her finger at her link to punctuate her determination. "You and the damned Guild."

She hurried on over her sister's open-mouthed image with, "And I don't know how to feel about your meddling in my life." An awful thought occurred to Sol. "Did you get me my commission or did I at least earn my captain's bars on my own?" Her heart trembled with the waiting.

Te's shoulders stiffened then she growled. "Damn it, Sol. You passed all the tests on your own. I did nothing but vote the way I felt on your advancements."

"Good." Sol spat just the one word and signed off before she said something to completely sever the ties with her only family. How much of her life had been manipulated by her sister? And for what ends?

* * * *

Just days after their heated exchange on the vid, Te' strolled into the Dante's Circus dancehall as big as you please. Sol was supremely thankful Te' had caved first, but hid her joy. She hadn't expected her stoic sister to give in; she never had in the past. But then, they had never had this serious of an argument before. Mist filled Sol's vision, but she stood at attention, her head above Te's. Te' didn't greet her or sit down. She just grabbed Sol into a quick embrace and held on. Sol felt her trembling over her own. After a moment, Sol relaxed and returned the hug.

Te's eyes glittered when she pulled back. "Sol, I can't stand the thought of you alone, pregnant and thinking the worst of me."

More worry lines bracketed Te's mouth. Shadows under her eyes testified that she hadn't slept much. Sol knew something terrible was wrong. Te's voice quivered a little too much to be caused by a spat with her sister.

"What's happened?" Sol demanded. "Tell me. Is it

Gabriel?"

Te' shrugged and hastened to reassure her. "Don't get too worried, Sol. There has been an interruption in communications. I'm sure it's just a delay—a glitch."

"How sure are you?" A lump gathered in Sol's throat. She fought to breathe.

Te's brows lifted. "I'm hoping?"

Sol's heart dropped. Oh god, what had gone wrong on Hydra?

Fifteen

"There hasn't been any intel in the last few weeks, so I don't know much about Merriweather's mission, success- or failure-wise. I only know that communication with the *Treaty* has been out for days." Te's keen gaze stared at Sol then she shook head. Her voice lowered. "You know that I can't tell you more until the investigation is over."

Sol snorted and held her temper, but it was with an effort. "Yeah, I know about Guild regulations and all that bullshit." She gripped her sister's arm, her glare steady. Her new emotional strength gave her courage. "Te', I've really got to know. Did you send Gabriel to Hydra? Was it on your orders?"

Te's flushed cheeks got redder, and she pulled from Sol's grip. She paced around Gellico's room, refusing to sit down and refusing to meet Sol's eye. "I'm not used to this, Soledad— your questioning me. What's happened to my little sister? When did you get so big that you doubted me?"

"Oh, I don't doubt that you love me as my big sister, Te'." Sol tilted her chin. "What I do think is that you personally sent the man I love into an unknown dangerous situation for the further edification of the damned Guild. Right?"

Te's shoulders slumped, all resistance drained out of her. She plopped down next to Sol and took her hands. "No, I didn't send Merriweather out on a whim. It's important that we end this mess on Hydra." She took a deep breath. "A few years back, after the debacle of 1251, I sent an operative to Hydra with the last bunch of prisoners to search out anyone of value and to form a working alliance. This operative—" Here Te' paused. She struggled for her next words, and Sol saw the brilliance in her gaze. Her stoic sister fought tears. "This operative is very important to me. I didn't know just how important he was until he left on the mission. Now, I find that I'm slowly going mad with worry."

"You sent Gabe more for word of this operative than for the colonization of Hydra." It was a statement rather than a question, and Sol stared at Te' in amazement. Her sister had never been involved with anyone as far Sol knew. When had this attachment started?

Te' avoided her gaze. "Yeah, I'm afraid my motives weren't exactly pure, although the Guild was petitioned for settlement. Lots of people want the misery of the prison ended." Sol almost missed the implied, "And lots of people don't."

"Well, it's good to know you're not such an ice queen after all." Sol hugged Te' to soften her words. Te' pulled back and frowned at her.

"I am *not* an ice queen." She glared then there was a faint twist to her lips. "And I'll freeze anyone who says so."

With Te' halfhearted laugh, the tension finally eased. But both sisters were teary-eyed—Te' in frustration, bound by Guild policies, and Sol in irritation, torn between loyalties. She hated her sister's involvement with the Guild.

"Would you have come home more often if you had known about my empathic ability?" Te' asked, then shook her head to answer her own question. "No, I don't think you would have. I think you would have been disturbed by my talent and stayed away. You wouldn't have accepted your own tranq talent either—to say nothing about my Guild involvement."

Sol gazed at her sister, stunned, and laughed. Te' knew her too well, and she didn't have to be an empath to know how uncomfortable they both felt after their one and only fight. A tight muscle loosened in Sol's chest. "I think, perhaps, you read me too well, Te'. You're right. I probably would have stayed away, especially knowing that you are the Guild's temporary governor. And that wouldn't have helped either of us."

Te' frowned. Sol heard the concern in her voice. "You won't stay away after the baby gets here, will you?"

"No, my darling sister, I'll come as often as I can." Sol, wanting to keep the new found peace with Te', wisely didn't mention Gabriel and his involvement. Her sister would just have to learn to accept him being in the picture because Sol wasn't going to give him up.

Nagging worry hovered in the back of her mind. Gabe had to be okay. He had promised to return to her. But after days of waiting, there was still no communication from the *Treaty*.

With a twinge of misgiving, Sol recalled her last conversation with Te', over tea in the safari splendor of Gellico's room.

Te' smiled over her cup, and Sol felt that, perhaps, they were on the way to their former closeness, but Te's next question caused her heart to skip. "Do you think the baby will have either an empath's ability or a tranq's?"

Shocked, Sol remained at a loss for words. She'd never given the idea any thought. Finally, she exhaled a long breath. Bloody hell, she hoped her son had neither. She had answered Te' with the inane response that all she cared about was that the baby was healthy.

For several hours after Te's departure, Sol's mind spun with the possibilities of what her offspring might inherit from two Chakkra bloodlines. The idea was disturbing, but maybe not so bad. An empath would be like Gabe and a tranq would be like her. Suddenly, she laughed. Either way, she could live with it. Then her worry centered on what Gabe might be facing at this very moment. Her heart raced at the thought of the danger on Hydra. That—that man. Oooh, just wait until she got her hands on him again. She stomped around Gelli's rooms, mad at her and then at Gabe for leaving her behind. He needed her protection, the bloody diplomat. He didn't know what he faced on Hydra. Never had she worried for so long over things beyond her control. She hadn't been herself since that night at the Pleasure Dome.

A sharp kick to her ribs brought Sol out of her misery. Her eyes widened with a sudden enlightening thought. She really should be thanking the Pleasure Dome, Gabe, Te' and the clinic, and, yes, even her wormhole dyslexia. If just one thing had been different, Sol might not be carrying the precious bundle of joy in her womb. Another sharp jab stole her breath. Sol ran her hand in a circling caress, and swore she felt a comforting response. Perhaps it was just wistful thinking on her part. She again recalled Te's goodbye. Somehow, her sister's words rang false.

Te'angel had smiled knowingly, smoothed her already

perfect, slick-braided hair and kissed Sol on both cheeks. "I've got to go, kiddo. Take care; I'll call you as soon as I know anything."

"You're going home?" Sol questioned.

She hadn't liked the way her sister averted her gaze or the way she hedged, "Soon, yes." Te's had given her another quick hug. "You'll hear soon."

After Te left, thoughts of the future kept Sol from thinking too hard about what could be happening to Gabe and his mission, but nighttime became the time for nightmares. And Soledad was always a great one for nightmares. She sank deep into them.

Cordite gasses filled the Guild's ship's corridors with the remnant of spent explosives. Confused bellowing and frantic yells rang out. In the chaos, grim-faced Marines ran through the narrow byways, followed by a frantic Gellico and Asher. All carried a full accompaniment of battle gear. Guns, knives, lasers, and radio helmets bounced on tense uniformed bodies. Their thick boots pounded out a cacophony on the ribbed decking. What had gone wrong? Where was Gabriel?

Asher's voice boomed through the mayhem. He snarled into his shoulder radio, "I don't care what it takes, Brubaker. Find him. That ship had to leave a signature behind. Get a fix on it, Lieutenant!"

The man's radio reply of "Aye, aye, Sir!" was barely audible over the scream of alarms and thumping through the corridor. Gellico knelt next to a spray of dark fluid that spattered the pristine military green in front of the ship's air lock. And there was a lot of spray, too much to come from just one man, one commander. But some of it was most assuredly his. Gelli ran her finger through the spots then raised dark eyes filled with dread to Asher's. Her voice shook.

"Sol's going to kill us for letting him get hurt."

"We may not be alive for her to kill when this is over, Miss de Marco." Asher's voice reflected the grimness of their predicament. "I don't know how those convicts could

*have gotten their hands on a galactic battle cruiser, much
less, why they felt the need to snatch the commander."* He
shook his head and thumbed off the safety on his rifle.

*"Did they know Merriweather was coming with a treaty
offer?"*

Asher shook his head, *"No. We weren't in transmission
range of Hydra yet. But someone knew."* His icy eyes
narrowed. *"Someone doesn't want us to succeed with this
mission."* His speculative gaze grew even more thoughtful,
more chilling. *"We have to rescue Gabriel—then go after
the sonofabitch that doesn't want this treaty. We owe him
that much."*

"Easy for you to say, Major."

*"What's the matter, Miss de Marco? Not up to the
challenge?"* A hint of humor colored Asher's words.

Gellico laughed; a hollow sound in the ship's corridor.
"I'm up to anything you are, Major. Lead the way." Her
dark gaze grew more haunted.

Asher ducked into the loading bay of a fighter with
Gellico on his heels. Blackness surrounded them.

Sol jerked awake. Her nightshirt stuck her skin. This was
just another nightmare. Right? It had to be. She cursed the
dream and tugged her sweaty clothes over her head. *Just a
nightmare, right?*

She swore again and threw her nightshirt across the room.
"Damn you, Gabriel Merriweather. So help me, if you get hurt,
I'll kill you myself."

Sol was still grumbling when fatigue overcame her in the
last hour before dawn. This time her sleep was free of
nightmares.

* * * *

Gabriel swiped his bound forearms across his forehead,
flinched at the sting and blinked his sticky blood from his vision.
Impossible to stop the head wound's steady blood flow entirely,
but he could alter it by tilting his head. Now the blood dripped
more to the side of his face than into his eyes. His head throbbed
abominably. His thinking remained clouded, surreal. Had he
called up his Chakkra blood and lost himself in battle against

overwhelming odds? Did he really let warrior haze overtake him after all these years? The last time Gabe had felt such pain, done such violence, was long ago. Had he fought Chakkra in truth or were they ghosts from the past?

Gabriel gave himself up to the oblivion of memory and was drawn back to his childhood on Chakkra.

There was no safe place on Chakkra's savage world for a half-human boy. Heavy-armed, ham-fisted, vicious dark warriors surrounded Gabriel on all sides for everyday of his existence. Punches, kicks and slaps became his daily routine. No warrior let the opportunity to inflict pain on him go by. Over the years, every limb on Gabriel's body, including his nose, was broken. His bottom front teeth grew in crooked from shattered baby teeth. His heart turned bitter, and still he persevered. Even the medic who treated Gabe's broken body managed to inflict more pain than necessary when setting his bones. The only reason the medic helped at all was because the king commanded it.

The great king, Gabe's grand sire, actually believed Gabe was just a clumsy, weak-limbed human boy despite his half Chakkra lineage. Gabe never told the king any different. In fact, he conversed as little as possible with all of them. He knew the warriors waited for him to flinch, to cry out or beg for mercy, or better yet, for him to petition his grand sire for help. Gabe didn't give them the satisfaction.

In silence, for every bruise he suffered, he learned avoidance. For every broken bone, he stored up his hate. For every drop of spilled blood, he kept a tally. All his injuries taught Gabriel battle hardness.

In their cruelty, the warriors unintentionally showed Gabriel their best skills. Gabe gave them only a token battle. He fought just enough for the warriors to become disgusted with his weak defense and lack of aggression, and they left him alone in Chakkra shame. But as Gabriel gave the Chakkra one thing, he took another. He learned warrior fighting techniques from the best of them. In his teens, he perfected his newly acquired empathy and learned to read the warriors like an open book. And Gabe never forgot his parents or the manner of their deaths. He was determined that someday, when he grew big enough, all of Chakkra would pay.

For years, Gabriel practiced their battle moves in secret and honed his skills. He learned to control and call up his great hatred. He used it to call on battle rage. Finally, when he was nineteen, the longed for day arrived—it was time.

Fresh from a battle victory, jubilant warriors surrounded Gabe, poking him with their great war weapons and laughing from their lofty heights. He absorbed as much as he could, letting his anger slowly build. Steadily, his hate grew, and using his anger to their taunts, Gabe called on his warrior rage. His hot blood surged through his veins. Red filled his vision. His muscles swelled with power. Finally, with a savage roar that shook clouds of dust off the high rafters, Gabe drew himself up to the full height he had grown into, not quite as tall as the others but formidable. Twin, sharp, curved blades danced in his nimble fingers. As a half-human, Gabriel was more adept with his hands than the blunt-fisted warriors. The curved short swords he'd welded were different too. He had adapted them from the Rigelian traders' weapons that the Chakkra scoffed at, but Gabe knew better than to scorn something just because it was different. His Chakkra battle rage was also better. Years of stored hate had honed it to perfection.

As he slashed and danced among the crowd of warriors, Gabriel's blades flew like butterflies and stung like bees He neither felt the cuts that nicked his body nor cared if he lived or died. He also felt no remorse for the great globs of warrior blood and flesh that flew from his blades. Chunks of Chakkra warriors littered the floor, but Gabe kept carving, even as he slipped and slid on the gore. Shrill cries rent the air, roars of the wounded, but Gabe heard nothing until his grand sire fired the staff of justice. The staff boomed amid the roaring in Gabe's ears.

In the sudden quiet, the red rage finally faded from Gabriel's vision although his pulse still throbbed in his hearing. His chest rose and fell, and he desperately sucked air into his lungs. His bloody kin, those still standing, glared at him. They moved together and, as one, stepped toward him. Gabe sucked in another deep breath, knowing this was his last.

"Enough!" the old king bellowed and pounded his long official staff. Again it boomed. "By the gods, enough. What is the meaning of this?"

No one spoke. None dared. Finally, Gabriel stepped in front of his grand sire. Blood dripped down Gabriel's body with stinging reality. He heard the collective breath of the Chakkra standing behind him draw in. They were afraid.

He turned, giving them a crooked sneer over his shoulder. "Why we're only having a training lesson, Grand sire. Your warriors have agreed that I am well trained." He gave a mocking snort. "Well enough, in fact, to leave Chakkra." He stared blandly at the warriors who stared back, dripping blood and holding body parts that were sliced and diced.

"Isn't that true, my teachers?" His throbbing sight narrowed on them until several heads nodded mutely, although no one looked up. Gabe's grand sire looked from the littered floor to the wounded warriors then to Gabe.

"Chakkra do not fight among themselves. Nor do they leave their home world."

Gabe gave a bitter laugh. "Is that so? Then why did you kill my father, my mother?" The old warrior flinched and swayed. Gabe knew that the king had ordered no one to repeat the tale of his birth and the slaying of his parents. Gabriel shook his head bitterly.

"I was born aware, old man." Gabe ignored the shocked gasp of those around him. "I know—I felt—what you did to them, your own son, my father and my gentle mother who should have had diplomatic protection. I knew them better than you. I also knew they had done nothing to you." Gabe was relentless in his hasty speech, sure that

all heard the soul-wrenching pain, the condemnation in his voice. "They only wanted to live and love in peace. And for that, you killed them—your own offspring. Just because his way wasn't your way."

Gabe stopped. He fought the trembling that had started in his voice. He had been saving this rage since his birth. On a deep inhale, he continued, just as strong as when he started. "I hope all of you rot in the decay of my hatred."

He swept the area with his glittering gaze. In disgust, he threw his bloodied blades down at his feet. Several warriors jumped. Gabe's sneering laughter sounded strange even to his ears. He realized that in his entire lifetime, he had never laughed once. Just for the joy of it, he did it again.

The crowd drew farther back, but just the same, all heard Gabriel tell his grandfather. "I am leaving Chakkra. It is not my home. I won't come back. If you, any of you, ever come after me—" His words gathered until they soared. "If I see any of you again, I will kill you on sight. Then I will come back here and wipe out every member of your family. Understand?"

"Go then." His grand sire grunted in a harsh whisper. "You abomination, get you gone." His white head never rose, and the ruler of Chakkra left the room before the warriors shuffled out. Not one Chakkra looked at Gabriel. And no one stopped him from taking a scout ship.

Half a light year from Chakkra, Gabriel vomited until he had nothing left to come up. His ribs hurt from the violent strain of his beating, but he ignored his cuts and bruises. He may have disgraced his mother's gentle admonition to "do good, learn and to work for peace," but he had appeased his father and his Chakkra blood that called for revenge for their deaths.

Gabe never returned to Chakkra, nor had he even thought of those warriors for all these years. Why did he think of them now? In the distance, his darkness was brightening—

Gabe awoke with a startled jerk. The past retreated with

his awareness of the present. He was on Hydra. Had he really heard Chakkra spoken in the *Treaty's* corridors, and had he actually fought warriors of his kind? His head wound bled, hurt, but other than that, Gabe doubted his wounds were serious. He really did have a hard head.

Awareness flicked through him. The ones, whoever they were, who attacked him on the *Treaty* didn't fare as well, and for that Gabe was truly sorry. And he knew he had left dead behind him. He had killed in a fit of Chakkra rage.

Dear gods, he was a diplomat, and he had to keep reminding himself of that fact through the resurgence of his remembered hatred. His pounding pulse still spoke otherwise. After leaving Chakkra, he had vowed to follow his mother's wishes for peace. He even took her last name of Merriweather. Through the years, he had curbed his warrior instinct and honed his empathy senses to become a bringer of justice and of peace. Gabriel had sworn to never take another life and he hadn't—until now.

When he was jumped in the *Treaty's* corridor, Gabe was overpowered by unidentified armed men. They spoke in what his mind recognized as Chakkra war speech, and when one warrior stuck a blade to his throat, ordering him to submit, Gabe had reacted as a full fledged Chakkra warrior. His enraged battle haze had wiped out all vows of peace. As surly as he knew his name, Gabriel Merriweather knew he had killed two, possibly three, captors. Three more were left wounded before someone knocked him out with a cowardly club from behind. Evidently, he had cracked his forehead in the fall to the deck.

Gabe swallowed guilt against a swollen throat. It wasn't cut, but his neck muscles were swollen and bruised. Even a half-breed Chakkra was hard to take down. He remembered little of the final outcome, awakening to his present state of a throbbing head and bound arms and legs.

For a long time, Gabe wandered in a dream where Chakkra kicked him in the head to make him fight. But now, in the present, when he regained his senses, Gabe felt sick about the loss of life. He recalled the spark of life fading from the eyes of the men he had killed. He jerked in his chair.

"Don't move." The burly man sitting across from Gabe

glared at him over the barrel of his old fashioned pistol. "Don't you move one little bit." The guard straightened and gripped the shaky weapon until his knuckles went white. His voice rasped. "Don't try any funny mind tricks either. We know about your evil ways, Mr. Empath."

Fear radiated off the man's sweaty scent, and Gabe fought to keep from wrinkling his nose at the sour odor. He also tried blocking out the miasma of conflicting emotions that bombarded him from his surroundings. Over and over, he attempted to engage the suspicious guard in meaningful conversation. No such luck. From what Gabe gleaned from the man's emotions, the guard lacked a high intelligence. Only fear and distrust flowed from him.

Finally, Gabe tried again, keeping his voice level. "I don't practice evil, Mr.—" He waited for the guy to supply the name, but again, the man only squirmed on his seat. "Really, I'm not a bad man." Gabe shrugged his bound shoulders. Metallic ropes tied him to his chair so tightly that Gabe couldn't do more than wiggle. If they had been fashioned of natural fibers, he could have dissolved the molecules in a snap. But any manufactured metal resisted Chakkra atom-releasing manipulation. Gabe couldn't even open his hands so that he could show empty palms in a peaceful gesture. "As I've told all of you over and over, I'm an ambassador for the Guild's Diplomatic Corps. I'm only here to offer the people of Hydra a treaty with the Guild."

"Yeah. Sure you are." The man squinted and nodded sagely. "I've passed those lies on. And they are surely lies. That's why we were warned about your attack. You killed some of our friends on your ship." His eyes glittered dangerously. "But we're ready for you now. We've got other friends in high places. Friends who will take care of you."

Truth rang in his words, and Gabe wondered who had so distorted his mission. Someone "in high places" wanted them to fail. Someone who knew Gabe was an empath and had warned the prisoners of Hydra to beware.

Finally, the door behind his guard opened and a trio of men in black uni-dress trooped in. The big guy in front tapped Gabe's guard on the shoulder. "We'll take over from here, Smithy."

Smithy rose slowly and backed out the door, never taking his frightened eyes off Gabe. Gabriel squelched the notion of scaring the guy further with a fierce glare. The superstitious guard would probably believe Gabe had the power to curse him with the evil eye. But not this new guy. No, this lean convict was made of tougher stuff. Gabe got no reading at all from him. Tranq? No, there was no dampening of the emotional field that swamped the place. Still, the man controlled himself well. Gabriel couldn't get a clear reading, and he assessed Gabe with the same intense scrutiny.

"Now, suppose we get down to business. I've been told you are Commander Gabriel Merriweather of the Diplomatic Corps?" The tall man with silver winging through his cropped dark hair took the seat that Smithy had vacated. His dark gaze remained neutral, calm. His jet-colored eyes shone solid black with no pupils. He placed his elbows on the table, laced his fingers together and rested his chin on the square knuckle joints. "We're not here to harm you further. Do you understand?" His baritone voice was indeed all business, but Gabriel could read the man's sincerity without his empathy talents. Gabe gave an affirmative nod.

"I'm Thresher, Marcus Thresher, and I'm the elected leader of Asylum," the man said. He stared intently into Gabriel's gaze as if to drill home his point. "We no longer think of our home as Hydra, Commander. We haven't been a prison for a long time."

Gabe nodded again, deeper this time, but stopped the motion quickly. Such movement made his head hurt worse. For a moment, his vision swam and he saw two images of Thresher. With shallow breaths, Gabe willed the pain away so he could think. His diplomatic skills came in handy while he sorted through the facts. Even without his empathy senses, Gabe knew the man in front of him had a lot more to say, and he really didn't want to interrupt.

"I don't know why you've come here, Commander, but I think it's for something other than what we've been told." Thresher leaned forward, nearer Gabe, and his eyes glittered like black ice. "I have a feeling we're being used. Both of us. And I, for one, don't like being used." He leaned back, and some of the tension left his stiff shoulders. The guards behind him relaxed a margin but didn't leave their protective positions. Thresher waved his hand in a forward rolling motion. "So tell me, Commander, what's your story?"

Gabe straightened in his chair and kept a wary eye on the two guards. Blind obedience emanated from them. Easy to read. No matter what, they would take their lead from Thresher. Gabe ignored the throbbing in his temples and kept his head tilted so his gaze remained clear. He flexed numb fingers. The blood flow wasn't entirely restricted.

His voice came out steady when he said, "I'm sorry about the men who grabbed me on the *Treaty*. I didn't know who they were, and with a blade to my throat, I reacted badly."

Thresher shrugged. "They weren't my men. I didn't give the order to nab you. It came from outside Hydra."

Gabe lifted one brow and waited for him to continue. When nothing came, Gabriel decided to reveal more than he had been cleared to. "In addition to being Commander of the Diplomatic Corps of the Spacing Guild, I'm a master empath, Mr. Thresher." Gabe waited for confirmation that the man understood that their information had been correct.

Thresher blinked a slow-eyed answer and sat straighter in his chair. His voice remained neutral as he said, "I'm familiar with empaths. And at least part of our intel on you is true." He inclined his head and made another forward roll with his fingers. "Continue."

While Gabe considered how he should respond, he twisted his neck in an attempt to ease the knot in his tense joints. They creaked, but some of the pressure was released. Finally, he decided truth—the whole truth—was the best way out of this situation. Thresher was still hard to read, perhaps due to his so called experience with empaths. Only an odd tranquility came from the man, and it was something Gabe had never encountered before. Was the man some kind of tranq?

"Mr. Thresher, this would be easier if I knew what you've been told—and where you got your battle cruiser."

"Tell me your truths first, and then I'll decide what information I'll share with you. And for the record, it wasn't our cruiser that attacked your vessel."

Thresher didn't seem to be in a hurry, but Gabe was. How long had he been here before he had awakened? The crew of the *Treaty* would be fast on his heels. Gabe had to head them off before an unnecessary war broke out. Enough people had died on Hydra already. This was supposed to be a peaceful meeting. *Damn it!* Gabriel jerked upright and flinched at the blinding head pain.

He couldn't keep excitement from his voice as he said, "That must be their plan. Whoever set my abduction in motion hoped that it would lead to a battle between the Guild and the people of Hydra—uh, Asylum—before we met and understood the situation." He hurried on at Thresher's deep scowl. "They don't want a treaty with you. Don't you see? They don't want you in the Spacing Guild for some reason. They don't want Hy—Asylum to become a free colony." Gabe wanted to grip Thresher's fists and make the man see his reasoning. Instead, he flexed his bound hands and waited.

Color flushed Thresher's face, and a broad muscle jumped in his rugged jaw. His black eyes narrowed. Gabe knew someone would pay for the deceit.

"Send for Tyner," Thresher ordered over his shoulder without turning around. One of his guards left. The other shifted closer, his hand nearer his weapon. "Now, tell me about your plan for the Guild's offer."

Gabe hurried through his treaty's outline. He'd do more of an in-depth review later. As Gabe spoke, some more tension drained from Thresher's features. He pursed his lips into an all business moue. His rugged expression fell deeper into thought, although his dark eyes reflected such fathomless depths that Gabe was still at a loss to read beyond them. He knew Thresher was willing to listen, but apparently that was all he was prepared to do until after he spoke with this Tyner, whoever he was. Gabe squirmed in his seat and fought the ropes that bound him to the chair. His splitting headache was beginning to blur his vision.

"We will have an ambassador, a say in Guild business?" Thresher stated after mulling over Gabe's hastily listed treaty offers.

"That's right. You will have trade restored immediately upon signing the treaty. Livestock and any colonists who want to settle here will have arrangements made for them." Gabe stared intently at Thresher. "But, you do know that before females come here, laws and bonds will have to be posted."

A pained look flickered over Thresher's hard features. "We are well aware of our black past, Commander. I wasn't here then but the perpetrators were dealt with long ago, although the wicked tale will never die." For a moment, the man stared at the rough hewn table beneath his scarred palms. Then he raised his solemn gaze to Gabe's. He had to clear his throat, but his words still rasped. "Did any of the rescued captives from 1251 survive? I know of the few who were hospitalized on Delta Three. Did they make it?"

"Yeah, a few." Gabe found his voice was just as husky as Thresher's. Funny, the guy had access to information that only the Guild and the survivors knew. "But you won't want to meet any of them." Gellico's image flashed in his mind, and Gabriel was sincerely glad he wasn't in Thresher's shoes. Any minute now, he expected Gellico and the *Treaty's* crew to show up.

Hurry, hurry he silently repeated in a mantra to the man sitting across from him.

Suddenly, Thresher untied Gabe and ordered his wounds treated. And as quick as his order, a grizzled medic came in and treated Gabe with a stinging solvent and a rough pressure bandage that irritated the skin around his head. Beyond the crude medicines, Gabe noted that most of their furnishings were also crude parodies of modern amenities. Feeling better, he gave the room a thorough once over. Thresher nodded in agreement to the question in Gabe's eyes.

"We've come a long way since 1251, Commander, but we've a long way to go. We could use the help in establishing a colony. I'm sure the Guild colonies always need the farming trade." His gaze lowered. "And I'm also sure I would not want to meet the dancers who survived that terrible year." Thresher seemed lost in the haunted past.

"I wouldn't recommend it." The words barely left Gabe's mouth when the door to their room blew off its hinges. Gabriel, Thresher and his men managed to drop to the floor before lasers blasted. He hadn't felt his rescue team's approach over the diverse emotions that swamped the room—almost a fatal mistake. But his men knew better than to fire into a hostage's location. What had gotten them so out of control? Scorch marks rimmed the walls. Sparks pinged off metal. Gabe's heart was pounding so hard that he barely identified the frantic thoughts of the troopers who were rushing into the room. They were definitely his men and bent on violence.

"Cease fire! Damn it! Listen to me!" Gabe heard Asher yell over the lasers that were still pinging and the returned blasts from Thresher and his men. Someone had supplied the convicts with antiquated firepower, Gabe realized. They were using old MK-15s.

"Hold your damned fire!" Gabe recognized Asher's frantic voice, and he breathed a sigh of relief when the firing stopped. He slowly rose from behind the shattered table that they had used for shelter. Thresher rose just behind his shoulder. The man wisely kept Gabe in front of him and his men.

"This is the speaker for Hydra, Major Jones," Gabe hurried to tell Asher, who took a menacing step forward. "Someone doesn't want this treaty and tried to sabotage our meeting. It wasn't him or his men."

"Got that, Commander." Gellico stood to the left of Asher with her laser still leveled at Thresher and his men. Her eyes glittered dangerously. "Who?"

Asher and his men stepped back, way back, from her. Gabriel shook his head and flinched at the motion. Dizzy, he staggered. He knew he had to save the situation before it got ugly—well, uglier than it was. He clenched his jaw and grunted, "Not these men, Gelli. It wasn't these men." Now he knew who had stirred his Marines to heated battle rage.

Her eyes remained narrowed, her stance rigid. Her finger tightened on the laser, and Gabe felt his heart rate notch up. He didn't dare move or Thresher was a dead man. This close,

Gabe wasn't sure that he wouldn't be one either.

Behind Gabe, Thresher muttered for Gabe's hearing only, "They were hired mercenaries, Commander, and we didn't hire them. Tyner was the only contact."

Gabe dropped his voice into his diplomatic reasoning mode. "It wasn't these men, Gelli, now or back in 1251. Do you hear me, de'Marco?" He watched Gellico's face for signs of returning reasoning. None came. Her eyes remained wild, savage in their intent.

She hesitated with her laser still on her shoulder and Gabe felt the memories that threatened to overwhelm her. She shook her head from side to side as if weary. "This Hydra isn't the same nightmare that I left, is it?" Her voice sounded lost, her eyes black pits of pain.

"No, Gelli, it isn't even Hydra anymore. It's called Asylum." Gabe used his voice to calm her. "Did you see the farms with their crops? And all the buildings?" He hurried on, "This isn't the same place or the same people. Do you understand, Gelli?"

She rubbed her chin against her rifle stock but didn't lower the weapon. "Everything in the place is turned around. I thought I would never forget it."

"It's time to put the past away, Gelli. You need to rest. You never have to remember Hydra again." Gabe wanted to wrap this up quickly. He noted that Gelli had blood dripping from the arm holding her rifle. "Gellico, does your arm hurt? Wouldn't you like medical attention? They fixed my head." He tried grinning at her.

"Nothing will fix your head, Commander, but—" Her rifle swung in Thresher's direction.

"He's not one of them, Gelli. Thresher's not, and none of the men here are the ones who held you captive. Do you understand?"

She snorted, "Of course, I do. But do you understand that Sol is going to be mad at both of us." She laughed and her hold on her laser loosened. Gabe tried to signal Asher to leave off his advance, but the Major stepped up close behind Gelli.

"Gellico, listen to me. It is all right now. Put down your weapon before this escalates and someone is killed. There will be no peace, no treaty this way." His reasoning was soft and calm, but he came no closer and made no move to take her weapon away. Gabe held his breath. Perhaps Ash could reach her when he couldn't.

"Honey, I'd rather you weren't hurt again. I want to take care of your arm. Doesn't it hurt?" Asher persisted, even touched her shoulder lightly with his fingers. "Let me take care of you, Gellico. I won't hurt you. I promise on my life that no one will hurt you ever again. Okay, sweetheart? Just lower your weapon." His fingers tightened on her shoulder. When she made no move to comply, Asher's voice hardened with command. "Put down your weapon, soldier. That's an order."

Gellico slowly lowered the laser as if it had suddenly had become too heavy. Its barrel rested near the floor. "You're not my superior, Major," she snarled at him over her shoulder. Her voice echoed in a weak parody of her normal sharpness. The sight of Asher's gray eyes with their amused wrinkles obviously annoyed her further. She frowned just before her rifle slipped from her fingers. Her knees buckled.

Asher folded her neatly into his arms and nodded to Gabe. He held Gellico tenderly but glared at Thresher's men at arms who hid their smiles at the way her long body draped in his short stature.

Gabriel wisely didn't comment other than to say, "I believe my aide has the situation under control, gentlemen." Gabe turned, let out a held breath and caught Thresher's eye. "I hope you can understand Ms. de Marco's apprehension. She was one of Hydra's captives back in 1251."

"Good god, man, why would you ever bring her back here?" Thresher's dark eyes were incredulous. He ran a shaky hand over his scalp.

"She insisted that I needed her help, and at the time, I let other opinions influence me.' Gabe paused and took a deep breath, then blew it out. "Now I'm not so sure it was a good idea."

"Definitely not." Thresher glared at him. "Just think how it would have looked if we had shot her."

Gabe snorted at the thought. "Yeah, almost as bad as you

taking the Guild's diplomatic commander captive." Gabriel showed his teeth in his best feral grin before he added. "Someone really doesn't want this treaty to happen, do they?" Not waiting for an answer, Gabe continued to speculate. "Just where did the Guild battle cruiser and mercenaries come from?"

The name Thresher freely gave caused a chill to run up Gabe's spine. He had expected someone in the Guild, but not someone so highly connected. And not someone who had connections with Chakkra.

Sixteen

Gabe paced his quarters and waited for word on the renegade cruiser. True to his commander, Asher reluctantly left Gellico's bedside to lead the chase. It was only a matter of time before they closed in on the heavier mystery ship. She might have more firepower, but the *Treaty* was no slouch. And she was a much faster vessel with a commanding officer more devious than the average warship commander.

A sharp knock rapped his door. "We have the ex-Guild cruiser, *Tristin,* in communication range, Commander."

"On my way." Gabriel felt a quirk to his lips. So it was a decommissioned Guild ship that had attacked them. He'd had his suspicions for a long time. The traitor's time was up. Retribution was at hand.

* * * *

All heads at the conference table turned in his direction when Gabriel entered the ready room. In the days after the *Tristin's* capture, the Guild's ruling ship, *Battlestar One*, had arrived for a Guild meeting on-board the *Treaty*. They again orbited above Asylum, the prison world formerly known as Hydra. Gabe was hit by a gauntlet of emotions from the seated members. Confusion and speculation vied for dominance among the heads of state. Calm acceptance came from Marcus Thresher. If there was more treachery among the Guild members they hid it too well for Gabe to find. This was the first meeting in a long time that he had actually looked forward to holding.

"Madam Governor," Gabe nodded a proper greeting to the acting governor of the Guild. He started at her faint smile. Suddenly, the stern-faced woman, with her broad cheekbones and her square face, looked more familiar to Gabe. But he didn't take time to ponder who the Guild's governor reminded him of. Over the years, countless confrontations with the stubborn woman had left Gabe frustrated more than once. But he had learned that the acting governor ruled the Guild board with sharp intellect and sharper wits than most of the other members. Even the times he disagreed with her, the governor had turned out to be correct in her ruling.

"Proceed, Commander." She nodded toward him. Even her evenly modulated voice sounded more familiar. Again, he couldn't quite put his finger on who she reminded him, and his head pained him if he thought on it too long.

The other members at the table were looking at Gabe expectantly. He began on a deep breath. "Thank you all for coming on this momentous occasion. Today, we end a tragedy and begin a world renewed with purpose. Past sins are forgiven, deadly indiscretions forgotten, past wounds healed with this new colony."

Gabe motioned for Marcus Thresher to step forward and introduced him. "Mr. Marcus Thresher, ambassador for this world, will present his case for colonization of Asylum, formerly known as the prison world, Hydra. Marcus—"

Gabe sat down, and a newly attired Thresher stepped up in his place. Freshly groomed, with his silver-laced dark hair trimmed and dressed in a sharply pressed suit, Thresher appeared a different man. His first words floored Gabriel.

"First of all, let me properly introduce myself. True, I am Marcus Thresher, representative for Asylum, but I'm first and foremost an operative for the Spacing Guild. I was sent here undercover years ago by the acting governor."

Several Guild members gasped and looked at each other. Gabe felt their questions. Why didn't they know of this? Had the governor overstepped herself this time?

Gabriel focused on the Guild's governor. The woman didn't even blink. Her gaze softened as she stared at Thresher, and Gabe was reminded of what Marcus had told him—that he was familiar with empaths. Could it be?

As if she had heard his unspoken question, the woman suddenly winked at Gabe. He was getting a sneaking suspicion. Gabe sat straighter and focused on Marcus's words.

"I was sent to Hydra on a vital mission with the last of the prisoners to be incarcerated here. Since then, I, along with others of like minds, have weeded out the unsalvageable criminals, set up a working form of government, and established law enforcement necessary for all to live semi-normal lives—such as they can here."

He paused and looked each member in the eye before he continued, "Asylum is still not a perfect world and never will be. But then there are no perfect worlds in existence, gentlemen and lady. We take our perfection where we find it."

Marcus nodded to the governor and she inclined her head for him to continue. "But a colony can survive here with the Guild's help. All my findings are in the reports you have in front of you. Asylum is ripe with fertile farming ground. Many fruits and vegetables grow here with only a minimum of care. Our people hope you will consider Asylum's application for colonization."

Thresher nodded to the governor whose cheekbones bloomed with color under his intense gaze. An idiot could see that the two shared a history, and Gabriel was curious to know more about them.

"We will adjourn soon to consider Mr. Thresher's findings, and we heartily thank him for his long and dangerous service," The governor said, her words ringing with authority. "While we ponder that problem, we have our next business to consider. Treachery has been afoot in the Guild. There has been a traitor working in our midst." She turned to the Marines who stood guard and ordered, "Bring in the prisoner."

Gabe gasped along with the rest when the guards ushered in their charge. He caught the waves of hatred that surged off the man as the guards forced him to sit facing the group.

"What do you have to say for your actions, Deputy Assistant Dushaw?" Before Dushaw could speak, the governor added, "For those of you who haven't heard the rumors, *Mr.*—"

She now ignored Dushaw's official rank and stressed the lesser title. A quick glance around the room assured Gabriel that no one had failed to grasp the significance of the slight. Dushaw had already been judged and was on his way out. "—*Mr.* Dushaw took it upon himself to hire Chakkra mercenaries to capture Commander Merriweather and sabotage the Diplomatic Corps's orders to establish peaceful contact with

Hydra."

The governor placed her hands on the table and leaned over the cringing, gray-haired Dushaw. "Why?" Her voice demanded a reply.

"Because—" The man hesitated, then suddenly found misplaced courage and sprang from the chair, only to have the Marines pin his arms. Spittle flew from his mouth and his eyes rolled. "Why? Because you are a vicious bitch, that's why. I've taken orders from you for years, and I'm tired of you and your sanctimonious Diplomatic Corps. You're all soft-hearted fools." Dushaw drew himself up and puffed out his thick chest. "The Guild could rule the galaxy. We could be magnificent if given to proper leaders." He sneered at the governor. "We need a male to run the Guild."

The governor lifted one elegant brow. "Oh? Perhaps a male such as yourself?" The governor's scorn was a palpable scent to Gabe. His lips twitched. Dushaw was a stupid, braying ass that didn't know to keep his ignorant thoughts to himself. If Gabe could read him so well, the governor was getting a mindful. Her golden eyes glittered. "How did you get the mercenaries you hired?"

"I paid them with my own credits," he fired back, then shook his head and muttered in disgust, "But right when success was at hand, the cowardly bastards turned tail and ran from the battle. They kept screaming about some prince and how they had damned their families. Idiots! We could have won except for them!"

The governor actually laughed. Gabe heard real mirth in the sound, but his thoughts were focused on Dushaw's revelation. He *had* heard Chakkra language in the *Treaty's* corridors. He had fought his kinsmen again—and killed some of them. They must have picked up their dead and wounded when they fled. Perhaps they thought he wouldn't find out who they were. Like he would ever fulfill the threat he had left behind on Chakkra.

The governor's derisive snort jerked Gabe away from his thoughts, and he heard her say, "I doubt that, *Mr.* Dushaw. Your battle was over before it even started. The Guild has been watching you for quite awhile. It was only a matter of time before you slipped, but we never expected you to go so far. You crazy fool, you thought to discredit me?" Her words echoed strongly in the shielded room.

"Take him away." She ordered the Marines who grabbed the wilted Dushaw under the arms and jerked him to his feet. He struggled against their grip, and no one spoke while Dushaw was taken, kicking and screaming, from the room.

"Now, there is one more piece of Guild business remaining," the governor announced. "Commander Merriweather, please come forward."

As Gabriel rose and walked toward her, he frowned and wondered what the governor had on her mind. He stopped in front of her. She had to look up since she wasn't as tall as he, but Gabriel had never been so ill at ease under her intense scrutiny. And he had been under that hard gaze more than once.

A corner of the governor's mouth twitched, and again Gabe wondered at the faint familiarity of the gesture. Then it hit him. She reminded him of Sol. Indeed, the resemblance was so strong that she had to be Sol's sister! The breeder whose records were so heavily sealed. How had he not seen the resemblance sooner? Even her voice held the same sexual resonance as Sol's when lowered in sincerity. With a jerk, he realized she was still speaking, a wicked twinkle in her gaze.

"In addition to enforcement, it is also the Guild's duty to recognize her officers when they have gone above and beyond. Commander Merriweather, for your many years of dedication and service, you are hereby awarded the Medal of Peace and the Cross of Valor."

With lips still twitching, the governor placed both ribbons with their heavy golden circles of commendations over Gabe's head. When she kissed him on the cheek, she whispered in his ear, "Welcome to our family, Prince of Chakkra."

Gabe stared at her, stunned, and she winked at him again. Then the damned woman stepped back as if there had been no breech of protocol. The wicked gleam in her golden eyes shouted her identity as much as her stubborn jaw line: Soledad Scott's sibling. There was no doubt that he had guessed correctly. By the gods, what had he gotten himself into?

Seventeen

After another long, dream-filled, sweaty night, Sol's lower back ached, and her temples pounded. When the hell was Gabe getting back? Sol refused to believe anything had gone wrong with his mission. But feeling both angry and annoyed with Gabe, she wept worried tears because she loved him so.

Weak, weak, weak woman. Sol chided herself, remembering all the times she had captained galactic war ships.

Lost in memory of her glory days, she was taken totally by surprise when Cheri burst through the door. The little dancer nearly skipped as she announced, "They're back. They're baaack. The *Treaty* is landing right this minute." Cheri clapped her hands and danced delightedly on her toes.

"Sonofabitch!" Sol gasped and folded over at the waist.

Cheri frowned and held onto Sol's arm. "Aren't you happy, mistress?"

"Yeah. I'm ecstatic. My water just broke.

* * * *

The moment Gabe stepped into the birthing room, Sol waved her hand that showed his ring encircling her finger at him so he knew she had accepted him as her lifetime companion. He fell to his knees next to her bed. He couldn't speak; he could only grab her hand and press his lips to its back.

"I take this to mean that you still love and want me." Sol chuckled, and he mutely nodded, fighting to see her lovely face through the irritating haze that filled his vision. "Well, say something." She demanded.

"I love you, my captain." He finally croaked.

"Oh, commander, we're going to have some great times."

"Promises, promises." He lost his grin when she arched off the bed and called him an ass. The doctor shooed him off with the assurances that she didn't mean it. She was just in labor.

Many hours later, Marco Scott Merriweather made his appearance amid cheers, shouts and cries, but no one was happier than Gabe. His baby's dark curls were exclaimed over, his long fingers unfolded and counted along with his perfect toes. Yep, he had all the right equipment, too. Gabe had checked that, just to be sure. And Sol, upon discovering him unwrapping Marco to check his plumbing, had called him an ass again. But this time she was smiling wearily before she drifted off to sleep.

Now Gabe lay next to them, watching over them as they slept. He still couldn't believe it. He had a family. Marco, a tiny warm bundle, was encircled in one arm while Gabe's other rested above Sol bright head. He gently stroked her cheek. He was beginning to understand the great depth of his parents' love for one another. He understood their love for him. Just as he knew Marco felt and knew their love for him.

The baby stirred, and Gabe was struck by the love he felt pouring from his son. Tentatively, he stroked a finger down Marco's cheek and was awestruck when his son responded by snuggling his face into Gabe's palm. He was so tiny, so dependent on Gabe for protection. Then and there, Gabe vowed that no one and nothing would ever harm his child or—he looked down at Sol—his mate. If he had to work for the rest of his years, he would make the universe a better place for them, a safer place than the one he had grown up in. Oh, he'd have help. Gellico, Marco's godmother, would be a pain in the ass, Gabe knew, but he recalled how her dark eyes had filled with awe. And Asher was a complete idiot, promising in baby talk that he was going to train Marco for the big, bad Marines. Gabe snorted and quickly whispered, "Sorry," to Sol who stared up at him with a one-eyed blink.

"You know you're on feeding duty next time he wakes up, don't you?" She frowned.

"Nope," Gabe shook his head. "I don't have the right equipment."

"Then you better not wake him up for at least another two hours."

"Yes, ma'am." Gabe tried to sound contrite.

Sol hum'mphed and turned over. He heard her soft "I love you, Gabe."

He grinned in the night and whispered. "Yeah, well, I love

you more."

Before he fell asleep, Gabe was considering sending a thank you to the Pleasure Dome for their mix-up. Quite a coincidence that Sol and he had ended up there at the right place and at the right time.

But he just didn't believe in coincidences.

Epilogue

Months later.

Gabriel Merriweather, Commander of the Diplomatic Corps, sighed and leaned back in the *Treaty's* padded but still uncomfortable chair. His ass was going to sleep, and this meeting was going nowhere. Neither group could agree on a peaceful settlement, and he was sure that at least one ambassador, maybe more, was only there to agitate the group. Perhaps even to try an assassination attempt on another ambassador. *Shit.*

The door snicked open behind him. His civilian aide entered and spoke with just a hint of disrespect in her voice, "Commander, the Deputy Commander needs to speak with you."

Gabe always sat with his back to the door, a sign of his complete trust in his crew to keep him protected. He didn't need to see Gellico to know that she wore some outrageous outfit. The hungry look on the ambassadors' faces made it clear that she was running true to form. Her smoky voice carried through the sudden hush that had followed her appearance in the ship's conference room. Gabriel was continually surprised that Gelli's blatant female sexuality could do that even to a bunch of alien species.

Sometimes, Gabriel wished the former dancer would wear more clothing, and sometimes, like now, when she strutted her stuff in front of everyone, he was just happy watching their reactions to her jiggling breasts and quivering ass. Inattention would bring their guards down and he'd be able to discover just who was here to disrupt the meeting.

"The Deputy Commander needs to see me now?" Gabe looked over his shoulder at Gelli and raised a brow. What could be so important that Soledad would interrupt such an important gathering? Not that he wasn't glad for the reprieve.

Gellico snorted. "Yeah. Right now—sir." Her face gave no hint of what the important matter could be, but she stepped closer to the Marine aide who stood at attention on Gabe's other side.

Gabe sighed deeper this time and rose. Both military and civilian aides marched smoothly at his side, escorting him to the door where Gabe hesitated before turning back. Thoughts swirled behind him. The others' angry, vicious thoughts brought blood throbbing in a thickened response, but he willed it away. He would deal with the treacherous ambassadors later. The rest of them had better work out a treaty.

"Gentlemen, perhaps while I'm gone you can reach an agreement without killing each other." He glared around the room. "Because when I return, honored ambassadors, if you have not done so, the Guild will be more than happy to annex your borders and divide them among the Alliance of Free Worlds. Then all of you will lose. Suit yourselves."

He gave them a grin that held absolutely no humor, turned and walked out the door which slipped close behind him with a slight hiss. Gabe wished he could have slammed something just for further emphasis.

"Watch them," he ordered the two sentries at the door. The tall Marines slipped inside where Gabe knew their stony-eyed stares would be enough to keep the dignitaries in line.

"Where is she?" he snarled at Gellico.

"In your quarters." Not a nerve twitched in her stoic expression, but the former dancer of Dante's Circus rolled her eyes at Asher. The gray-eyed Marine fought to keep his upper lip from twitching. He failed.

"She wants me in our *quarters?*" Of course, Sol waited for him there in the only shielded room on board ship. Sol always stayed in their quarters when Gabe held a meeting. He couldn't use his empathy if she was near. Of course, if Sol was in any room, Gabriel couldn't think with anything but his dick.

He sighed and walked toward their quarters, ignoring Gelli and Asher who automatically fell into step beside him. What could Sol want? She knew he was busy with this treaty today, and Marco was fine, as healthy as any growing child. Gabe could think of nothing that was urgent enough to interrupt his work.

Mumbling under his breath, he entered his quarters and waved his laughing guards away. It was damned hard to keep protocol when those two were together.

"Sol, where are you? Damn it, what's so important that you'd interrupt—" The rest of his words died in his mouth. Sol danced toward him in that damned Arabian Nights outfit that always gave him a hard-on. Inside their quarters, sultry music drummed in the background, keeping time with Gabriel's suddenly rocketing heartbeat, which also matched his mate's thrusting hips.

"I've been waiting a long time for you, Commander. My patience is at an end."

Some kind of heated spice scent floated through the air. Seduction was surely afoot. And was there a little something added to the scent? Gabriel snorted at the waste of good pheromones. Sol didn't need anything other than her natural smell to turn him into a slobbering idiot. He knew he should tell her he didn't have time for this, but he couldn't take his eyes off Sol's hips—rounded, white hips that dipped and swayed, beckoning him to come closer and touch the naked flesh he glimpsed through her silken scarves. He could scarcely get his thick tongue to form words. The blood had fled from his brain.

"Damn it, Sol. This isn't fair. Now isn't the time." Gabe swallowed noisily. Never. He would *never* have enough of her.

"Yes, it is the time." Sol swayed closer and caressed his groin with one hand while she grabbed his ass with the other. "This says it is." She rubbed him where he tented the front of his uniform, and laughed when his cock responded with a twitch.

Gabe slammed her hard against the wall and covered her with his body. He held her wrists above her head and leaned in close. Sol felt warm and soft in all the right places. Her quick breaths rose and fell against him. Gabe measured his with hers. He kissed the hollow of her throat, licking up her taste with his tongue. Her gold-dusted eyes sparkled with laugher and something more.

He couldn't speak above a harsh whisper. "I have only a few minutes. It'll be hard and fast."

"Sometimes I like hard and fast." She gave him a slightly evil grin, and he knew she had something on her mind. *Damn it!* For all his expertise, Gabriel couldn't read her. They had discovered through exhausting research in the Guild records that mixed Chakkra and Terran bloodlines resulted in some offspring being born with empathy talents while others received tranquilizing defense mechanisms. Gabriel had been lucky to find Soledad. She completed him—and tormented him—at the same time.

Sol rolled his bottom lip between her teeth before she whispered. "I like slow and easy, too, partner. But right now, I'll settle for anything I can get."

She tugged her hands which were still tightly held in his grip. After a moment of wry speculation, Gabriel freed her. With that golden gleam in her eyes that spelled trouble, she clasped Gabe so tightly around the neck that he couldn't breathe for a moment—then lost his breath entirely when Sol slid down and knelt in front of him. She mouthed him through his pants, then blew her hot breath through the damp cloth. A groan escaped, despite Gabe's intention of not giving in. The heat and moisture from Sol's sweet mouth through the thin material of his uniform made him lightheaded. His searing response to her blew his good intentions all to hell.

"You'll leave a mark, Deputy Commander," he warned, his voice barely above a whisper. He lacked the strength to speak louder. His fingers tangled in her silky hair. He held her head close to his groin.

"There's already a mark, Commander." Sol laughed, and her sparkling gaze lifted to his. She pointed to the dark spot in the gray of his uniform. Not all of the moisture was from her.

Gabe couldn't stop his own joy-filled laughter. Ripping at stubborn cloth, he jerked his uniform off, then grabbed for Sol. After giving him only token resistance, he thought he had won her only to have Sol toss him over her shoulder with some kind of martial arts move. She pinned him to the bed with a quick one-armed maneuver worthy of the best of Gabriel's Marines. He didn't care. He'd lose a fight to Sol any day.

The two of them rolled on the little bed, giggling in a

definitely undignified way. Then, Gabe stilled for a moment and cupped her face in his hands. "I love you, Soledad Scott Merriweather. I'll never get enough of you."

Her strong chin rested in his palms, and he stroked the bridge of her wide cheekbones with his thumbs. His fingers joined behind her neck and tangled in that soft, flaming hair. There was no teasing in him now. The steady gaze of her whiskey-gold eyes softened, and Sol turned her head to kiss his palm. That one gentle touch of those sweet lips went straight to the pit of Gabe's stomach. His balls tightened. His cock danced against her leg.

"And I love you, Commander."

Those three words seemed to come easier to her now, but Gabe knew them for the great gift they were. He admired and respected this woman who gave such comfort. She was brave and selfless beyond measure. Duty came first to her, but never before their love. Gone was the woman who had seduced him with enticing videos and raging emotions. In her place, Gabe had gained a cool-headed partner who commanded with an iron fist, but who never asked her crew to do something she wouldn't do herself. It frightened Gabe sometimes to think that Sol would put herself in danger to save another, but he accepted that this was her way. She wouldn't be who she was without her selflessness. Gabe made sure that the Diplomatic Corps knew her worth. Sol was a prize beyond measure. And she was all his—well, his and their son's.

Gabe swiftly swept the area with his mind and got a sleepy response. Marco was in his Aunt Te's temporary quarters resting. Gabriel sent him his love and told him to sleep. He got a mumbled reply from Marco and a terse, "Go away, Gabriel," from his sister-in-law. Te' was unhappy with Gabe's recently exposed telepathic ability. Somehow, the now elected governor, had gotten the idea that only she both that talent and her empathic abilities. Gabe knew Te' was also out of sorts with him because he continued to refuse to take diplomatic offers to Chakkra. Eventually he would have to give in, but Gabe wanted to delay that meeting for as long as possible. Te' was also angry with Marcus Thresher. Gabe pitied the man. Anyone who fell in love with the Guild's governor was in for a rough ride.

And speaking of rides—Gabe decided that he did have time for Sol after all. Perhaps the time spent here with his mate would give the ambassadors the incentive to agree to Gabriel's offer.

But even if it wasn't enough incentive, it was certainly a treat for Gabe to see some of the old Sol from their sparing days. He parted the jeweled material that barely covered her breasts, and her nipples puckered for him. They had stayed big from their child.

Another warm glow flooded Gabriel. Sol had not only given him a son, but a life worth living—a life filled with all the things he had denied himself. He no longer damned his Chakkra blood. Perhaps it was that very bloodline that had led him to Sol in the first place. And by the gods, he owed her so much.

Gabe tongued the circle of one of Sol's nipples, watching her eyes. With a chuckle, he nipped. Her pupils darkened in their fields of gold. Her arms tightened around him, and she drew his head up to her mouth.

"Make love to me, Gabriel," she whispered.

"Your wish is my command, Captain."

"It's Commander."

He laughed and then tongued her sweet mouth. "Whatever."

* * * *

And in the beautiful Straits of Tralarie, the Pleasure Dome continues on, along with all the other forty-some pleasure houses. In the future, as in all things, other "mistakes" will continue to be made.

But there really are no coincidences in life—anywhere.

Printed in the United States
212825BV00001B/2/P

9 781933 417455